A Field of Fireflies

Merry Christmas!!!

A Novel by

JOEY JONES

Copyright © Joey Jones 2018
All rights reserved.

This book is a work of fiction. All content, including but not limited to names, places, characters and incidents are the product of the author's imagination or are used fictitiously. Any similarity to actual events, locales or real persons, living or dead, is coincidental and not intended by the author.

ISBN-13: 978-1-948978-02-6 (mobi)
ISBN-13: 978-1-948978-01-9 (epub)
ISBN-13: 978-1-948978-00-2 (print)

For my mom.
You're my hero.
One of my best friends.

Also by Joey Jones
A Bridge Apart

A Bridge Apart, the debut novel by Joey Jones, is a remarkable love story that tests the limits of trust and forgiveness . . .

In the quaint river town of New Bern, North Carolina, at 28 years of age, the pieces of Andrew Callaway's life are all falling into place. His real estate firm is flourishing, and he's engaged to be married in less than two weeks to a beautiful banker named Meredith Hastings. But when Meredith heads to Tampa, Florida—the wedding location—with her mother, fate, or maybe some human intervention, has it that Andrew happens upon Cooper McKay, the only other woman he's ever loved.

A string of shocking emails lead Andrew to question whether he can trust his fiancée, and in the midst of trying to unravel the mystery he finds himself spending time with Cooper. When Meredith catches wind of what's going on back at home, she's forced to consider calling off the wedding, which ultimately draws Andrew closer to Cooper. Andrew soon discovers he's making choices he might not be able, or even want, to untangle. As the story unfolds, the decisions that are made will drastically change the lives of everyone involved, and bind them closer together than they could have ever imagined.

Also by Joey Jones
Losing London

Losing London is an epic love story filled with nail-biting suspense, forbidden passion, and unexpected heartbreak.

When cancer took the life of Mitch Quinn's soulmate, London Adams, he never imagined that one year later her sister, Harper, whom he had never met before, would show up in Emerald Isle, NC. Until this point, his only reason to live, a five-year-old cancer survivor named Hannah, was his closest tie to London.

Harper, recently divorced, never imagined that work—a research project on recent shark attacks—and an unexpected package from London would take her back to the island town where her family had vacationed in her youth. Upon her arrival, she meets and is instantly swept off her feet by a local with a hidden connection that eventually causes her to question the boundaries of love.

As Mitch's and Harper's lives intertwine, they discover secrets that should have never happened. If either had known that losing London would have connected their lives in the way that it did, they might have chosen different paths.

Acknowledgments

A Field of Fireflies, my third novel, reminds me that anything is possible. There are a plethora of wonderful people who helped make this book become a reality. First and foremost, I would like to thank God for His grace and the gift of writing. Branden, my oldest son, inspires me to be my best self. I am grateful to have him in my life. Parker, my baby boy, brings joy to my days. I am eager to lead him on this adventure we call life.

I would also like to thank my awesome family. My parents, Joe and Patsy Jones, helped mold me into the man I've become, and I hope I leave a legacy that makes them proud. My dad now lives in Heaven, and I miss him dearly. My Mom, my breakfast partner and one of my best friends, is the most humble person I know. My brothers and sisters, DeAnn, Judy, Lee, Penny, and Richard, are some of my closest friends. Their support is, in many ways, my foundation.

My editors, Erin Haywood and Krisann Blackwell, are incredibly talented at polishing my writing. My graphics designer, Meredith Walsh, has done a fantastic job with all of my novel covers. Polgarus Studio made the intricate process of formatting the interior of this novel a breeze. Bob Peele (Sozo Fine Art Photography) is responsible for my author photo—he somehow made me look presentable!

Lastly, I would like to thank some people who have been influential throughout my life. Some for a season, but each for a reason. Thank you to Amber Gray, Andrew Haywood, BJ Horne, Billy Nobles, Cathy Errick, Diane Tyndall, Jan Raynor, Jeanette Towne, Josh Haywood, Josh Towne, Kenny Ford, Kim Jones, Mitch Fortescue, Nicholas Sparks, Ray White, Rebekah Jones, Richard Banks, Steve Cobb, Steven Harrell, and Steve Haywood. It is a privilege to call each of you my friend.

A Field of Fireflies

1

Like many other people, Nolan Lynch had learned the hard way that love truly is thicker than blood. Twenty-four years ago his biological mother had left him at the county hospital after spending nine months carrying him in her womb. She had endured the natural physical pains of childbirth, then walked away. As he understood it, she wasn't a druggie or an alcoholic or a promiscuous woman. She simply had chosen not to raise a boy who would often lay in bed at night wondering what kind of people she and his father were. What did they look like? Where did they live? What did they do for work? That's what all children who are abandoned for whatever reason end up doing. Even if they are loved and treated like family, there is a hole that burrows deep down inside of them, one that even answers might not be able to fill.

Over the years Nolan had discovered that color was only skin deep, but that didn't mean there weren't also roots and branches. The man he called Dad and the woman he called Mom had taught him many such life lessons. He tried his best to treat every human being with the same respect regardless of their sex, race, age, or religion. That didn't mean that he liked every one of them or agreed with their beliefs or opinions. He had his own beliefs, and he often wished people would treat him the same way. Some did, but many didn't—or maybe *hadn't* would be a better word. He had been called every name in the book: *Cracker, Oreo*, and even the N-word. For some reason the latter seemed to carry the most weight when it slapped society in the ear, but truth be told, words in and of themselves weren't what caused pain, it was the ignorance and intention behind them that did.

Nolan had dated white girls, black girls, mixed girls, and even an Asian girl while in college at East Carolina University. He had his preferences but he didn't rule out anyone. Growing up, all he had ever wanted in life was to find one woman to fall ridiculously in love with and for the two of them to spend the rest of their lives together making memories worth more than all the possessions in the world. It didn't matter if they lived in a shack or had a gorgeous home with a picket fence, he just wanted to be married to someone he could call his best friend and his soulmate. Maybe they would have two kids and a Labrador Retriever. Maybe not.

As a little boy he had always had dreams of marrying a woman just like his mama. As he grew into a man, she often reminded him of their walks to the river and how he had always wanted to hold her hand and would often tell her that he would marry her one day even though she explained that a boy couldn't actually marry his own mother. In time he understood that, and now days it often made him laugh to think about the silly ideas that children concoct. More so, however, the silly ideas that adults concoct made him laugh out loud.

Six years ago life had changed dramatically, and Nolan's mindset when it came to the idea of settling down wasn't quite what it had once been. Some things hadn't changed, though. He still didn't care how much money he made, if he ever became famous, or even if everyone liked him. His life's track at one point had actually been headed toward fame, but then life threw him a curve ball. Even though things in his life had always been black and white, he'd often felt gray. People that didn't really know him wouldn't understand what that meant.

This morning, these thoughts had been trickling through Nolan's mind as his feet forced the two pedals on his new bicycle in a circular motion. Steering toward Beaufort County Community College, he could feel sweat beads beginning to form on his forehead. It was a warm mid-August day in Washington, North Carolina, but surprisingly it wasn't hot enough that he would have to apply a new layer of deodorant upon arrival at his first day at a real job. He wasn't dating anyone right now, and he was completely fine with that. Everything else in his life seemed to be settling into place. This past spring he had tossed his cap into the air in Minges Coliseum at ECU and then spent much of the summer interviewing at colleges up and down the East Coast. He felt fortunate to have been offered a position at three different community colleges, but ultimately this small town that most out-of-towners often confused with the nation's capital, was where he signed the dotted line. His brother flew in to help him move the belongings he had accumulated during six years at ECU, but his things didn't entirely fill the two-bedroom house he was renting near campus.

Once on campus, Nolan slid his front tire into a metal-framed bicycle rack near the building where he would be working and bent down to secure the lock he had recently picked up at the downtown bike shop. The employee who had helped him pick it out boasted that it was made of Kryptonite or made by Kryptonite or something like that. "Which means even Superman can't steal your bike," had been the climax of the guy's sales pitch. Kind of dorky, but it must have worked because Nolan now found himself affixing the U-lock around a shiny black pole.

The woman at the other end of the bike rack must not have picked out her equipment from the same shop because she'd been struggling with her lock ever since he had come rolling up with a backpack strapped over his shoulders.

"You need some help?" Nolan decided to offer, wiping his brow with his shirt sleeve as he spoke.

When she glanced up from bended knee, Nolan all of a sudden found himself temporarily trapped in the most beautiful set of eyes he had ever looked into. He felt lost in a moment that would undoubtedly become etched in his mind for all of eternity. His entire body felt flooded with a calm surge of emotions, and in some strange way, he felt like he had known this woman his whole life.

Emma Pate had never had a problem finding words, but as she stared upward at the stranger standing above her, she felt a connection as strong as the rusty old chain marking up the palms of her hands. It wasn't that she couldn't muster up a response, she just didn't feel the need to say anything as she watched him kneel down beside her and begin to offer a clean hand.

"You might not want to touch this thing," she finally warned, opening the palms of her hands so that he could see what he was about to get himself into as the links clanged on the blacktop.

Nolan picked up the chain and began to work at the knots she'd been working at herself for who knows how long. As he twisted, turned, and tugged he couldn't help but let his eyes dart in her direction as they chatted easily.

"I think this chain is older than me," Nolan teased. The lady hadn't seemed overly irritated by the problem at hand, but he figured he would offer up some comic relief anyway. In college, he had figured out that women liked a man with a good sense of humor.

"Ha, ha," she chuckled. "It was my dad's. The bike was, too."

Nolan took another glance at her bike and imagined it probably had more miles on it than the car he had left parked in his driveway. The yellowed white-wall tires, less than straight spokes, crooked iron basket in front of the handlebars, and rusty springs below the banana-shaped seat had all seen better days. On a positive note, the contraption had one of those nifty retro looks that had come back into style.

"It has character," he pointed out with a grin.

"That's the nice way of putting it," she replied.

"Hey, it got you here, right?"

Cliché, he knew, but not as cliché as if he had said the first thing that had popped into his mind: *I'm a nice guy*.

Smiling sideways, Emma shook her head.

Eventually, Nolan straightened the chain and held it in place as Emma clicked a padlock to connect two of the links.

"I don't think it is going anywhere now," he assured, letting go.

"Thank you," she offered. "By the way, my name is Emma." She paused, then added, "Emma Pate."

"I'm Nolan Lynch," he reciprocated. "I would be a gentleman and shake your hand, but we might both need to find a sink first," he suggested with a smile, wondering how any rust could possibly remain on the chain as he inspected the layers of orangey and blackish gunk covering his skin. The feel of grit on his hands made him think of how an auto mechanic's hands must feel all day.

"Oh, why not," she suggested anyway, letting her hand collapse into his before either of them could think twice about it. "I'm the one who started this, remember?"

Nolan wasn't sure who had started what, but he knew that something amazing had just happened. He imagined himself trying to explain this encounter to his brother, but he knew Norman wouldn't understand it. *Norman and Nolan*—he had heard their names paired together thousands of times over the years. It only made sense, though, because not only were they brothers but they'd been born on the same day, grown up wearing matching clothes, and done most everything else that twins do. Yet, they were different. Quite different in some people's eyes.

Nolan found himself wondering why he couldn't take his own eyes off Emma Pate, but he was more intrigued by the fact that she hadn't taken her eyes off him. He knew Norman would be more interested in the physical description of the woman now holding his rust-filled hand: Red hair. Striking eyes. Tanned skinned covering a body worth painting. Nolan noticed all of these things yet somehow he had also seen right past them as his mind suddenly recalled a Shakespeare quote: *The eyes are the window to your soul.* He had never seen as deeply into a person he didn't know as he had with Emma. Something on the inside appeared even more attractive than what was visible on the outside, which was somewhat difficult to fathom. He had instantly recognized that he liked her taste in clothing—a pair of leggings were covered by a simple gray dress with thin blue horizontal lines. He figured the two of them were close in age, although if he had to guess he would say she was a year or two older. His dad taught him never to ask a woman her age, and he knew if she were to ask him how old he thought she was he would guess a year or two in the other direction just to be safe. He found himself wondering if Emma Pate was an instructor or if she worked in administration. He was almost certain that she didn't work in his department since he'd been to several meetings since taking the position as a health and physical education instructor at BCCC. He'd spent some time exploring the campus and met a lot of the staff members. Most had been kind to him, except for Clay Bell, the instructor that had informed him of the staff bicycle rack, which in fact had been the only polite thing the guy had done for him. Every time Nolan had been around the man, he felt like a freshman in a fraternity.

"You're new here, aren't you?" Emma asked as they walked side by side toward one of the light-colored bricked buildings that dotted the campus.

Emma took note of all the students filing the sidewalks like ants marching with a purpose. The first few days of classes were always like this; most people were more concerned about figuring out where they were going than mingling with friends and hanging out in the courtyards. By this time next week, there would be groups clustered across the grassy areas taking in the sun and having fun in their own way. Some would have out their guitars, some skateboards, some books, and others wouldn't be here at all. The latter group would decide that college wasn't their cup of tea and they'd move on to the next thing in life. In a small town like Washington, good paying jobs were limited especially if you didn't have a college degree. A lot of the guys she'd known in high school became commercial fishermen—a relatively hard life but good money nonetheless. A lot of the girls became stay-at-home moms. Some of her friends took off and joined the military. She had never viewed any of these choices as right or wrong, just as choices.

Nolan wished he was still holding Emma's rusty hand, and he had made sure to glance at the other one to make sure she wasn't wearing a ring. He couldn't think of a better way to walk into his first day of being a college instructor than with a beautiful woman by his side.

"How could you tell that I'm new?" he wondered aloud, his brow slightly furrowed.

"I think I would have remembered you if I'd seen you before," she admitted.

Nolan smiled way more on the inside than he portrayed on the outside, but every woman he'd ever dated had told him he wore his emotions all over his sleeves, so Nolan was almost positive Emma could decipher he'd taken her comment as a compliment.

"The campus is relatively small, and I've been here long enough to recognize most of the people," she added.

His smile sunk a little as he held open the glass door and watched her walk through. When they reached the restrooms and headed for separate doors, Nolan wondered when he might see her again.

"It was nice to meet you, Emma," he made sure to express.

"Likewise," she said. She nearly pushed open the door but then decided to ask Nolan a question. Life hadn't been going her way lately, and she needed something good to happen. She missed her dad. Missed her routines. Missed the life she had known for so many years. "Nolan, would you like to have coffee with me?"

2

Nolan walked the halls for the first time with students buzzing around. The conversations amongst them all blended to make one loud constant hum that sounded something like the roar of the ocean. In a way, being in the midst of the flow of students felt no different than it had this time last year when he had been in their shoes, except now he could no longer get away with wearing flip-flops to class. He also had a new I.D. in his pocket that read *Faculty*, which somehow seemed to cause his shoulders to stand just a little taller. As a P.E. instructor, he could justify wearing a sleek pair of wind pants and a comfortable solid-colored Dri-Fit shirt with a collar—his outfit of choice for day one. Such attire kind of came with the territory. "The other instructors will be jealous that you don't have to dress up," the dean of his department had informed him the first time he'd given Nolan a walking tour of the campus. "I'm even a bit jealous," he added in the midst of a loud chuckle that vibrated his rather large belly. Wearing this outfit worked out well since Nolan had decided to ride his bicycle to school for the workout. If he were wearing dress pants and a suit coat, he would look more like a religious missionary, and he probably would have been sweating profusely. *Is it Mormons or Jehovah's Witnesses that ride around on bikes?* he found himself randomly contemplating. Maybe he would ask Clay if he ran into him today. That guy seemed to know everything about every topic that came up at meetings, and he talked way more than any one person needed to talk. His mouth was like a water faucet that someone had forgotten to turn off.

Inside his classroom, Nolan began to set out the contents as he pulled them from his book bag. He had spent a reasonable amount of time on his computer laying out the syllabus, and by now he almost knew it word for word. He'd settled in on the brown Italian leather couch in his living room for hours at a time the past few nights making sure he had every word memorized. He had no idea if the sofa was authentic Italian leather, but the lady who sold it to him for a mere fifty dollars swore it was the real deal. Honestly, it didn't matter all that much to him—it was comfortable, and it didn't have a foul odor. Furniture often had a way of telling about a person's story—whether they smoked, had pets, and so on. Nolan flipped through the pages of the outline he had prepared to discuss following his review of the syllabus with the students. All of this proved to be a bit intimidating, and he could feel the nervous tension rising in his blood as the pages dangled loosely from a staple in the upper left corner. Right now he was sitting alone in a classroom filled with empty desks, but within the next fifteen minutes there would be people occupying the seats and all of their eyes would be fixed on him.

Twirling a pen between his fingers, Nolan thought about Emma Pate. He still couldn't quite fathom the idea of her asking him out for coffee. It hadn't been the first time a girl had asked him out, but he still wondered how he had been so fortunate. His college buddies often told him they wished they had his nonchalant demeanor. They'd noticed that something about it seemed to drive women wild. He was the guy at the party that just had fun. It didn't matter to him whether he left with a woman or not; he would constantly tell all his friends that they were trying too hard and overthinking, and that females had a way of smelling fear in a man.

At the moment, Nolan found himself wanting to think of nothing other than Emma—relive their brief encounter and imagine how a conversation with her over coffee might play out—but he needed to focus. He needed to make sure he managed to get everything for the class set up as planned. *Set your mind on something else*, he thought to himself just like he used to advise his friends.

A blue dry erase marker—the scent as strong as perfume—soon squeaked across the whiteboard as Nolan wrote out a few notes that would apply to all four classes he would teach today. He would only cover the basics, he'd decided. The professors who jumped right into the action on the first day were the ones that had always driven him crazy in college, which is why Nolan made a pact with himself to never put his students through such torture. He also wouldn't give them homework today or ask them to stand up in front of everyone, state their name, their favorite food, their major, or some other mundane fact about their life. Chances were that absolutely no one would remember anyway.

As students began to trickle in, Nolan introduced himself to each one as they stepped through the doorframe. He knew he would rather mingle than to sit impassively at the metal podium at the head of the classroom. It somewhat caught him off guard that some of the students were twice his age, although he could tell that many were recent high school graduates. Some were talkative, others passive. Some were in shape, and some needed a new diet. Nolan himself wasn't in tip-top condition, at least not in relative perspective to which he had been during his baseball playing days as an ECU Pirate, but he had managed to fit in several workouts per week over the summer months. His sessions were simple compared to the rigorous training a college baseball player endures on pretty much a daily basis. As a pitcher, he hadn't lifted weights as much as some of the other position players, but he had done his fair share of toning in place of bulking. His strength and conditioning coach always stressed flexibility and range of motion, which meant stretching routines that the average person didn't even realize existed, and lots of cardio. The coaches didn't want the pitchers' chests being too tight, which sometimes aggravated Nolan and the other hurlers because they wanted to be able to bench press 315 pounds or more like the home run hitters. In the summer months when the college was on break, he would lift heavy anyway. Of course, the coaches always noticed the newly found bulk when he came back to Greenville in the fall, but to him, it was worth a brief scolding. Some of the other pitchers would choose the same path, so he was never the only one reprimanded, and the coaches mostly just told them to cut back and start getting ready for the season. What else could they do?

The workouts Nolan would implement in the classes he would teach would be simple compared to what he was accustomed to, but he knew it was all relative to the individual. He would have each student set goals of their own, and he would help them achieve the objective with a balanced plan. He hoped to introduce fun ways to be active and methods of keeping track of progress.

The first class of the day went well. Speaking in front of a room filled with strangers hadn't been as intimidating as Nolan had imagined. None of the students fell asleep, a handful asked essential questions, and the group even laughed at a few of his corny jokes. He led off with an icebreaker, a joke he'd made up a while back: "You've heard of the candy Junior Mints, right?" he asked rhetorically. "How come there isn't a candy named Senior Mints?" He then opened up the floor for guesses but only received blank stares. "Because no one would want to eat old candy!" he finally said with a snicker. Most of his friends had told him repetitively to stop telling this particular joke, but to him, the reason it was funny was that it was ridiculously silly.

Between classes, he wandered back out into the hallway where the roar of conversations was bouncing off the walls. He wondered briefly what other instructors did between classes. Some probably went to their office, he assumed, while others remained in their classrooms, and the social butterflies most likely roamed the hallways. Nolan didn't fit the latter category, but he had always been able to create casual conversation.

If he kept tilting his head back for swigs out of the bottle of water he'd brought along for the day, at the current pace, he would end up having to visit the restroom between each class. He went ahead and took care of that this time around so that he wouldn't feel the need to excuse himself in the middle of a lecture. That would be embarrassing, which he knew firsthand because it had happened to him during a student-teaching assignment. He'd recently cut out the consumption of caffeinated beverages altogether and planned to strictly drink water. Of course, he would have cheat days now and then, but he doubted he would have much difficulty sticking with this new routine. He'd never been one to be addicted to anything. He'd smoked one pack of cigarettes when he was sixteen, thought it made him look cool as he cruised the roads with his car windows down, but then remembered the torment his uncle had gone through as he slowly died of lung cancer. That's when Nolan decided cancer sticks weren't his thing. In college, he'd passed around a few joints at frat parties but eventually concluded that the mellow feeling wasn't worth the risk of getting kicked off the baseball team. Needless to say, the stench both habits left in their tracks was awful. He liked the taste of some beer, but he wasn't one of those men that felt like he needed one in his hand the whole weekend.

Class number two went much like the one prior. Not many students displayed a willingness to share their personalities this early in the semester, but one middle-aged man did take a stab at the answer to the candy joke. "Dale Earnhardt, Sr. wouldn't promote the candy, so the company asked Dale Earnhardt, Jr. to be their spokesperson," he expressed in one of the thickest Southern drawls Nolan had ever heard. Figuring that to be an answer one would only offer in this part of the country, Nolan laughed respectfully. People in the area loved NASCAR, and the diehard fans figured everything in life had some connection to the sport. The answer reminded Nolan of the race he'd attended in Darlington as a youngster. It amazed him when the speed of the cars coming around the turn near his family's seats caused his hair to blow as if a gust of wind had just swept across the asphalt and through the chain linked fence. The roar of the engines sounded a lot like thunder, too.

After dismissing class, Nolan headed to his office to file paperwork. On his way through the community area—relegated to the instructors in his department—he discovered a few random documents tucked in his inbox, but nothing of real importance. He checked the phone on his desk for messages only to find that not a single one awaited his attention. Nolan had brought a lunch from home but had yet to decide whether he'd eat in his office, outside at one of the picnic tables in the commons area, or in the campus cafeteria. He had no idea what to expect of the food there and he didn't know how many healthy options they would have, so he had chosen the safe route: a turkey sandwich, an apple, and a granola bar.

Across campus, Emma Pate headed for the cafeteria with a small lunch bag draped across her shoulder. Her classes had gone well this morning, but she was nonetheless excited about a break in the midst of what she knew was going to be a long day. So far Emma had worked through the familiar first day routines: mingling with students, talking with instructors, and thumbing through the syllabus of each class. The drill was always the same even though she'd only been at the college for a few years. To her, it was fascinating how quickly the new wore off of most everything in life. She could vividly remember her first day here and how she had wondered if she would ever make it in this world, but this was supposed to be her ticket to leave behind the restaurant where she had been waiting tables since high school. "Don't become a teacher," her father had warned her when she sought out his guidance on what major to select in college. "Teachers often have to hold a second job just to make ends meet." A sad fact yet often accurate which is why she had initially chosen psychology as her major, but a few classes into the program she decided that trying to figure people out wasn't in the cards for her. Her dad had also raised her to be independent and not to depend on a man or anyone else to take care of her, especially financially.

She had plans to get out of this place, to move on to something bigger and better, most likely a university which would provide more opportunities. However, when her father passed away this past winter, it felt as though a wrench had unscrewed every plan she had ever imagined possible and now she had no idea what would happen next in her life. She had been taking care of him for years and she had known that one day his liver would completely shut down, but all the mental preparation in the world hadn't been enough to buffer the pain of burying her dad alone. Her mother had never been around; she'd abandoned her family before Emma smashed her face into her first birthday cake. Her dad had told her the story about the cake-dive a hundred times—before he could even light the candle and start singing the words to *Happy Birthday*, Emma had chocolate icing dripping from her chin. Her dad had never remarried, so she didn't have any brothers or sisters.

Emma met her best friend Lisa at one of the outdoor tables under the oak trees where they ate lunch and chatted about Nolan. Emma found herself hoping he would happen to walk by so she could introduce him to Lisa. Instead, Lisa had to paint a picture in her mind as Emma described him one word at a time, adding emphasis to his desirable qualities. "Handsome. Lean. Toned. Helpful. Funny. Single." Emma smiled big and Lisa, holding a sandwich, giggled. "Oh, and mesmerizing green eyes," Emma added.

When the time came for Emma to leave campus, she noticed Nolan's bicycle still parked in the same slot. She unfastened the lock holding her front tire in place, set the chain in the basket, and pedaled toward home.

3

Nolan had ventured downtown quite regularly over the summer, often riding his bicycle from his house in the Washington Park residential district which was a little less than two miles away. Most days he took the scenic route along the streets that paralleled the Pamlico River. The stroll through his neighborhood included towering pine trees and narrow one-lane roads divided by a patch of grass and well-manicured shrubbery.

This afternoon he opted to drive rather than pedal since this would be his first date with Emma Pate. Thinking about how that thought rhymed, he smiled on the inside as his tires came to a halt in a small gravel parking lot. This morning when Emma had asked if he would like to meet at Coffee Caboose, he immediately knew the spot although he had never actually visited the place. He had asked what time she would finish with classes for the day, and when they figured out that their schedules matched up reasonably well, they set a time. Now, Nolan found himself walking up to a long, narrow building—the wood exterior painted red to mimic an actual caboose, and it even featured a charming little brick chimney on one side.

Nolan made sure to arrive early so that Emma wouldn't end up being the one waiting for him. A quick peek inside the squeaky front door confirmed that she had yet to arrive, so he parked himself on the wooden bench out front. An array of chalkboards made up the décor on the front exterior wall of the shop, detailing things such as hours of operation, specialty drinks, and other menu items. He studied the selection, not yet sure what he would order.

After sitting for a few minutes, enjoying the breeze and the simple sounds of downtown life in a small community, Nolan watched Emma's bike roll to a stop on the sidewalk beyond his flip-flops.

"Do you ride that thing everywhere, Lance Armstrong?" Nolan teased, wishing he knew a female cyclist's name he could have tossed out instead. Maybe later he would google the idea and be better prepared for his next opportunity.

Emma laughed. "Aren't you the comedian?" she asked rhetorically.

"Corny comes naturally," he admitted. Emma laughed again. "If I had known you were going to ride your bike I would have ridden mine, too." Nolan imagined a bike ride around the downtown streets after coffee would have been an excellent option to suggest.

"Maybe next time," she replied, pushing her bicycle to the rack on the chimney side of the coffee shop as if she had done so a hundred times in her life. "Before we go inside, I need to warn you of something," she mentioned.

Nolan felt his brow furrow, wondering what might come next. "Oh, yeah?" he uttered slowly, waiting for her to enlighten him.

"I'm a professional coffee drinker," she offered somewhat proudly.

He flashed a smile. "I will buy as many cups of coffee as you can drink," he offered with a smirk.

Another laugh echoed beneath the awning above their heads. Nolan liked her laugh. A lot.

"Professional in quality, not quantity," she explained further.

"Well then, since we are giving warnings, I have a confession to make."

This time a wrinkle formed on Emma's brow. "Yes . . . ?"

"I am not a coffee drinker," he admitted.

"Then I can't date you," she fired back immediately, stretching out a grin to ensure him that she was merely kidding, yet surprised. *Who doesn't like coffee?* She decided to keep the thought to herself.

Nolan responded with his own witty banter. "Who said this is a date?"

"Me," she said simply and convincingly.

He shrugged his shoulders. "I'm good with that," he responded nonchalantly, finding the assertive part of Emma's personality attractive. He had first noticed it this morning when she shook his hand and introduced herself. Then, of course, she had been the one to suggest coffee.

Once inside, they placed an order at a relatively tall counter and made their way over to a set of bar stools to wait for their beverages. One of the first things Emma said when they nestled in was, "I can't believe you ordered green tea."

"Green tea is delicious and relatively healthy."

"Yeah, but this is a coffee shop."

"A coffee shop with green tea on their menu," he pointed out.

"Water is on the menu as well, but who orders water at a coffee shop?" she quizzed.

"I've ordered water from a coffee shop," he countered.

Emma didn't hide her surprise. "Really?"

"Sure. No law states you have to consume caffeine in a coffee shop," he joked. "Plus, I bet my tea will taste better than your coffee," he offered.

"I doubt it. The coffee here is amazing."

Nolan had to admit that even though he didn't care for the taste of coffee, he did find the coffee aroma, floating heavily in the shop, quite refreshing.

"I think I'll tell the owner that you said her green tea isn't good."

"That's not what I said." Emma paused for a moment. "And do you even know the owner?"

"Nope, this is my first time here, but she's probably the woman making our drinks."

"Wrong. That's not the owner. And if you've never been here then that means you've never had green tea from here either," she said, emphasizing the word *green.*

"True, but I guarantee you I'll like it better than I would the coffee." Nolan liked how the two of them were having fun debating this topic that in the grand scheme of things didn't mean a hill of beans.

Emma pressed her lips tightly together. "I fear this is going to be our last date," she said with a flirtatious grin.

"What are you doing this Friday?" Nolan asked.

"I'm not sure, why?"

"We need to plan our second date," he said with a smirk.

Emma snickered. "You're too funny, mister."

"You already used that line earlier," he pointed out with a grin on his face.

"You're wrong—again. Earlier, I said 'Aren't you the comedian.'"

"I think the word 'just' was sandwiched in there as well," he zinged.

There was no telling what the next things out of Nolan's and Emma's mouths might have been if the barista hadn't interrupted the conversation by delivering Emma's coffee along with a napkin and a wooden stirring stick. Emma held the cup—warm to her fingers—near her lips to test the smell and temperature before taking a swig. A few moments later the barista handed Nolan a fresh cup of green tea and asked if they needed anything else. When they acknowledged that they were all set, she made herself busy again. Following a steady stream of casual banter and a few sips from their respective beverages, Nolan mentioned the idea of moving their date to the outdoor tables. Emma found the idea quite pleasant, and she followed him out the front door.

The weather outside was nearly perfect, and even though Emma had primped a bit for the occasion—applying a thin layer of makeup and painting her fingernails—she wouldn't have to worry about the wind whipping her hair around since she had put it into a ponytail before hopping on her bicycle to head here. She was pleasantly surprised when Nolan pulled out a chair for her at one of only a few tables nestled between the coffee shop and a weathered wooden fence that surrounded the front lawn of a small apartment next door. Their conversation outdoors seemed to flow just as smoothly as the one they'd enjoyed indoors. "How long have you lived here?" Nolan queried.

"All of my life," Emma answered.

His eyebrows raised at her response. "Really?"

Emma nodded her head but didn't elaborate. "How about you?"

"I moved here earlier this summer."

"Where from?"

"Greenville."

Emma was somewhat surprised to hear that he'd moved here from Greenville since most of the time it happened the other way around. Young adults were eager to leave small towns like the one she'd grown up in and head to the bigger cities. Greenville's population didn't rival Raleigh's or Charlotte's, where many of her friends had moved for college and to start careers, but it was the closest city that offered a nightlife, decent shopping, and a wide variety of chain restaurants. It was typical for her to venture in that direction once a month or so, usually with a group of girlfriends, but sometimes she'd go alone just to get away.

"What made you choose to move to Washington?"

Nolan swallowed a sip of tea. "I like the idea of living in a place where I can actually enjoy a drive through town rather than sitting in traffic while pedestrians walk at a faster pace than my vehicle moves."

Greenville traffic wasn't really like that, Emma thought quietly, except for on Saturdays during football season. The Pirates had drawn large crowds for as long as she could remember. She'd grown up watching massive players in purple and gold uniforms roam the turf, and had always assumed she would go to college at ECU. "You should be safe here," she acknowledged.

Only a few cars passed by the Coffee Caboose as Emma and Nolan chatted between sips of their beverages about things such as the differences of life in small towns and large cities.

"Did you grow up in Greenville?" Emma eventually asked.

"No, I didn't."

She waited a moment to see if Nolan would elaborate, but when he didn't, she figured she might as well dig a little deeper as he absent-mindedly pushed the condensation down his cup with his thumb. "Where are you from originally?" she inquired.

"A big city," Nolan remarked with a smirk.

"Which one?" She'd been trying to figure out his accent since this morning. She'd told Lisa that he definitely wasn't from up north. Plenty of people from New York and Connecticut and everywhere else up the Eastern seaboard had sold their homes and retired to little towns all over the south including Washington, and she could pick out a Northern accent as quickly as she could the taste that nominal coffee left on her tongue.

"Phoenix," he replied.

Now it made sense why his accent was difficult to pinpoint; he was from Arizona. As she asked a few more background questions and listened to him talk about growing up there, she could hear a mixture of dialects—a little bit of Texas mixed with a dash of California.

"Do you go back home often?"

"Not much."

"How come?" she wondered aloud.

"I don't have many reasons to," he admitted.

Emma kind of felt like she was prying, but her dad had always taught her that the only way to get to know a person was to ask questions, especially the difficult ones—the ones that most people skate around.

Nolan shifted in his seat, wondering why she wanted to know so much about his past but trying not to come across as closed off. He tended to live a private life, keep things to himself until someone he had come to trust needed to know something in particular. There weren't many people he'd let get close to him since he'd moved off for college. None, actually.

"What about your parents?" Emma asked. "Do they live in Phoenix?" As the question rattled off her tongue, she found herself hoping that his parents were still living. But how else would she find out? It wasn't like new people she met frequently asked her if her dad was dead. That would just be weird.

"Yes, but we're not that close." Nolan hoped that answer would close the door to this conversation for now. He didn't like to talk about his parents. It brought up other subjects . . . ones that he didn't care to discuss with anyone.

"I'm sorry to hear that," Emma answered sincerely. She wanted to ask more questions, but she could tell that he was starting to shut down and she knew when to leave well enough alone. He would reveal more when he felt comfortable, Emma figured, and until then she knew she would probably find herself thinking of all kinds of reasons why a person wouldn't want to see his parents. She would give anything for one more day with her dad, one more cup of coffee with him—like the one she'd been sipping on as she caught the first glimpse of something less than a perfect life in Nolan Lynch.

4

As Emma and Nolan discovered the bottoms of their cups, Emma found a way to use her spunky personality to help Nolan swim out of the deep end where she seemed to have inadvertently pushed him. First, she turned the theoretical spotlight in her direction and shared a personal vulnerability by admitting that she didn't have a relationship with her mother. The circumstances, Emma assumed, were different, but she felt like the gesture would express some common ground. She chose not to linger on the subject but instead offered to ride on the handlebars of her bicycle if Nolan felt strong enough to pedal them both around to some places she wanted to show him.

Nolan thought about asking if she would rather hop in his car, but he sure as heck wasn't going to turn down a challenge he knew he could handle. He had been building his calf muscles all summer long, which Emma noticed as he nestled in on the seat and asked her to climb aboard.

"Have you done this before?" she checked.

"Not in flip-flops," he admitted.

"Oh, my," Emma exclaimed as she stepped to the front of the bike. Facing the same direction as Nolan, she reached her arms back to find the handlebars so she could pull herself up onto them using her hands.

Nolan couldn't help but notice specific curves as Emma straddled the front tire. He held on tightly to the handlebar grips as she lunged like a gymnast on a balance beam over the basket and onto the metal frame between his thumbs. In order to keep the bicycle steady, he couldn't help but let her thighs settle onto the inner edges of his hands, sending a sudden surge of adrenaline through the rest of his body. It felt like that moment when you sit beside a girl in a dark movie theater, and your hand touches her hand for the very first time.

Nolan soon realized that the cliché saying *It's like riding a bicycle* also applied to riding a bike with someone sitting on the handlebars. As soon as Emma settled in, he leaned toward her from the standing position he'd assumed to steady the wheel. Then Nolan pushed off the sidewalk with his right foot, exerting pressure on the left pedal with the opposite foot. He expected that his feet might slip due to his choice of footwear, but surprisingly they glided off without a glitch.

Emma let out a screech made up of excitement and anxiousness as they began to roll and then pick up speed. She was smiling even though Nolan couldn't see her face, and she couldn't help but wonder what his face looked like and what he was thinking at the moment. Emma could feel his hands pressed against her body, the muscles on them clinched to balance the two-wheeled vehicle. She hadn't even thought about such a thing happening, yet under the circumstances, it didn't seem awkward. She asked him to steer them toward the river, and in a matter of moments, the bike was bouncing slightly on a bricked sidewalk where only a black metal fence separated them from small waves slapping against rocks and a concrete barrier. Emma pointed out the old train trestle to their left which stretched across to the opposite shore. The track featured a rotating bridge that could open to let boats cross through.

Since moving here, Nolan had yet to see a train cross the tracks in that spot, and he wondered if the railway was even still in use. He was about to ask when Emma made a wisecrack about his driving abilities, and just before turning slightly right to follow the path, he threatened to stay straight, ram into the railing, and throw her overboard into the water. She shouted, "You better not," as if he actually meant what he had said, then she laughed at herself realizing how serious she sounded and how silly it must have looked when her grip tightened and her shoulders tensed. Nolan couldn't help but laugh out loud both at and with her.

Seagulls were swarming in the air, squalling and searching for food left behind in and around trashcans, and landing their webbed feet on the light poles and railing and wherever else the creatures desired. Emma thought about how delightful it must be to live the life of a bird—free to fly wherever it pleased and do whatever it wished. In a way, she actually felt like a bird in this very moment as a steady wind brushed against her face, and to be completely honest she had felt free ever since Nolan had begun to pedal. Even though he'd gone in every direction requested, he was in control, like a strong wind pushing a bird with or against its will. Sure, she could hop off anytime she wanted, but it felt nice to give up control and let someone else do the work since her legs had pedaled more miles on this bike than she cared to admit.

Nolan maneuvered around pedestrians, and most of them smiled as their paths crossed. He imagined that the older folks found it cute to see a couple of young adults having fun in a way that they most likely enjoyed when they were young, when life moved at a slower pace, especially in Little Washington. He figured many of the people they came across were tourists and would end up in one of the waterfront restaurants in the historic buildings to their right. Between the water and the buildings, there was a grassy area, a street, and a row of parking spaces. The ones here didn't have meters like the ones in Phoenix, though,

Nolan had recognized shortly after moving here. Parking pretty much everywhere downtown was free, and he liked that. No need to purchase a parking pass or carry coins in his cup holder.

Every so often Nolan and Emma would hear the sound of a splash made by a fish jumping in the river, but more than often they didn't catch a glimpse but only saw the after effect—small or large ripples depending on the size of the fish.

As Emma pointed out random things only privy to the locals, Nolan figured out how to slow down the bike by finding the perfect balance between pedaling slower and wiggling the front tire left to right so that he could hear her well enough to take in the story. Over the course of their time spent together today, he had noticed that Emma's normal tone leveled out a notch more emphatic than the average person's, which seemed to match her spunky personality. Thankfully, her voice by no means came across as overbearing. Loud people drove Nolan crazy, especially obnoxiously loud people. Emma didn't seem to fall into that category, though, he recognized as her strawberry hair swished back and forth every time he twisted the handlebars.

"That boat right there," Emma motioned, referring to an old sailboat docked at one of the slips protruding out into the river, "never moves from that spot."

Each of the wooden docks around the boat slips only held a handful of vessels. The floating structures took on the shape of the letter *I* from Nolan's and Emma's vantage point, but probably more closely resembled the letter *H* to the folks in the yellow helicopter flying parallel with the river. Nolan had heard the steady rhythm of the aircraft off in the distance a minute or so ago, even before he'd been able to spot the object against the blue sky background. He and Emma had been watching it and chatting about it ever since. Eventually, it slowed down and ended up hovering almost directly above their heads, the force from the blades creating enough downdraft to cause their clothes to flap.

The effects were visible on the water, too, as the wind forced it to ripple.

"That looks fun," Nolan mentioned, but he immediately realized Emma couldn't hear him. A moment later she turned her head just far enough for him to study the side profile of her face, and he could see her lips moving, but couldn't pick up any sound whatsoever. Earlier he had caught a glimpse of a freckle on her nose that at first sight resembled a tiny nose ring. It was cute, he'd decided immediately, and that thought crossed his mind once again as he spent the next few deafening moments reveling in the beauty of her perfect imperfections. He didn't yet feel comfortable saying anything about that particular feature, but he hoped that once he did, she would take it as a compliment.

As the helicopter continued to linger in the air over the downtown waterfront area, Emma motioned toward the ground. She had figured out that Nolan could no longer hear her and she hoped he would be able to interpret her implied sign language.

When Emma pounced off the front of the bike, Nolan felt the muscles in his arms tense up. He struggled momentarily to balance the frame in order to keep himself from falling onto the walkway in front of scores of strangers. People were scattered throughout the area, participating in various activities. A group of teenagers threw a Frisbee back and forth. A few couples were sitting close together on park benches. A handful of people were laying out in the grassy area, some reading books and others appearing asleep. There were also people jogging, hanging out on boats, and many merely standing around taking in the scenery: birds and water and boats and the helicopter that seemed to have temporarily silenced all communication at the waterfront.

Once Nolan brought the bicycle to a halt, Emma walked up close to him and raised her voice. "I couldn't hear a word you were saying," she confirmed in his ear. It had taken her a moment to catch her own balance, so she had missed the short show Nolan had put on behind the handlebars.

Nolan figured since most people had become focused on the helicopter only a few had seen his near mishap, but it didn't bother him all that much anyway. He just laughed at himself instead.

"Were you laughing at me?" Emma quizzically accused.

When Nolan explained his reason for laughing, she laughed with him and then went on to holler out why she had missed his humorous moment. He yelled out that he'd seen her from his peripheral vision but that he hadn't been able to take in her dramatic landing fully.

"I wish the helicopter would just land, too," Emma said.

Nolan laughed, realizing she'd actually heard what he said but instead of acknowledging such, Emma inserted a play on his words.

Shortly thereafter, the helicopter disappeared into the distance and Nolan asked Emma about the boat she had begun to talk about.

"I was just telling you about the old man that lives on the boat."

"I bet that was an interesting story," he said with a chuckle.

"I'll tell you on another day when we walk by or ride by or whatever," Emma promised, realizing the story wouldn't be as good since they'd traveled far enough where Nolan could no longer see the boat.

"Oh, so *now* you've decided you want to go on a second date?"

"Maybe," she teased, turning her shoulders where he couldn't see her blush.

When he had chartered the helicopter, he intended to map out several plots of land to add to his investment property portfolio. Years ago, he had started this real estate endeavor by purchasing a few run-down mobile homes at a ridiculously low price, fixing them up just enough to pass inspection, and then renting them for what at the time seemed like decent profits. Now he owned over three hundred acres of real estate in the area and was acquiring more on a consistent basis. The business was lucrative, and he loved the challenge of finding a piece of land or a building that he could develop. Lately, he had been focusing on and around the downtown area. The town had invested a good deal of money into sprucing up the waterfront and surrounding areas which boded well for his wallet.

Just today, he had located two plots of land on which he planned to place a low ball offer, but he had spotted something else that interested him even more. Actually, it did something other than interest him—it irritated him. That's why he'd had the pilot steady the helicopter over the boat slips and hover as low as possible so that he could get a better visual. He wished he had thought to use the camera on his phone to shoot video of all of the frustrated people down below which had been somewhat of a sideshow. Hats flying off heads, picnic blankets blowing like leaves in the fall, and even some pedestrians hurrying off as though they thought they were about to be bombed by a harmless little yellow helicopter. However, his attention had been on something else entirely—what was Emma Pate doing with that guy?

Nolan and Emma spent the next eight hours of life together, and the time flew by like a fighter jet rather than a yellow helicopter. They walked side by side for a while longer, Nolan pushing Emma's bike until they decided to hop on board for another adventurous ride. She showed him the famous Bill's Hot Dogs restaurant, and she couldn't believe that he hadn't eaten at the historical landmark since arriving in town. He mentioned that he'd heard of the place, and she said, "Yeah, pretty much everyone has. It's been here since 1928, and people from all over visit

Washington just to eat hot dogs." Nolan went on to explain that hot dogs didn't fit into his diet regimen and that he preferred eating healthy. This didn't surprise Emma because she had assumed as much as soon as he'd ordered green tea at the coffee shop. He did agree to eat a hot dog with her one day if she would try his zucchini pasta with grilled chicken. "Sure," Emma complied. She made sure to inform Nolan that she didn't sit around all day drinking coffee and eating hot dogs, which Nolan could see clearly by the size of her waist. She appeared to be just as fit as him, which helped in the attraction department.

As they carried on about food and diets, they wandered in and out of a variety of shops on Main Street. They passed under the colorful marquee that adorned the iconic Turnage Theater. At nighttime, the vibrant red, white, and blue sign attached to the historic building sparked flashbacks to an era in the history books. Inside one of the clothing stores, Nolan and Emma used their phones to take silly pictures of each other trying on hats and scarves and all types of accessories. An antique shop they visited had tons of old baseball cards which Nolan glanced through while Emma stood nearby admiring doll houses, reminding each of them of their respective childhoods. They tinkered with many of the old items, trying to figure out what some could have been used for, poking fun at others, and once again strolling memory lane as they came across familiar items such as Pepsi cans and Teenage Mutant Ninja Turtle figurines.

By the time they made it back to the coffee shop parking lot, Nolan had talked Emma into letting him squeeze her bicycle into the trunk of his car so he could give her a ride home. At first, he thought it might not fit but after some finagling, the two of them found a way to wedge it in without breaking anything.

Nolan found out that Emma's house was only a few miles from downtown. They crossed over a short bridge that led to River Road—the main road that bordered his subdivision—and passed by his usual right turn. The route was the same one that Nolan took when he headed to the college from home, and he was always amazed at how quickly the scenery changed from retail establishments and paved streets to cornfields and farmhouses. Emma lived down a dusty road where only a few other scattered houses nestled in amongst a variety of crops and clusters of ancient oak trees. She invited Nolan to sit with her on the porch as blue sky gave way to nighttime and eventually the only visible light came from distant porches and twinkling stars. He agreed to a sweet tea since Emma promised she made the best around and then he laughed when she offered to put something green in it—"like green beans or maybe even green grass," she teased. "I have plenty of both out here on the farm."

"It's absolutely breathtaking out here," Nolan said for what seemed like the tenth time. He couldn't quite get over the unhindered serenity of the atmosphere. Crickets chirping. Owls hooting. Fireflies floating loosely through the air.

Much of their conversation fell into the casual category, but at the same time, each of them felt like they were learning a lot about each other. Maybe not as much in the detail department, but more so about character and perspective on life and things that mattered. Ironically, work hadn't come up even one time the entire evening which surprised Nolan since they had met at the college. He kind of liked it that way. Work seemed to define way too many people these days. As an adult, he'd noticed how most often the first thing other adults asked when they first met was *What do you do for work?* Sure, it was an easy icebreaker question, but that was the problem with it—people didn't want to take the time to ask something with more meaning. Like *What do you enjoy most about life?* or *How do you spend your weekends?* Such questions sparked much more meaningful conversations than finding out the person in front of you is named Bob, and he's been a banker for fifteen years, and then listening to him ramble about one of two things: how much money he makes or a career he wished had been something else. Sometimes both.

"I'm fortunate to have lived here my entire life," Emma responded. There had been a time when she wanted to leave Washington, but when her dad passed everything changed.

Nolan picked up on something in how she'd spoken the words, a particular sadness on which he couldn't quite put a finger. He figured that maybe she would elaborate at some point, but he wasn't going to ask any questions about it now. Instead, he asked, "What do you enjoy doing on the weekends?"

Emma smirked. "Well, what I do on the weekends and what I enjoy doing on the weekends are two *entirely* different things."

Nolan's eyebrows lifted. "How come?"

"I work a lot on the weekends," she explained.

Well, I was wrong this time, Nolan thought to himself—what he considered to be a meaningful question had still led back to the topic of work. He almost laughed out loud at her answer but was able to pinch his insides to hold in his amusement.

"That doesn't sound fun," he pointed out.

"Nope, not really, but a girl's gotta do what a girl's gotta do."

"True," he agreed, a hint of a laugh escaping through his nostrils.

Many educators, even at the college level, spent a good part of their nights and weekends grading papers, planning lessons, and working on the overwhelming amount of mundane paperwork that had become a part of life in this field. Nolan imagined that Emma most likely poured her heart and soul into teaching just like the vast majority of teachers tend to do. Most didn't take on such a position for the money because the money just wasn't that great. Especially in North Carolina. Thankfully salaries had been on the rise but at one point in the not so far past teacher's income in the state had been very near to the bottom in the United States. Of course, it was inevitable that some states had to be at the bottom of the barrel, but as a teacher you never wanted one of those to be your state. Many of the community colleges had cut way back on hiring full-time instructors and were now paying adjunct instructors to teach classes at a fraction of the pay with no benefits. It saved the institution substantial funds on the front end, but the flip side is that it essentially lowered the quality of the education. Most of the people who took these part-time jobs did so for extra spending cash or to add a nice blurb to their resume. Their primary focus was on their real career and truth be told most didn't have the needed time to devote to students.

"What work do you find yourself doing on the weekends?" he asked even though he was pretty sure he knew the answer.

"The work I do isn't anything to write home about, but it helps pay the bills—I wait tables at Central Pork."

Nolan quickly realized her answer wasn't at all what he had expected. Not that it was all that surprising for a teacher to have a part-time job but for some reason, it just caught him off guard. The way she said it was as though she was embarrassed about being a waitress. As she spoke, her eyes had ventured to the wooden plank boards at their feet, and her voice had resembled their thin stature.

"A job is a job," Nolan said matter-of-factly. "I think people often get too caught up in what they do for work and they let it define them rather than just letting who they are speak for itself." He'd heard positive things about Central Pork, like not to let the name fool you, but he hadn't eaten there.

Emma appreciated the words he'd just spoken and even more so the way in which he had said them. She had already noticed that Nolan had a way of making her feel better about herself. Not because her self-esteem was running low, but it was always encouraging to hear a positive spin. The last man she'd dated seemed to spin everything in the opposite direction. He was a decent guy beneath the surface, but his outlook on people was so negative. He was more concerned about how much money people made and how well they dressed than with who they were on the inside.

"I'm a people person, so I enjoy being a waitress most of the time; I'd just rather be doing something else if you know what I mean."

Nolan nodded in an understanding fashion.

"I bet you have a lot of great stories."

Emma intentionally lifted her eyebrows. "I have plenty," she said wearing a half-smile before pausing as if thinking through a mental queue of memories. "Some hilarious ones. Some embarrassing ones. Some crazy ones. Even some sad ones."

"You'll have to tell me some of those stories sometime."

"I would love to," she agreed.

Nolan and Emma talked on the porch until well past midnight. She never invited him inside—which with most women would have bothered him—but for some odd reason, he didn't seem to mind at all. He didn't attempt to kiss her goodnight or get all touchy-feely with her as they sat only a few feet apart in white rocking chairs. Somehow everything seemed just right, and he found himself wondering what tomorrow would bring for him and Emma Pate.

5

Tomorrow came way too soon. Technically, tomorrow had come while Nolan was at Emma's house last night, but he'd woken up in his own bed this morning to the alarm clock on his cell phone. He wanted to send it crashing through the window adjacent to his bed. That probably wouldn't be the best idea, though, since his cell phone served so many purposes. Not only was it his means of communication and his alarm clock, but it was also his camera, calendar, e-reader, GPS, flashlight, radio . . . the list could go on and on. He wasn't one of those individuals that couldn't function without his phone in his hand, but he often wondered how people had ever lived without such devices. Cell phones made life much easier in so many ways and saved people way more money than most realized. Many items were no longer necessary to purchase because of all the available apps.

Before Nolan had left Emma's house last night, he watched her plug his number into her contacts, and she was thoughtful enough to send him a text message right away so that he would also have her contact information. Then as soon as he pulled into his driveway he had taken the time to save her number on his phone just in case he somehow mistakenly deleted her message. He had never made that particular mistake before, but he had once lost a napkin on which a cute girl had written her name and number with lipstick. Nolan loved the sound of the name Emma Pate, and seeing it spelled out on his screen caused him to smile. He had wanted to call her on his way home last night to carry on their conversation, but ultimately he decided that would seem overbearing being as they'd just met and had only been on one date. She had asked him to text her when he arrived home so that she would know he made it there safely. "But not until your car is in park," she instructed. This request had come just after a conversation on texting and driving, and how much Emma despised people risking their lives, and others' lives, for mostly meaningless conversations. "I try not to even talk on my phone in the car anymore," she'd shared with him. He didn't concur nor debate with her about the talking part because he knew he was guilty of making phone calls while driving but he agreed with her about not texting while driving. The data on accidents caused by texting was staggering, and in his opinion, the selfish act was more stupid than drinking and driving. An idiot who chooses to drink and drive could at least point to the alcohol as a reason for not thinking clearly, although there was no excuse for either choice. Occasionally, Nolan would shoot a quick text message while sitting at a red light, but he wasn't even sure if that was legal. Most likely it wasn't, but he hadn't taken the time to research it yet. *Maybe I should ask Emma; she might know the answer to that question*—this thought had entered his brain late last night as his mind wandered while the moon hovered across the otherwise dark sky. He had found himself replaying the evening in his head, and he couldn't seem to fall asleep to save his life. He was high on Emma Pate and her delicious southern sweet tea.

Wish I was still sitting with you on your front porch! I made it home. Hope to run into you on campus tomorrow. Sleep tight.

Emma reread the text message this morning—the same one she'd read more than once last night. Nolan Lynch had made quite an impression on her in such a short time. They hadn't made specific plans for a second date, but it didn't seem like they needed to—it just seemed inevitable that they'd see each other again. Somehow they were both comfortable with knowing that there was more to their meeting than a friendship. That's what first dates usually defined. Within a couple hours of being around someone new Emma could figure out if she would want a relationship, just a friendship, or if she wanted absolutely nothing to do with the guy. There had been a few over the course of the years that had fallen into the latter category, but most just seemed to turn out not to be who she was looking for, which brought up the age-old question that women liked to ask each other: *What are you looking for in a man?* Of course, she didn't have the answer to that, and neither did any honest woman she'd ever met. It was typical to list off the romance novel fantasies—tall, dark, and ruggedly handsome. Then there were the qualities everyone seemed to want in a relationship—someone honest, dependable, supportive, and kind. This list could travel to Paris and back, but to her, a list never did seem like an acceptable way to define a relationship. Chemistry was vitally important, and she had to admit she'd felt more chemistry with Nolan than with any man she'd ever met. The spark had begun at the bicycle rack and the flames had burned steadily throughout their evening together. Most of her friends made this same comment about each new guy they met, but she had always been a little more guarded with her own heart. Infatuation had never been her thing. She prided herself on recognizing the red flags rather than overlooking faults. Of course, she had missed some in previous relationships, or maybe more honestly, she had overlooked them in hopes of change. But let's face it, she thought to herself, most adults don't change. They are who they are, and you get what you get. People on the surface are often like rainbows, but underneath they're usually black and white.

Nolan. She couldn't get the man off her mind as she sipped on her morning coffee. Not that she wanted to, not at all. For the most part, he had come across as black and white, but there were some other colors that he used to guard himself with, she'd noticed, which wasn't necessarily a red flag. Most people weren't an open book and that typically was a good thing, especially in the beginning. She knew she wasn't an open book either, and she didn't want to be with a man that talked only about himself and shared his entire life story on the first date. With Nolan, she had purposefully avoided the topics of college and work for the most part. She hadn't wanted to ask him about work because she didn't want to take the chance of feeling even more like a loser. It was silly for her to even think this way, she knew that, but it didn't change the fact that she did. She wished her circumstances were different. She longed for the day when she no longer had to walk on eggshells around a difficult boss, who one week would yell at her for dropping a few chunks of ice from the icebox and the next would help her clean up an entire tray of hot food off the floor with a smile on his face as he helped her throw his profits into a black trash bag. She never knew what to expect from the short man with bulging biceps and yellowing teeth. Then there were the customers. Many nice ones, but the bad apples always seemed to stand out. There were the town drunks who wandered in and harassed her until her boss literally pushed them out the door. That, she always appreciated. Then there were men in suits who thought they'd literally earned the right to talk to a woman provocatively just because they assumed their wallet was thicker than her skin. She'd been pushed beyond her limits a few times and she'd stood up for herself, but it was different now that her daddy wasn't alive. Most people in town knew her father, knew he was an old-school farmer who had no problem dragging any man outback that belittled his only daughter. He'd done as much a time or two when she was a teenager. One of the men he'd bloodied up had called the police, but one of the nice things about living in a small town is that proper butt kickings were often overlooked, even appreciated. Women were expected to be treated with decency and respect in Little Washington, and when one wasn't, a respectable man would typically stand up for her. People from other parts of the country could complain about the South being behind times all they wanted, but Emma felt like they had it balanced out pretty well. Women here had all the same rights as women anywhere else. They could vote, they could join the military, and most of the time they were treated relatively equal when being interviewed for a job. The difference in this part of the country was that most men were still gentlemen, a quality that seemed to be becoming a lost art unfortunately. *Nolan* . . . Nolan who'd moved all the way to Eastern North Carolina from Arizona—maybe to distance himself from his parents—seemed like a real gentleman.

Nolan Lynch and Emma Pate spotted one another at precisely the same moment, and although their mouths weren't literally gaping open, each of them knew what the other was thinking. *There is no way this is happening. Absolutely no way.* How had this newfound realization not come up in conversation during all the hours they'd shared together yesterday?

Emma was the first to look away. She found herself staring down at the classroom floor where white blocks outlined with a fine black line and speckled with the same color dots became her focus. Suddenly, she felt like she might get sick to her stomach.

Nolan froze. He didn't know what to do or what to say. At the moment he knew he couldn't say anything. Not here, not now. It wasn't the right place. He had imagined seeing Emma today at the college, but he hadn't imagined finding her sitting in his classroom amongst a class full of students with a book bag at her feet and the textbook he'd handpicked for his students on her desk. He wasn't even sure how he'd spotted the thin blue covered book from his stool nestled behind the podium where he'd been sitting for less than a minute now. Today most of the students had beaten him to the classroom, only because he had lingered in the halls throughout campus hoping to cross paths with Emma Pate. Now, he wanted to think that she had ventured into his classroom just to say hello, that she'd merely sat at one of the desks amongst the students to see how long it would take him to notice her. However, this wasn't the case. His gut was shouting this to him, and he suddenly felt a feeling he didn't like—fear.

Emma's mind raced back to the moment she had met Nolan. She had been leaning down next to her bicycle tire, her knee digging into the dirt beneath her from the pressure she'd been applying to that darn chain. In her peripheral vision, she had noticed someone coming her way, but she hadn't taken the time to look up because she was too focused at that moment. Then Nolan had spoken to her, and she had glanced upward. He was handsome, that was the first thing she had noticed. The next thing was that Nolan was wearing comfortable clothing, nothing like what a college instructor would wear. Not that the latter part of this thought had crossed her mind at that particular moment, but not for one instant had she ever assumed he might be an instructor. She'd simply thought he was a new student—he looked younger than her for God's sake.

Nolan considered asking Emma to meet him out in the hallway for a moment, but then allowed his better judgment to take charge of the urge to immediately figure out this calamity. The other students would wonder what such a request was about with it being their very first class of the semester. It wasn't like he could pretend to be talking to her about an assignment or some other student-teacher confidentiality issue. His second idea was that he could inconspicuously nod his head for her to follow him outside the opened door hoping no one else would notice the gesture. That was too risky as well, he quickly realized. His mind continued to wander various scenarios, even the idea of just walking out to see if she would follow, but ultimately he came to the conclusion that he would have to wait this out. As difficult as it would be, he would have to spend the next hour and a half trying to introduce himself and the class plan while at the same time attempting to figure out how in the world he'd ended up spending intimate moments with a student last night. Thank God he hadn't kissed her or . . . although he sure as heck had wanted to, especially when she'd abruptly wrapped her arms around his waist before he staggered down her front porch steps like a little puppy with weak knees. Emma Pate had given him a very memorable hug, as corny as that sounded. It was one of those things a man would never admit to one of his buddies, but last night he'd found himself longing for the next time he could slip his arms around her back and feel her body pressed ever so loosely against his own. He had spent the entire ride here on the phone with Norman, telling him all about Emma. As Nolan had expected, the first question out of his brother's mouth was, "Is she hot, bro?"

Emma just now realized that there was more going on inside the classroom than the dance between her and Nolan's eyes. She assumed he had probably been thinking the same thing as her: how could they find a way to talk about this without having to wait until the clock on the wall just beyond Nolan—her instructor, as ironic as that now seemed—circled a time and a half. Emma thought about walking out, maybe to a place nearby where Nolan could find her or perhaps even to fetch her bike at the rack where they'd first met. Then she would pedal home as quickly as possible, fall face down on her pillow, and scream.

Why had Emma parked her bicycle at the faculty bike rack if she wasn't a staff member? Nolan didn't understand that. Sure, students and staff weren't issued decals for their bicycles like the ones they were required to display on their vehicles, but it certainly would be beneficial to help avoid sticky situations like the one in which he now found himself webbed. Did she not think that a staff member would eventually realize a student was parking there? Did she think she could park there all semester and no one would notice? The racks had been nearly full, and her bike was probably taking up a spot that another instructor would have liked to occupy. Nolan suddenly halted this trail of thoughts, realizing how stupid the conversation in his head seemed when considered logically. Who would care if a student parked at the faculty bike rack? Not him. Well, not ordinarily. It would sound mighty ridiculous to walk into the campus security office and say, "I need to report a violation," then go on to bring up such a trifling issue. He would look like a tattletale in elementary school, not an instructor at a college.

Emma had questions for Nolan, and she could feel herself getting a little heated thinking through the scenario that had led the two of them into this very awkward situation. Why had he not brought up the fact that he was an instructor? They had spent the entire evening together after meeting yesterday, and that would have been a very helpful tidbit of information to know prior to walking into his classroom and feeling like a complete idiot. Secondly, had he known she was a student? If he had, then *he* was an idiot. The college had rules that forbid staff and students to date. Even hanging out one-on-one on campus, and especially off campus, was frowned upon for obvious reasons. Maybe he had assumed she was also an instructor. Emma hadn't mentioned that she was a student, but she *had* told him that she was a waitress. Why in the world would an instructor also have a job as a waitress? That made no sense at all. If she were an instructor, she wouldn't be behind on all of her bills. She wouldn't be afraid of losing her house and all the farmland her family had accumulated over the years, which she didn't need to think about right now. That made her want to cry even more than she already wanted to at the moment.

Nolan found it hard to be still as he addressed his students. Throughout the class time, he ventured back and forth in front of the board behind him, and he found himself turning slightly and glancing out of the corner of his eye to periodically check the clock. He tried not to make eye contact with Emma, but he couldn't help but look at her from time to time, especially when he opened up the floor for questions and comments from students. That was the only time when all eyes weren't on him. Emma, he had noticed, hadn't looked at him very much. When he would catch her looking his way, she quickly glanced back down at the unopened book on her desk. She hadn't taken any notes or asked a single question or responded to any of his questions. He'd almost decided not to encourage student participation, but then he had no idea how he would fill the allotted time frame. His joke about Junior Mints came across unconfidently, and no one even snickered. As he spoke, he found himself wondering if his face was a shade of red as deep as Emma's hair. Today, he definitely felt like a rookie teacher. A naïve one, too. One that hadn't even asked a person he'd met at the college whether her I.D. displayed the word *Student* or *Faculty*. No one had taught him that trick in college, although his ethics professor had warned of the dangers of getting personally involved with students.

Emma had barely heard a word that Nolan had spoken the entire time he'd been standing at the head of the classroom. She wanted to sink down into her chair and disappear every time she thought about sitting with him on her porch last night or riding on the handlebars while he pedaled the two of them along the riverbank. Emma couldn't even look at him without thinking about them being something they now couldn't be. When he told his joke about the candy, she found herself thinking how funny it might have sounded if he had shared it with her last night. She actually loved Junior Mints and always enjoyed having a box when she watched a movie at the theater. *Great*, she thought, now she would think of him every time she ate that candy. Or maybe she'd never eat another piece again, she considered. Right now she couldn't imagine eating anything at all; her stomach was still in knots even as the clock approached the one hour mark. She'd noticed Nolan glancing at it just as much as she had been, and in a way, she felt terrible for him since he was the one up there having to talk.

Nolan knew that no one would think anything of him for letting class out thirty minutes early, so as soon as the big and little hand met at the top of the clock, he dismissed the students. He inconspicuously watched as Emma took her time packing up her bag as some of the other students lingered in the classroom to chat amongst themselves. A few came up to him—two of them to suck up to the instructor and one to tell him about a job that might interfere with his class schedule at times.

When the last person in the classroom besides Nolan and Emma exited through the doorframe, Emma was the first to speak, and her voice wasn't nearly as low as Nolan would have preferred given the circumstances. "You are my instructor!" she exclaimed.

Nolan could feel his chest rising and falling. There were people in the hallway but by no means was it bustling with foot traffic, which meant anyone out there was within earshot of a conversation inside the classroom. *His* classroom. Protective mode instantly kicked into high gear, and he said nothing in response to Emma as he walked toward the doorway.

"You're just going to walk away?" she sounded, a notch louder than her first outburst.

With his back turned to her, Nolan felt his eyes close and his jaw clench as he tried to steady his breathing. He took three more steps and reached for the door, letting it latch before he turned to speak. When his body rotated, Nolan discovered Emma standing as still as a statue—her left knee kicked out, arms folded, book bag draped across her shoulders, and her gorgeous eyes staring a hole in him. "Hey, Emma, how are you?" he spoke in almost a whisper, hoping to calm the situation.

She squinted her eyes and allowed her face to express how dumbfounded she was by his choice of words. "Let's just skip the pleasantries," she suggested. "Just because you are the *teacher* and I'm the *student* doesn't mean that you are in control here; so don't treat me like a child by trying to settle me down with your psychological garbage," she huffed.

Nolan felt his eyebrows climbing up his forehead. In unison, his eyes bulged. He noticed how she'd made sure to emphasize the words *teacher* and *student*. "So you want me to raise my voice at you just because you raised your voice at me?" he said using a more normal tone this time.

"No, Nolan . . . or should I call you Professor Lynch?" she asked rhetorically without giving space for a response before continuing her rant. "That's not what I was inferring. What I'd prefer for you to do is not attempt to de-escalate this conundrum that you and I now face."

Without even realizing what he was doing, Nolan interrupted Emma, and his comment escaped quickly and with intensified volume. "You really think I don't realize this is a big deal?" he said, not eliciting a response. "My job is on the line here, Emma. This is my first real job, and on the first day of it I met a student, flirted with her, and went on a date with her that ended up at her house." He shook his head. "Your house," he clarified as if for some reason he needed to.

"Did you know I was a student?" she wanted to know.

"No. Absolutely not."

"Why didn't you ask?" she wondered aloud.

Nolan threw his hands in the air. "Probably the same reason why you didn't ask if I was an instructor. I just assumed you were a staff member."

"Why did you assume I was a staff member?"

"Because you parked your bicycle in the faculty bike rack."

"I did what?" she exclaimed, apparently confused by his comment.

"The bike rack where we met is for faculty only," he pointed out.

Emma sneered. "No, it's not."

Nolan wasn't sure how to respond.

Realizing he didn't know what to say next, Emma decided to clarify the issue. "There are no assigned bicycle racks for students or faculty. I've been parking my bike on that rack for years." She paused. "Are you serious about this whole bike rack thing or are you just trying to wiggle your way out of a sticky situation?"

"Yes, I'm serious," Nolan responded, openly embarrassed. "A staff member who noticed I sometimes rode my bicycle to the college told me about the faculty bike parking." As soon as Nolan made the last comment, he started backtracking in his mind, realizing which staff member had told him such, and now he began to feel stupid for more reasons than one. It appeared he'd fallen for that clown's shenanigans and this time it might end up costing him dearly. All Emma had to do was report him to his superiors, and he would probably lose his job. Even if Emma wasn't the type of person to do such a thing, anyone could have seen the two of them together downtown yesterday. News traveled fast in small towns. Heck, news even traveled quickly in big cities, a fact he'd learned the hard way. He wanted to think Emma wouldn't turn him in, but he could be wrong—he hadn't imagined she would lose her cool like she just had.

"Who told you that?" Emma wondered aloud.

"Clay Bell."

At the mention of Clay's name, Emma turned, walked to the door, twisted the handle, and hurried out into the hallway without saying another word.

6

As Emma had walked out of Nolan's classroom, he almost spat out the words *You're just going to walk away!* He decided at the last second that retaliating with the exact words she had thrown at him a few minutes earlier might only add insult to injury. This situation sucked, Nolan realized again, it really sucked. He liked Emma a lot, and he also liked his new job. Nolan knew he couldn't have both, and he knew the choice he had to make. However, it appeared as though Emma had made that decision for him, which now left him hoping that he wouldn't lose both his position at the college and his chance of getting to know Emma Pate.

Nolan gritted his teeth. He wanted to storm down to Clay Bell's office and punch the arrogance right off the clown's face. Up until now, the guy had just been a pain in the rear, but now it had become personal. Sure, Clay most likely hadn't imagined that tricking Nolan into thinking there was a *Faculty Only* bike parking area would lead to a situation like this, but it had.

Nolan spent fifteen minutes sitting in his small office trying to figure out what to do next. Maybe he should just take a step back and play the waiting game, he considered. That seemed logical, but he knew that route would be more mentally taxing than trying to unravel this scenario. *Why did Emma storm out like that?* He squinted his eyes as he wrestled with this question. Instinct had nudged Nolan to follow her, ask her more questions, and talk about the best way to handle this. Then he realized the last thing he needed was a scene in the hallway including a student with whom he'd crossed the boundaries.

On the desk in front of him, Nolan's computer screen had been glowing since he opened the browser window that now displayed the list of his classes along with the names of the enrolled students. He thought back to when he had read over the rosters before the semester had begun, but at that time the name Emma Pate had no reason to solicit a red flag. *Now* it sure as heck did. He found himself wishing that when she had first introduced herself at the bicycle rack her name would have triggered something in his memory. He couldn't beat himself up about that, though. There were nearly a hundred names on the lists combined, and to his knowledge, he had never met a single one of the students. If only he had glanced at the names this morning, Nolan thought momentarily; he knew he would have caught it then. This morning, though, he had slept in until the last possible minute because of staying up so late with Emma last night, and he ended up rushing to class. After following that train of thought for a moment, Nolan eventually realized that knowing this morning wouldn't have changed anything other than the fact that he could have possibly initiated a conversation with Emma well before she sat down in his classroom.

Next to the class roster, a second window framed Nolan's work email inbox. His opportunity to be proactive was now, he decided. It would be in his best interest to send an email to the dean even though he didn't want to. He felt hopeful that Jerry Small would appreciate him being upfront about what had happened between him and Emma. He hadn't had time to get to know the gentleman well enough to be confident in how he might handle the news, but so far Jerry had come across as calm, understanding, and helpful. Being honest seemed like the right thing to do, which is what Nolan's parents had always taught him. He recalled his mama instructing him on more than one occasion with words of wisdom. "I'd rather you be honest with me about a mistake you've made, Nolan, than try to cover it up with lies only for me to later find out you were hiding something," she'd say with curlers in her hair. At least that's how his memory pictured her in regard to that particular grouping of words. As a kid, sometimes he took his mama's advice and sometimes he didn't. His recollection of such events reminded him that he usually found himself in less trouble when following her advice, and when he did, he didn't lay in bed worrying either. He accepted his punishment, usually got mad at one or both of his parents for a little while even though *he* had made the mistake, and then life eventually moved on as if nothing had happened.

Nolan started and stopped typing the email to Jerry about five times. Now, he sat staring at the keyboard, unsure how to explain everything, and he found his fingers on the delete button more than the letter keys. Nothing sounded quite right. Finally, he decided that a conversation in person might be more appropriate even though he felt like the email would give him the opportunity to word things more accurately, which only made sense if he could figure out what he needed to say. Who knows what he might say when standing face-to-face with the dean, he considered. He might get nervous, might say something that he would later regret. He might even further incriminate himself somehow. However, if he decided on the email then the news would be in writing, and he assumed this situation would be more likely to be added to his file whereas a conversation might remain confidential. Maybe Jerry would keep it entirely off the record if nothing else came of it from Emma.

Great, Nolan thought, *I have no idea how to handle this.* He dialed Norman's number on his personal phone but ended up only hearing his brother's voicemail greeting. He chose not to leave a message as the wheels on his chair guided the seat below him all the way to the wall at his back. Then Nolan pushed out of it and headed for the closed door. Before shutting it behind him he made sure to sign out of his email account and close all of the windows on his computer. He doubted anyone would be snooping around in his office, but he didn't want to take any chances.

A few hallways with a couple of glass entranceway doors in between led Nolan to Jerry's office. He temporarily stared blankly at the closed solid door that he feared might lead to his dismissal. He seriously considered turning around and heading to his classroom where he would need to be shortly anyway to greet his next group of students. No need to glance over that roster since he hadn't had any other inappropriate relationships with potential students—Nolan made himself laugh at that thought. Instead of walking away, he raised his knuckles and knocked three times in a steady rhythm.

Emma tossed the last shirt from her dirty clothes laundry basket into what had to be one of the oldest functioning washing machines in America, and then shut the lid. Since leaving campus on her bicycle in a hurry, she had been attempting to keep her mind off this situation with Nolan by busying herself. So far she had made a sandwich and eaten half of it, swept and mopped the kitchen floor, and taken out the trash. These were the things Emma had planned on taking care of last night, but she had ended up spending the entire evening with Nolan. Now the realization of what all needed to be done around the house reminded her of why it hadn't been accomplished, which ultimately reminded her of him—the person she didn't want to think about right now.

As the tires on her bike had ground into the pavement earlier,

Emma had seriously thought about going back to talk to Nolan, but she kept convincing herself it wasn't the best idea. She didn't want him to get into any trouble with the college which is why she had just walked out in the first place. In hindsight, Emma knew she should have taken the time to explain that to him, but she didn't, and now assumed he was probably mad at her. She planned to just sweep all of this under the proverbial rug. Who knows, maybe once she graduated in the spring they could go on that second date. Until then, Emma would just treat their relationship like she always had with her other instructors. She would be professional about what had happened.

Upon returning the clothes bin to its proper place in the bathroom closet, Emma peeked at the clock on the wall which reminded her that she would need to finish up her chores soon so she could take a shower and make it to work on time. Her boss was a moving target when it came to punctuality. Sometimes an employee could show up thirty minutes late, and he wouldn't say a word; and then other times if one of them clocked in three minutes later than scheduled he'd flip a lid. One positive aspect of working tonight was knowing that waiting tables would keep her mind occupied. Tourist season wasn't technically in full swing now that most schools and colleges were back in session but retirees, especially folks from up North, pretty much streamed in and out of Washington year-round. Some came South in search of a quaint warm-weathered town where they could purchase a home for a fraction of the price for which they would sell their residence in places like New York while others were visiting time-shares or just touring the coast.

A few minutes before five o'clock, Emma inserted a paper time card into an old-fashioned time clock. Behind her boss's back, the employees often joked about how cheap he was when it came to improving the restaurant, especially when it involved technology. The establishment had only started accepting credit cards a few years ago, which she was confident had lost them a ton of business up until that point. These days you were more likely to hear someone ask "Do you accept cash?" than "Do you take cards?"

Emma's first customers of the evening ended up being an elderly couple visiting from Philadelphia who ironically paid with cash and left her a relatively sizeable tip. Menu prices at Central Pork—its name a play on words—were relatively steep. Doug, the owner, moved from New York after falling in love with Eastern North Carolina barbecue. His career to that point had been in the chain restaurant business, but his lifelong dream had been to open his own establishment. When he hired an employee or met a new customer, he would explain the concept of the name Central Pork. While living in New York City, he loved to take walks, run, and bike in Central Park, where he ended up meeting the love of his life. This, of course, had become another running joke amongst the staff, who had nicknamed his wife Central Pork. To Emma's knowledge, Doug didn't know anything about this, and she tried to steer clear of inconsiderate humor even on days when she was as mad as fire at the man. His wife was one of the sweetest ladies Emma had ever met, but even Emma had to admit that the two of them were an odd couple, to say the least. Doug was an exercise freak and his wife was a pleasantly plump woman with a boisterous voice. Emma often felt bad for her, not just because of her nickname at the restaurant but because it seemed her husband treated her the same way he handled his staff. Emma assumed that one day his wife felt like a queen and another day an ant—but not the queen ant.

Tonight, everything in the restaurant had been running smoothly, and Doug had been pleasant although his mood was subject to change without notice. The front door had opened and closed a hundred times which meant that the tables were full, and every time one emptied, the bus boys hustled to clean it so the next people on the waiting list could be seated.

"What do you recommend?" a guest who had just nestled in at one of the corner booths asked Emma.

"Everything on the menu is delicious," she responded—it was her go-to answer to this popular question. It also happened to be the truth. In addition to barbecue, the restaurant had become well known for a variety of dishes from seafood to steaks to pasta.

"What's your favorite item on the menu, Emma?" the gentleman's wife asked.

Emma had taken notice of the lady reading her nametag while she'd sat them. She always appreciated customers taking the time to care to know her name. The question the wife asked was another typical one, and Emma again responded out of familiarity. "When I am in the mood for seafood I often eat the shrimp and grits. All of our seafood is fresh catch," she touted, and she noticed the gentleman's eyebrows raise as she spoke. "If I want something a bit simpler, our bacon cheeseburger is about as juicy as fruit." Emma nearly laughed out loud as her mind caught up with the sound of the last comment that had exited her mouth. She often recommended the burger, but this was the first time she'd called it juicy fruit, which instantly caused an image of the chewing gum to pop into her mind, which for some odd reason made her think of Nolan's Junior Mints joke. It wasn't the first time Emma had thought of him tonight, and if she were honest, she would have to admit that she hadn't been herself the entire evening. She'd been making small mistakes and saying things she didn't normally say. As she was jotting down the couple's order, Doug suddenly appeared at the table and stood next to her.

"Emma, I need to talk to you when you finish up here."

The couple in the booth looked up at Doug with an expression that read *Who are you?* Emma hated when he did this. Why couldn't he just wait until she made her way into the kitchen, which would probably happen in less than two minutes? If the tables had been turned and she had interrupted Doug, he would have had a cow.

"Yes, sir," she answered with a forced smile.

Doug glanced at the patrons for the first time. "How are you folks tonight?" he asked, flashing his teeth.

Emma noticed the subtle difference in the tone of his voice when he addressed the customers. Whether or not the customers picked up on it, she always did.

The couple responded conventionally, and after a brief uncomfortable conversation, Doug disappeared. Emma finished taking their order, delivered the ticket to the chef, and then started searching for Doug who had said he would be in his office. Of course, he wasn't there, and now she had to decide whether to look for him or head back out to check on her other tables. With the mood shift she'd just recognized from her boss, she figured that whichever choice she made would most likely prove to be wrong. She asked a couple of coworkers in the kitchen if they'd seen him and received the usual answer. "He was just in here, and he went that way," one person said, pointing to the back door which led to the dumpster, employee parking lot, and a picnic table where employees often escaped for refuge. The other employee said, "Last time I saw him, he headed to the front of the house." Front of the house in the restaurant industry meant the area where the customers dined. Doug spent a lot of time out there, which typically proved to be good for business because most of the customers liked him—except for the ones who had witnessed him making a rear end out of himself.

Emma opted to focus on her tables while keeping an eye out for Doug as she refilled beverages, brought out plates, and entertained guests. Thankfully, all of her customers had been treating her well this evening, and she could feel the bulge in her apron starting to grow. One of her rules, though, was never to count her tips until the end of the evening. Once her shift ended she always transferred the cash to her purse, which during work hours remained locked up in a locker inside Doug's office.

Eventually, she brought out a plate of shrimp and grits along with a plate of barbecue to the couple from Philadelphia. As she'd checked in on them, they'd asked her a few questions about her boss's unusual behavior. As usual, she attempted to play it cool. Later in the evening, she found out that Doug had left to take dinner to his wife and may or may not be coming back to the restaurant tonight. He liked to leave his presence up in the air like that so the employees would be on their toes. Probably a good idea, Emma had always thought, but it would have been nice if he had told her he was leaving since she was the head waitress. This title basically meant she had way more responsibility than the other waitresses—including managing them and their ever wavering personalities—and that Emma got paid a dollar more an hour. It didn't afford her any benefits such as health insurance or retirement even though she was considered one of three of the restaurant's managers along with the head chef and the marketing guy named Alan. Alan also handled a customer service role including checking in on guests to make sure they were satisfied with their meal and service. He worked more hours than he got paid for and he constantly sucked up to Doug. Every night at closing Alan would offer to drive Emma home so she didn't have to ride her bike. At first, this seemed like a nice gesture, but on a few late nights and rainy nights when she had taken him up on his offers, she found out he wanted to do more than just take her home. She never felt to be in any harm in his presence, but he was touchy feely, and he often crossed the lines she had attempted to establish with him.

"Emma, you need some help with that?" Alan queried as Emma pulled her apron string while standing at her locker. The front doors of the restaurant had been locked nearly an hour ago, and she was looking forward to hopping on her bike and heading home. Most of the workers had left, and now the managers and a few others were tying up all the loose ends.

"No, thanks," Emma answered frankly.

Without flinching, Alan reeled out another line. "I've noticed that you seem a bit off-key tonight. Would you like a ride home? I'd be happy to take you, and maybe we could talk about anything that's on your mind."

"I'll be fine, Alan, but thanks for the offer."

He touched her shoulder and held his hand there until she shot her eyes in the direction of his fingers. Alan pulled it back slowly as if it hadn't bothered Emma one bit and continued with casual conversation until she walked out the back door. Thankfully, he wasn't the stalker type so he didn't follow her outside and harass her about the ride or her personal business. He was keen enough to realize she had something on her mind, but it was none of his concern. In fact, it was none of anyone's business, and she preferred to keep it that way.

When Emma climbed on her bicycle the first thing she did was pull her phone from her shoulder bag, which she called her purse. Then she checked to see if she had any new messages or missed calls. She would be lying if she pretended she didn't hope that Nolan had tried to contact her. Even when a lady gave a man the impression that she didn't want to hear from him, it still made her feel good inside if he reached out in a respectful manner. Her eyes lit up when she discovered a missed call, but then her brow furrowed when she clicked on it and saw the name of the contact. Why had *he* tried to call her?

7

Nolan had spent the daylight hours of Tuesday evening wandering around Little Washington. He pedaled his bike from his house to the downtown district, trying to keep his mind occupied. There, he sat on one of the park benches overlooking the river for more than an hour watching boats and people—some moving, some stagnant. Nolan thought about Emma, but he thought even more about his mom and dad. He wished he could call them, talk to them about his life—the good, the bad, and the in between. Nolan hadn't spoken to either of them since he left for college, and it was eating him alive although he had a hard time admitting it on most days. Through prayer, he had begged his mom for forgiveness, even his dad, but he never felt the burden of what had happened six years ago lift from his shoulders. When he made it back home as twilight turned into darkness, he found himself inside at the desk in his office with only a small lamp illuminating the hundreds of baseball cards that filled the plastic sleeves nestled inside an open heavy duty binder. His dad had bought or given him most of the cards in his collection. The ones he stored in this book were some of his favorites, but they weren't the valuable cards. Those he kept in single hard plastic cases locked up in a small safe under his bed.

He could still remember his twelfth birthday when his father sat down with him at their family's kitchen table and pulled out Yogi Berra and Jackie Robinson autographed rookie cards. He vividly remembered his dad asking, "If you didn't know these two men's names, who would you see when you look at these cards?" Nolan studied the cards for a moment, mesmerized because this was the first time his dad had ever shown him these two cards, which until that very moment were merely folklore. The two of them had been collecting together for as long as he could remember, and Nolan had always begged his dad to show him these hall-of-famers' cards. His dad would buy him cards for his birthday and Christmas and other special occasions, and Nolan would save his allowance so that when they went to the store he could get a new pack of cards.

His father had always been a philosophical man, and the answers he searched for were rarely the ones that seemed obvious. "I see two baseball players," Nolan replied that day. He watched a proud grin grow on his dad's face. "That's right, son. Many people would say I see a black man and a white man, which isn't necessarily wrong or right, but when a man chooses to see the color of the man before he sees the man himself, he displays ignorance." His dad often talked to him about race and how society needed to look past color and love one another unconditionally. His dad had taught him so much about life and baseball, and Nolan knew things that even most avid baseball fans didn't realize, like the fact that Moses Fleetwood Walker was the first African American man to play professional baseball way back in the 1880s.

Sitting below the light at his desk all these years later, Nolan realized that the thought of eye color had sparked this memory of his father. The day his dad had shown him those baseball cards he said something else very profound that had stuck with Nolan until this day. "A man's skin color is just a color, like the color of his eyes or his hair. It's okay to notice the differences between a black man and a white man or a man of any other color, just like it is okay to notice the difference between a person with blue eyes and a person with brown eyes. We all notice profiles every day, but our profiles are just visible characteristics, they don't define who we are. A man is who he is on the inside."

The ironic thing was that at this very moment Nolan couldn't even remember the color of Emma's eyes. Brown, maybe? Or were they blue? Heck, he couldn't even rule out green. It amazed him how he could feel so connected through that first look they shared yet not remember the color of the eyes that had mesmerized him. He smiled, knowing his dad would be proud.

Nolan realized he didn't know Emma well enough to know if she'd treat him as well as his mother had treated his father, but he knew he liked what he did know about her which made knowing that he couldn't date her even more difficult. In his twenty-four years of existence, no one had ever told him he couldn't date someone. However, when he'd signed the papers to become an instructor at the community college he'd understood that it was more than frowned upon for staff to date students. This rule made sense at the time, and even now in the mindset of rational thinking, but he still felt the desire to spend time alone with Emma Pate. Nolan had heard that men are attracted to women whose personalities remind them of their mother. He didn't know of this to be an accurate fact, but in the moment he found himself wondering what his biological mother was like. He wondered if she was decisive like the mother who'd raised him, and like Emma.

On Wednesday morning, Nolan went through the same motions he had gone through the first two days of classes. He ate breakfast at home, rode his bicycle to work, and parked at the rack where he had first met Emma. Nolan hoped to discover her dilapidated bike parked there again today, but to his dismay, neither it nor she was anywhere in sight. He figured she had probably driven her car or decided to park her bicycle elsewhere.

Maybe at the student bike rack, he whispered sarcastically to himself in an attempt to make light of the situation. He shook his head and walked straight to his classroom.

Throughout the day the only places Nolan moved between were his office and classroom. He didn't eat lunch in the cafeteria nor wander the hallways hoping to bump into Emma. The entire day he feared a visit from Jerry, but time passed by and eventually work came to a close.

That night Nolan stayed home and spent most of the evening looking through his baseball cards again and thinking more and more about his parents and his brother. Over the years he had found himself questioning everything. Why were his parents so proud of him? Why did they love him so much? How had they always treated him and Norman just the same? Thinking of Norman, he knew a call to his brother would probably help ease his mind.

Thursday rolled around, and Nolan found himself growing nervous as he waited for the students in his class—in which Emma was enrolled in—to fill the room. He had decided that it would be hard to keep his eyes off the most beautiful woman he'd ever met, but he was going to make it a point to treat her like every other student. As Nolan watched the students trickle in, he wondered why certain students sat at specific desks. He hadn't considered implementing a seating chart since this was college and he was teaching adults, even some that were older than him which still seemed kind of awkward. On day one, Nolan had informed his classes that they could sit wherever they preferred, and so far most of them had continued to sit in the same spot as they had on their first day. A psychology course he'd taken in college had taught him that humans crave structure for the most part, and he realized that was true as the desk where Emma Pate had sat on Tuesday remained empty for an hour and a half today as he outlined the workout plan for his students. Nolan allowed them to fill in their current status and the goals they wanted to achieve from taking his class. When he began visiting each individual at their desk he was amazed by some of the goals they set. One lady wanted to lose forty pounds during the four-month class. "It's doable," Nolan said in an encouraging tone, "but you'll definitely have to stick with a strict diet and exercise a lot outside the class." The student actually asked if she could read her goals out loud to the class which Nolan agreed to and in fact thought to be very courageous. Then he used her plan as a teaching moment by saying, "We will have to keep a close watch on the overall health of anyone who wants to lose a lot of weight quickly. A lot of people that lose weight fast do so in an unhealthy fashion. We will want to avoid that."

The way the college had allowed him to structure his class, the students would spend time exercising each day and—rather than sitting around in a classroom setting for any period of time—Nolan would do most all of his instruction as they worked out. He was both comfortable and confident with this plan. He knew there would be times that he would have the entire class pause their workouts for him to explain something, but for the most part, he wanted to work with students one-on-one. He also planned to pick out a few mentor students in each class that would be able to come alongside him to help some of their classmates who might not be accustomed to working out and eating healthy. He had already taken mental note of a few that might be a good fit—a young guy who'd played soccer through high school, a part-time yoga instructor, and a woman who on her first day of class had shared with everyone how much she loved to cook. People nowadays were so much more educated on which foods were healthy and which ones weren't so healthy than the adults were when Nolan was a kid. The flipside was that people now tended to allow meals to be determined more out of quickness than quality—which meant eating fast food too often when out and about, and when at home not investing their time in preparing a healthy meal. Cooking, it seemed, was becoming a lost art, which he found to be sad. One of the fondest memories Nolan had from childhood was when he and Norman would help their mama in the kitchen. She would grow fruits and vegetables in the backyard, and the three of them would frequently tend the gardens, and when the time came they would pick. Picking was Nolan's favorite because then he was able to help his mama cook the items they'd selected. There was nothing quite like watching your food from seed to kitchen. "Boys, you've got to find the silver lining in the cards that life deals you and your family. Our family's heritage includes working the fields, where they learned how to grow all the food a person could ever need to survive. They worked hard, and they've passed down these traditions through the years. Our ancestors worked for some good people and some bad people. They didn't always get treated fairly, but sometimes they did. We never live in the past, though, we learn from it and move forward with wisdom." At the time, Nolan had no idea his mother was talking about slavery. Now, he was old enough to know that some of his parent's ancestors had been slaves. He'd seen pictures of some of them throughout the years—of the grounds on which they'd lived and the fields they worked.

When Nolan dismissed class, he walked out of the building and toward the wooded area that paralleled the entire backside of the college grounds. Last night while he struggled to sleep he'd had a random idea about a project that included the woods, but it would include a lot of hard work and approval from the powers that be—which meant another trip to Jerry's office.

Emma had purposefully skipped Nolan's class today, and to be honest, she didn't know if she would be going back at all. It was a big decision because if she dropped the course it would make graduating in the spring, as planned, more difficult. Common sense had told her to just sign up for another elective, but upon an impromptu meeting with her advisor this morning she was reminded that health and physical education was a requirement for her degree program. "Is there another instructor that teaches the same course?" Emma inquired. This question elicited a contemplative stare from her advisor, and as soon as Emma recognized the look she wished she'd gone about this a different way.

"Is there an issue with Mr. Lynch?" her advisor queried.

Emma's mind churned as she attempted to think quickly on her feet. "No, not at all." She hoped her facial expression or tone didn't reveal the contradictory story. "The time of the class just isn't working well for me," she finally uttered.

"I see. Well, unfortunately for your case, Mr. Lynch is our one and only health and physical education instructor. So far I've heard nothing but great things about the gentleman. One of Mr. Lynch's students even told me that he was looking forward to a hands-on class where he could see immediate benefits. You know what, Emma, maybe I can move you to one of his other class times," she suggested, shifting her attention to the computer screen to search for that information.

Emma began to wiggle in the padded chair beneath her. "My work schedule is tight, and I'm so busy taking care of the house and the farm that I'm just not sure I have any other availability, but . . ." She held on to the rest of her thoughts, deciding to let her advisor share the times with her so she wouldn't suspect anything more than she probably already did.

The last thing Emma wanted to deal with was another suspicious person. The voicemail she'd listened to Tuesday night after work had freaked her out: "Emma, how have you been? I was just thinking about you, and I wanted to check in on you. I noticed your porch light was on late last night and I didn't recognize the car that left out of your driveway when I was sitting on my porch drinking a beer. By the way, you should come over for a cold one sometime. I'm sure that wouldn't be a big deal. We could just sit on the porch, something casual, you know."

Emma didn't like anyone being in her business, especially him. It just so happened that he was her closest neighbor—the porch light she could see from her own front porch. Thankfully neither of them could see the other's actual porch from their own. One of the things that bothered her was that she doubted he had called out of concern—he had called because he was prying into her social life. Like Alan, this guy wasn't a stalker or anyone to be worried about for reasons of physical harm, but he did hold certain things over her head. Things that made her not want him to find out who had been at her place Monday night. For now, no one needed to know that.

8

The next week sped by for the most part, mainly because Emma stayed busy with work and school and managing the farm. Ever since her father passed away, she hadn't worked in any of the fields nor hired employees of the farm to handle the crops. Instead, in the aftermath of funeral arrangements and in the midst of sleepless nights, she had made a poor emotional decision to let Clay Bell lease the fields to local farmers on her behalf. At the time it had sounded like the perfect plan. He promised to take care of every aspect including advertising the property, showing the fields to interested farmers, keeping an eye on the tenant's upkeep once the land rented, and collecting monthly payments. Honestly, from that standpoint, things had gone relatively well. All she'd had to do was fill out paperwork and approve the farmers that wanted to rent the land. Every single acre had become spoken for, and Clay had handled it all just like he said he would. Of course, he got his cut of the rent, but the fee was worth not having the hassle and pressure on her shoulders. Now, though, the stress came from dealing with Clay.

Just a few minutes ago, Clay had knocked on her door, but she hadn't invited him inside. Instead, she joined him on the front porch with a cup of coffee.

"Clay, I've asked you not to show up unannounced."

He glanced toward the tree line at the front of her property and pointed in that direction. "Emma, we're neighbors. That's what neighbors do; they stop by to say hello."

"Well, hello, Clay," she said bluntly. "What do you want now?"

Ever since Clay had left the message last Tuesday night while she was at work—snooping into her business—she had been avoiding him. This was the second time he had shown up on her doorstep since, and during their last conversation, she had told him that her guests were none of his business. "Well, when you didn't call me back I felt like I needed to check on you, Emma," he'd said that day. "You're a young single lady, and now that your dad isn't around, I feel like the big brother you've never had." At that comment, she'd rolled her eyes.

"A big brother wouldn't want to date his sister, Clay," she'd reminded him. Clay was clever with the way in which he worded things to his advantage when it helped his cause at the moment, but she wasn't going to let him get away with playing the brother card. The two of them had spent ten minutes talking about that then, and now here she was having another conversation with him that she didn't want to have.

"I know you don't want to rent out the cleared field in the middle of your property, Emma, but we really need to consider putting it on the market. Given the potential options it could be used for, I think it will be a lucrative choice."

"No," she said sternly. "Not a chance. That field has a history that I will not ever allow to be erased."

In the 1800s and 1900s, Emma's family had leased her home and the acreage surrounding it from the Bell family. In the early 2000s, her father had made a deal with Mr. Bell—Clay's father—to purchase the property so that the Pate family heritage here would be secured. Emma's father had discussed with her on many occasions how important the legacy of the land was to their family.

He'd feared that once Mr. Bell passed, Clay would decide to terminate the lease and build a subdivision or strip mall on their property. Since their family had leased the land from the Bells for so long, Mr. Bell offered them a personal loan with no interest rather than making them go to the bank for the loan. In so many ways this favor was a gift from God, but now the issue Emma faced is that she had to hand a check to Clay every month. The deal was in writing inside a legally binding contract, but it stated that if at any point the Pate family was unable to make the payment they would have ninety days to catch up on the amount owed or risk losing the property.

Clay looked her straight in the eyes. "If you don't earn every penny you can from this property, you're going to end up losing it. I've been running numbers lately, and what you're making off the leased farmland, even combined with your earnings at the restaurant, isn't going to be enough to make your mortgage payment."

Emma closed her eyes. She knew Clay was right. The only way she'd been able to make ends meet up until this point was by using cash her dad had stored away for a rainy day, as he'd put it. She'd hoped the extra money would last long enough to get her through college so she could get a better paying full-time job, but her dad's savings had run out last month. She'd seen it coming, which is why she'd chosen to let Clay lease the land that her father had worked his entire life. She'd grown up working the fields, too, but now she just didn't have the time, and unfortunately, there wasn't nearly as much profit in farming as there once had been. She could remember picking tobacco on summer days when it was so hot outside that she didn't even feel like drinking water from the gallon-sized milk jug she'd kept nearby at all times. This farm had survived through the blood, sweat, and tears of her family and many others that were just like family for as long as she could trace back in history.

"Clay, I realize this. I can do the math." She paused to collect her thoughts and to attempt to control her emotions. "Can't you just cut me a break until I finish college?"

"Emma, I wish I could, but I have investments to consider. Just like you, I have payments to make." He shared a semi-concerned look with her. "But the bank isn't as flexible with me as I've been with you, so I can't just let you pay whatever you can and cover the rest for you. Maybe if you and I were still together, I could work something out . . ."

Emma turned her back to Clay Bell fast enough for her red hair to flip all the way around and slap her own face. She should have slapped him, but instead, she slammed the door in his face and headed straight to her bed.

Emma cried into her pillowcase for fifteen minutes straight before an echo bounced off the walls of her house, interrupting her thoughts. She'd been contemplating questions like, *What in the heck am I going to do*? She didn't want to let her family down by losing the farm. At the same time, she also hated the idea of quitting college now to acquire a full-time job, but it seemed like it might be her only option. Emma had already given up her plans to transfer to a four-year college. Her father was supposed to live longer. Long enough to watch her walk across the stage to accept a bachelor's degree. She'd already watched that dream die right along with her father, and now she was afraid she wouldn't ever even be able to finish her associate's degree. The plan had been for her dad to maintain the farm while she went away to finish college, and then she'd move back home to help him with bills and cooking and anything else he needed. He'd always taken care of her, and that time was supposed to be her chance to return the favor. Sure, she'd helped him as much as possible all these years, even put off college to save the farm a few times in the past, but this wasn't the way things were supposed to turn out. She shouldn't have had to sell her car and her father's car this summer to pay Clay, but she had. She had sold other belongings, too. Basically, anything that didn't have real meaning, she'd watched go to the highest bidder. The emotions attached to all of the things flickering around in her mind were boiling inside her as she walked swiftly toward the front door preparing to give Clay Bell an earful. Like he often did, she knew he would come back to apologize then only end up saying something else that would cut even deeper.

Emma slung the door open just after a second knock echoed, a little louder this time, and before the man on the other side could catch a glimpse of her tear-stained, make-up smeared face, she began her rant. "Clay Bell, you are a piece of . . ."

At the site of Nolan Lynch standing on her front porch, Emma halted her stream of words in mid-sentence, which left her mouth gaping completely open. She felt a sudden surge of shock, and for a moment neither she nor Nolan spoke.

Nolan could feel his face changing colors. He had been nervous about coming here in the first place and had no idea how to initiate a conversation with Emma, and now the tone of her voice had taken him aback.

"Um, I . . . well," he stammered. "Did I . . . come at a bad time?" He paused. Emma said nothing even though her mouth continued to hang open. "I shouldn't have come," he said. "I'm sorry," he concluded, letting his head fall slightly then turning with the intention of walking down the steps much more quickly than he had walked up them.

"Nolan," Emma spoke in a faint whisper.

Nolan heard her speak his name but barely. He wasn't sure he'd ever heard such a shift in the volume of a person's voice as he'd just witnessed. He thought about pretending he hadn't heard her, thinking maybe he could simply walk to his car and leave. Then, though, he would only continue to wonder why she had thought he was Clay Bell when she opened the door, which had instantly reminded him of her walking out of his classroom at the mention of Clay's name. What was going on? Nolan sure did want to know.

Emma's hand was still stuck on the doorknob, and her eyes had become locked on Nolan's feet. She'd watched his left foot drop to the first step, and his right foot was about to follow when she'd uttered his name. Now he appeared frozen just like her, and for some reason, she wanted nothing more than for him to turn around even though she knew it would probably be best for both of them if he just walked away. If he hadn't realized previously that Clay Bell had something to do with her storming out of his classroom, now he knew. She was sure of that.

Nolan hesitantly turned back. "Yes," he said simply.

"Hey," she said, her brow furrowed in embarrassment.

"Hello."

"How are you?" she asked sincerely.

"I've been better," he said honestly. "But I've been worse, too," he added. Once he'd said it, though, he wasn't quite sure why.

Emma laughed, but it sounded more like a quiet cough. "Yeah, me too," she uttered, her facial expression unaltered.

As soon as Emma had opened the door, Nolan had noticed that she looked like she had been dragged through the ringer, but somehow she still looked cute. "I know I probably shouldn't have shown up here unannounced, but I need to talk to you."

"Okay," she said, trying to inwardly calm the emotions that had been triggered by her previous unannounced guest. Now she felt like a hot mess.

"I talked with Mary," he said. "Your advisor," he clarified in case Emma didn't know Mary by her first name.

"You did?" Emma took a deep breath. "Why?"

"She visited my office the other day and asked if I knew of any reason why you might want to drop my class."

"What did you tell her?"

"I lied to her," he confessed, his head drooping as he said it.

"I did, too," Emma admitted.

Curiosity stole the sudden gloomy expression covering Nolan's face. "Excuse me?"

"I lied to her, too," Emma stated. "I told her that I didn't have time to take your class."

"Lying must not be one of your strong traits," Nolan suggested, smirking. "She came to see me because she thought there was more to the story than what you told her."

"I guess she is right, huh?" Emma said, subconsciously biting her lip.

Nolan felt himself wanting to step toward Emma, grab her by the waist, and kiss her lips until he forgot all about this mess that he had come here to discuss. It wasn't that easy, though. "She told me that if you drop the class it will make it more difficult for you to graduate on time," he acknowledged. "That's not fair, Emma."

"Life isn't fair, Nolan."

He could hear the pain in her voice, and in that instant, he realized she had been through some tough times. He had, too, and he wondered if Emma had or would see the same hurt in him.

"I don't want you to drop my class."

"That's *my* decision."

"I realize that, but we can make this work. I like you, Emma, I really do, and I'll be the first to admit that I felt something special between us from the moment I first met you to the moment I walked off your porch that Monday night. If I am honest, I haven't been able to get my mind off of you."

Emma stepped toward him and began to cut him off, but Nolan held up his hand.

"Please let me finish," he said in a gentle tone. "I need to say this." He started to speak again, but he didn't get to say what he had come to say. He was supposed to say that they were both adults and that they could be professional about what had happened. That she deserved to graduate as planned . . . but then Emma pushed her body flush against his, and before he could let the words roll off his tongue, her lips were sliding across his as one of her hands gripped the hair on the back of his head, and the other one became nestled tightly on the low of his back. At the moment, he couldn't tell a left hand from a right one. His mental balance became completely thrown for a loop, and in that instant, Nolan felt himself give in to the same urges that Emma had given into. He let his lips dance slowly over hers, feeling the moisture and savoring the electric feeling traveling from his head to his toes and back and forth at a million beats per second.

9

Emma hadn't planned on kissing Nolan, but she had loved the way their lips moved so succinctly to the sounds of the daylight hours in Eastern North Carolina—a variety of birds chirping in harmony and warm winds rustling the leaves dangling from nearby trees. It almost sounded like they were at a ballgame and nature was cheering them on. It felt natural, Emma couldn't help but think when her lips eventually fell from Nolan's.

Nolan couldn't recall the last time he'd been kissed so passionately. Staring into Emma's eyes, he was trying to catch his breath as her fingers slid down his neck and pinched the collar of his shirt.

Emma spoke first. "I'm dropping out of college for the semester," she abruptly informed him.

Nolan's eyes appeared to grow in size. "What? Why?" Kissing Emma was incredible, but he didn't want her to change her life plans because of him. He didn't want to think or say *What if this doesn't work out,* but that didn't keep the thought from entering his mind.

"I have to," she said.

"No, you don't, and I'm not going to let you do that," he demanded.

Their bodies were still touching, and Emma's eyes were set on

Nolan's, her hand hovering around his waist. "I've already made the decision."

"You can't, Emma." His mind flashed back to a statistic he'd learned in one of the courses he'd taken in college. "The majority of students that take off a semester of college never go back," he shared with her.

"I will go back," she promised.

Nolan carefully pulled himself away from her. "No. I can't let a student drop out of college because of something that's happened between us. I won't allow that to be on my conscience." His head moved side to side slightly as he spoke. "It's been hard enough dealing with this for the past week, and now to know that I'm hindering your education, well, that's the opposite of why I became an educator," Nolan said with a hint of fire in his voice. "If you feel as though one of us needs to leave the college because of what has happened, I'll leave."

Emma interrupted. "Nolan," she said, but before she could share her reasoning behind the decision, he began to speak over her.

"If you go through with dropping your classes this semester, the moment I see your paperwork come across my desk I will march right into the dean's office and offer my resignation." He thought back to the day when he had knocked on Jerry Small's door with plans to tell him what happened between him and Emma. Since then, Nolan had been so thankful that Jerry hadn't been there to answer that knock. After later talking through the situation in depth with Norman, the two of them had concluded that it would be in Nolan's best interest to wait it out. There was so much gray area since Nolan hadn't realized Emma was a student during the short time they'd spent together. Now, Nolan found himself wishing Jerry had been there that day, and then maybe Emma wouldn't be the one talking about quitting college.

"Please don't do that," Emma said.

Nolan shrugged his shoulders. "Why?"

"I'm not dropping out of my classes this semester because of what happened between us."

"You expect me to believe that?" He didn't.

"Yes, I do."

"Then you'll have to explain to me why you are suddenly dropping out during your next to last semester, after walking out of my class because you were shocked to find out that the man you'd gone on a date with the night before was your instructor," Nolan stated dramatically.

"If I don't drop out, I'm going to lose the farm," she unloaded abruptly, nearly in tears by this point. "Clay is going to take all of this from me," she added, holding her hands out and rotating her body like a wayward compass.

Caught up in the emotion of the kiss and then the debate about which of them would leave the college, Nolan had somehow temporarily forgotten all about Clay Bell. "So what's the story between Clay and you, and why would he take your farm if you don't quit college?"

Emma glanced in the direction of Clay's house. "Will you pull your car around behind my house?"

Nolan's forehead wrinkled. "I guess, but why?"

Emma pointed in the direction in which she was looking. "The porch light we could see the other night through those trees, that's where Clay lives."

"Okay?" Nolan responded in a questioning tone; then it suddenly hit him why she wanted him to hide his car.

"If Clay finds out we've been spending time together, he would love nothing more than to march into the dean's office on your behalf."

Nolan suddenly felt that this situation was even more complex than he'd initially imagined. There was so much he didn't know, he thought to himself, as he cranked his vehicle's ignition and followed Emma as she walked on the grass next to a dirt path that led to the backside of the house. Nolan was surprised to discover a tattered barn nearly as large as the house itself in the backyard. In fact, he was surprised he hadn't been able to see it when pulling in the driveway, but the last time Nolan had been here it was dark, and this time he had to admit his mind hadn't been exactly clear. Not that it was any clearer now.

Emma invited Nolan into her home for the very first time, and when the two of them walked through the screen door that led directly into the rustic kitchen, the hinges let out a squeal as if the door hadn't been oiled in a decade. Nolan's head jerked at the sound, and Emma giggled.

"That's my alarm system," she teased.

Nolan chuckled and then began to take in décor like none other he'd ever seen. A picnic style table twice the length of a standard picnic table, with matching unattached benches on either side, ran along the wall directly in front of him. It could probably seat a family of twelve, he figured, as Emma led him to it. Against the adjacent wall, the refrigerator was white with rust in a few spots and the countertop, made out of some type of real wood, looked like it had doubled as a cutting board for the last hundred years. Above an antique looking stove with iron burners, cast-iron pans adorned an array of hooks that made them look like ornaments dangling for decoration. After taking a seat at the table, Nolan's eyes swiveled, and spotted a potato bin in one corner, fruit baskets in another, and lots of cabinets—some with solid doors and others with thick glass panes. Eventually, Nolan noticed the hardwood floor he'd walked across. Even though it had creaked, and nearly everything in the kitchen looked as old as the outside of the house, it all still seemed stable and clean.

"Would you like some sweet tea?"

"Yes, please," Nolan answered without hesitation. Emma's sweet tea tasted better than any other he'd ever had, hands down. He had even craved it a time or two since the first and last time he'd sipped from one of her glasses. Since then, water had been the only beverage he'd consumed so even though he knew he'd be able to smell the sugar rising from his glass, he'd earned it. It only made sense that when she reached into the refrigerator she pulled out a glass pitcher with a rounded handle and hand-painted flowers. She poured each of them a full glass, sat across the table from Nolan, and spent the next twenty minutes explaining her history with Clay Bell.

Growing up on the same road, the two of them had been close childhood friends. They'd roamed the fields together, rode bikes down the dusty roads, and shared their first kiss underneath a large oak tree near the pond in the back corner of her property. She didn't mention the kiss to Nolan, but she did tell him that they'd dated off and on in high school but eventually broke up when Clay moved away for college. When he'd moved back home he'd become a different person, she explained, and she no longer had any interest in him as anything more than a friend. He'd asked her out a few times, and they'd hung out a little. But when he took a position at the community college, she used that as a reason why the two of them couldn't date. "How ironic, huh?" she said to Nolan. "Now from time to time Clay likes to suggest that we should be friends with benefits, but I'm not into that. I either want a friend or a boyfriend—one that's committed, not something in between." She paused, thinking about her conversation with Clay earlier today. "I'm getting to the point where I don't think Clay should fall into either category, especially the latter, of course. So that's why Clay would take pride in ratting us out."

Nolan brushed his entire face with both hands as if washing it under water. He ended up interlocking his fingers behind his head as he leaned against the wall at his back. "Wow," was the first word Nolan uttered since the moment Emma had started talking. "I think I need more sweet tea," he added, realizing his glass had become empty.

"I know that's a lot to take in." She'd also given a synopsis of the loan her dad had taken from Mr. Bell and why she now had no other choice but to temporarily quit college and take a full-time job.

"So your decision seriously has nothing to do with me?" Nolan wanted her to confirm again.

"It doesn't," she said on her way to the fridge. "Initially, I had decided to drop your class because I knew I couldn't spend every Tuesday and Thursday with you and not be tempted to be more than your student."

"It sounds funny when you call yourself my student," Nolan pointed out, attempting to lighten the mood.

"I bet it does, Professor Lynch," she taunted back, then squeezed his arm. "The positive thing about me deciding to drop your class is that it made me look more closely at my financial situation. I started checking to see if I could afford to push back my graduation one more semester, if needed, but then I realized that this idea made no sense because next semester, and every semester in the foreseeable future, you'll still be the health and physical education instructor. I then realized I had two options. Take your class—whether that be this semester or another semester—or take the same class at another community college, which I honestly don't have time for." She took a deep breath and then a swig of her tea. "With all that said, as I was looking at my bank account, I realized that I am quickly running out of funds to continue paying Clay the monthly loan amount." She took a moment to catch her breath before finishing. "If I drop my classes before the deadline, I can also receive a tuition refund."

"This is horrible news," Nolan acknowledged.

"It might get worse."

At this point, Nolan didn't want to hear how, but he couldn't help but ask. "How come?"

"Clay is nosy, and he admitted to noticing an unfamiliar car drive down our road the night you came to my house. He said he was sitting on his front porch, so he saw us turn into my driveway, and I wouldn't put it past him to have walked down the road that night to get a closer look."

"But we were sitting on the porch the entire time, we would have seen him," Nolan suggested.

"Do you remember how dark it was out there?"

"True, but with it being that dark he probably couldn't see my car very well either."

"We had the porch light on, though, so if he walked down the road he could probably see us," Emma pointed out. "However, my house is far enough off the road that I doubt he could make out that the man on my porch was you, but the mere fact that a guy was on my porch is enough to make him jealous."

"So what do we do now?" Nolan asked, realizing that Emma knew Clay much better than he did.

"We hope that he doesn't find out that we've spent time together outside of the college." She paused for a moment. "So, do you have plans tonight?" she asked.

Nolan racked his brain for a few moments. "Not that I can remember."

"Want to stay for dinner?" she asked. "We can hope that Clay didn't see your vehicle drive by earlier, and then you can sneak out of here with your lights off once it turns dark outside."

"Emma Pate, are you asking me on a second date?"

She cocked her head and let a smile run across her face. "Well, my hands are kind of tied," she admitted. "I see it more as me doing you a favor to help you keep your job," she teased.

Nolan smirked in response to her witty comment, but at the same time, he found himself thinking about how bummed he'd be if he were to lose his job. The thought of Emma dropping her classes this semester also made him feel uneasy. Sure, he now realized that Emma not obtaining her degree in the spring would have nothing to do with him, but that didn't seem to make this whole situation any less messy or unfortunate.

"I appreciate that," Nolan said. "Since you've been honest with me, I'll be honest with you. When you stormed out of the classroom that day, I thought for sure you were going to report me."

Emma couldn't be upset at him for thinking as much, but she did want him to know that she would have never done that to him. "I walked out because as soon as you mentioned Clay's name I wanted to do everything I could to protect your brand new career and your reputation. In hindsight, I realize I should have shared that bit of information with you, but I just freaked out, and I ran away from the problem rather than dealing with it." She took another sip from her sweating glass. "I'm sorry, Nolan. I really am. I know this has been stressful for you."

"Just a bit," he said, trying to downplay the thoughts that had consumed his mind this entire week.

"How about I make it up to you with a homemade meal and then we can watch a movie or something?" Emma suggested.

"That sounds nice," Nolan confirmed. "I'd like that."

With that decision made, Emma began opening and closing cabinet doors in search of options that she thought might lend themselves to Nolan's likings.

"How about ribeye steak, boiled potatoes, fresh green beans, and white rice?"

Nolan's eyebrows rose. "All of the above sounds delicious."

"I know it probably seems crazy for me to offer you steak after I just finished telling you that I'm broke, but my best friend's family raises cows. Once a month or so, Lisa will bring me meat that her dad packages especially for me."

"So you lied to me?" Nolan accused, assuming his response would elicit a puzzled look on Emma's face, especially since she'd been thoughtful enough to preface this subject with a blurb about a tight budget and expensive steak. He was right, her facial expression immediately became one of curiosity and concern, but he decided not to let her become too confused. He laughed and said, "Earlier, you told me you didn't believe in friends with benefits!"

Emma sighed, then giggled. She enjoyed his crackerjack humor but punched him in the arm anyway. "Very true. Steak is definitely a benefit. Lisa also shows up at my front door with her yoga mat once a week and gives me private lessons. So, I guess I am guilty of having a friend with benefits," she laughed.

As they chatted, Emma began to pluck out and cover the counter with bowls, pans, utensils, and all sorts of ingredients that seemed more like the workings of a master plan than a whimsical dinner. Nolan could immediately sense that she knew her way around a kitchen. Probably better than he did, which wouldn't be saying much about the average man, but the average man hadn't been raised by his mama. The woman could have made dirt taste delicious, and she'd taught him that idle hands don't belong in the kitchen.

"What can I help you with?" Nolan instinctively asked.

Emma liked that he said *What can I help you with* rather than *Can I help you.* Ultimately, it was just linguistics, but to her, his choice of words spoke volumes. It gave her the feeling that he genuinely wanted to help rather than asking only to be considerate.

"How about you just keep me entertained," she suggested, "and I'll do the rest."

"You sure?"

"Positive. You're my guest, you're not allowed to work in my kitchen," she said, nearly smiling as she spoke the words.

"Fair enough."

Showing a non-verbal response to Emma's comment, Nolan began noticeably surveying the kitchen walls. "Do you have a list of rules somewhere around here that I should read over?" he joked.

Emma laughed and played along. "Yes, I do have a set of house rules, but they're not posted." She twisted a knob on the back of the oven. "But I'm proud of you."

"Why is that?"

"You're doing your job—keeping me entertained."

Nolan snickered. "I like to be helpful however I can."

"I can see that."

Emma had made her way to the far corner of the counter, and from Nolan's vantage point, he couldn't see her face but was pretty sure she was smiling. He liked the way he felt relaxed in Emma's presence. The way he could let loose a corny joke in the spur of the moment and not wonder if she'd think he was nuts. She seemed to understand his humor, and he enjoyed her style of wit as well.

Neither of them spoke for a few moments as the sounds of cooking took over the air around them, but eventually, Emma spoke again. "You know, I wouldn't normally invite a man into my home for a second date, so you're lucky that our situation lends itself to privacy."

"Oh, so I'm the lucky one," he replied with a snicker.

With her hand clutching a spatula dangled over a boiling pot of water, Emma turned for an instant and grinned. That look was her response. She fancied having someone sitting at her kitchen table while she prepared dinner. She missed her dad sitting at the table—dirty, sweaty, and stinky from a long, hard day's work. Like Nolan, he often offered to help, but she wouldn't let him. He deserved to relax and enjoy the harvest after working from sunup to sundown six days a week. She'd grown up in a somewhat atypical environment having a father that cooked the meals rather than a mother, but she'd learned how to cook early in life from watching him do his level best. She could still remember the first real meal she prepared for her dad. It had been her birthday gift to him that year. He absolutely loved beef stew, and after eating hers, he raved for months to his friends about how delicious his eight-year-old daughter's special recipe tasted. Looking back, she knew she'd poured in way too many spices and herbs—mostly from their garden—but he loved it anyway. Most of the meals her father concocted as she'd grown up had been bland, so once she introduced him to spices he felt like a king. Lisa's mom was the one from whom Emma discovered how sprinkling in a little of this and a little of that could create heaven on a plate. Thinking of her father now, Emma reminisced about how he always removed his John Deere cap and prayed before meals while holding her delicate and growing hand in his rough and aging hand. She remembered how much she loved to trace the wrinkles on his palms with her fingers.

Nolan found himself wondering what thoughts were traveling through Emma's mind as she moved around the kitchen like a dancer on Broadway. Her movements were patterned and precise as she floated from the stove to the fridge to the cabinets and everywhere in between. He enjoyed watching her, but not just because the curves that outlined her body made a man think things that a man can't help but think. Her skin wasn't pale like most people with red hair, and he wondered if years of working out in the sun had defied nature of its normalcy. The sun also seemed to age people which made him curious to know Emma's age. Before knowing anything about her past, he had assumed her to be a smidge older than himself. He'd also assumed she worked at the college, but he'd been wrong about that. Racking his brain for a round-about way to ask Emma her age, Nolan came up with a decent approach.

"You said you grew up with Clay, but he looks a bit older than you. Is there a big difference in your ages?"

Emma didn't hide her laughter. "It must be his receding hairline," she teased. "I'm twenty-four, so that makes Clay twenty-six."

Nolan had pegged Clay to be at least thirty, which had thrown him off when Emma mentioned earlier that the two of them had dated in high school. Emma had been kind to label his hairline as receding; the guy might as well be bald.

"How about you, how old are you?" Emma asked, but then changed her mind about asking the question. "Wait, I want to guess," she said instead.

"Give it a shot," Nolan responded, happy that he wouldn't have to guess her age.

Emma appeared to be doing math in her head as she continued to stir the potatoes. "Twenty-five?"

"Close," he commented.

"Then I think you either have to be twenty-four or twenty-six, so I'm going with twenty-four since you aren't going bald yet," she laughed.

"Yep, same age as you."

Nolan and Emma immediately began to discuss the irony of them being the same age while technically being forbidden to date because of the student and teacher labels. When the conversation became a little tense, Emma rinsed her hands beneath the faucet and changed the subject. "Do you know any more jokes, in addition to the one about Junior Mints?"

"Why are stop signs read?" Nolan asked on cue, knowing she would hear the word *read* as *red.*

Emma wrapped the dish towel around a bar across the front of the oven and slid a hand to her hip, thinking. "Because red means stop," she answered with a smile, knowing her guess was probably way off.

"Because they can't be heard," he said adding the sounds and motions of a drumroll and a clashing cymbal.

Emma let out a laugh. "That's corny."

"So is your neighborhood," Nolan responded immediately, openly amused at his own wisecrack.

The instant Emma absorbed the punch line she laughed all

over herself, and Nolan rolled right into another joke. "Here's one you'll like—" he paused, trying to hold in his laughter. "Why did the bike fall over?"

Emma fired back with her own relatable antics. "Because it had a rusty chain lock," she responded, unable to keep from laughing.

"Good one," Nolan complimented. "But no," he teased as if she had been serious. "Because it was two-tired," he revealed.

"Another play on words, huh?" she pointed out, thinking about how *too* and *two* sound exactly alike.

Nolan just smiled. Every eye on the stovetop was in use, and the smells rising from the pots and pans covering them had been inviting his stomach to growl for some time. Watching Emma in the kitchen reminded him of his mama, of good memories like the ones he'd thought about recently of being in the kitchen with her.

Emma eventually gave in and let Nolan help set the table while she carried the cookware over and set it up like a buffet the same way she always had. She also asked him to top off their glasses and to leave the pitcher of tea on the table. These were the traditions Emma had come to love, and she did all the same things she and her dad had always done in steady rhythm, and before she realized it, she was eating a meal with Nolan Lynch for the very first time. For some reason, it hadn't surprised her when he'd said he didn't want steak sauce or ketchup with his steak. She had never cared for anything extra on her steak either.

"A good steak doesn't need condiments," Nolan confirmed.

"So you think my steak is good?"

"It's seriously one of the best steaks I've ever tasted," he said after a few bites.

"It helps that the meat is fresh, and I've had it marinating in seasoning all day."

"So you had this dinner date planned all along, huh?"

"Technically, I did . . . but Lisa was supposed to be sitting where you are," she shared, pointing to his spot with her fork.

"Oh, really?"

"Unfortunately and fortunately, she canceled on me. Said her classes are kicking her butt. One in particular, actually—you see, she has this new young instructor that likes to tell corny jokes and has a crush on her best friend."

Nolan perked up like a fawn caught in a pair of bright headlights. "Your friend Lisa is in one of my classes?"

"Yep."

Nolan forked a few green beans and dropped them into this mouth.

"Don't worry," Emma clarified. "She won't say anything."

"You told her about us?" Nolan quizzed, attempting to hide the sudden concern rising within him.

"When a girl meets a guy that sweeps her off her feet at the bicycle rack on the first day of classes, the first thing she does is tell her best friend," she answered matter-of-factly. "Lisa knew about you before I had any idea you were an instructor, and I couldn't lie to her when she kept asking me about you over the next few days while also telling me about her hot new instructor, mind you. I tried to play it off like you hadn't been who I thought you were, which by the way was true," she laughed. "But she knew better."

"You're sure she won't say anything?"

"Pinky promise," Emma guaranteed, offering her pinky.

The gesture caused Nolan to snicker a little as he realized he hadn't been asked to pinky promise since elementary school. Reaching across the table, he let Emma twist her pinky around his pinky.

"So she thinks I'm hot, huh?" he asked, their smallest fingers tied together like shoestrings.

"Don't get any ideas," Emma teased, yanking her pinky back in a playful manner. "Instructors are forbidden to date students."

"I would never do such a thing."

"Not knowingly, huh?" she said with a wink. "At least I won't be a student soon, and you'll be free to date me if you please."

"I like the idea of dating you, but I seriously don't care for the thought of you dropping out of college," he reminded her.

"I know, I don't like it either, but let's talk about something else—maybe a less complicated issue," she suggested. "Have you ever dated a black girl?"

Nolan nearly choked on a laugh. The question had come entirely out of left field, he thought silently. "I have," he answered swiftly.

"My friend Lisa is a light-skinned black girl. She's gorgeous, and she teaches yoga when she's not helping her folks at the farm."

A light bulb immediately blinked on inside Nolan's mind. "I know exactly who Lisa is now," he acknowledged. "When she told me she teaches yoga, I decided to ask her to be a mentor in the class." He watched Emma shake her head in agreement with the idea as she chewed a small bite of steak. "So, have you ever dated a white guy?" Nolan asked.

Emma covered her mouth as she laughed. "Yes, I sure have," she said after swallowing.

"My brother is black," Nolan randomly stated.

"You have a brother?"

"Yep, a twin brother."

"You have a twin brother that is black?"

"Or African American, if you prefer."

"Lisa doesn't like to be called African American. When she fills out a form that has African American listed as a race, she crosses out African and then checks the box."

The thought tickled Nolan. "That's funny. I'll have to tell Norman he should start doing that."

"Norman—that's your brother's name?"

"Yes."

"Nolan and Norman," Emma reeled off for the first time, just as many others had throughout Nolan's life, "has a nice ring to it."

Nolan figured Emma would jump right into a string of family history questions after finding out he had a black twin brother, but to his surprise, she didn't. She acted as if it was no big deal, and she kept on talking. "What is Norman like?"

"He's talkative, intelligent, and good looking like me," Nolan said with a straight face.

Emma smiled. "Is he single?"

"Do you date African Americans?" Nolan teased.

"I date Americans," Emma responded with a smirk.

"My dad would like that answer," Nolan mentioned.

"Your dad sounds like a great man."

"Why would you think that? I haven't told you much about him."

"Am I wrong?" she challenged.

"He is a great man," Nolan said simply.

"I bet he's proud of you and Norman."

"Maybe of Norman . . ." Nolan's mind drifted to Norman's accomplishments.

"But not you?"

"I'm not sure I turned out the way he expected."

"What does that mean?" she interrogated.

"He wanted me to play Major League Baseball." Nolan's mind froze for a moment, unsure of why he shared that bit of information with Emma. He usually didn't talk about baseball with anyone anymore.

"So you grew up playing baseball?"

"Yeah, my dad was always my coach."

"I'm sure he realizes that not every boy that grows up playing ball can make it to professional baseball," she offered as food for thought.

"I could have, though," Nolan explained. Then he paused, thinking about how he should change the subject like he normally would if anyone started talking about baseball, especially about his baseball career. The highlight that defined Nolan's career was one he'd been trying to forget for years, but instead, he relived it every single day. "The Boston Red Sox drafted me right out of high school," he divulged as if it was no big deal, looking down at his plate as he spoke.

"Really?" Emma reacted in surprise.

"I never played, though."

"Why not?"

"I went to college instead." It wasn't the whole truth.

"I'm sure your dad is proud of you for going to college."

"Yeah, probably," he answered nonchalantly.

"He hasn't told you so?"

"I haven't talked to him in a while," Nolan admitted. This was another subject he didn't talk about. Ever.

Emma could sense Nolan beginning to clam up just like he had the day at the coffee shop when the conversation had turned to family, so she rewound the subject slightly. "Did you play college baseball?"

"I did."

Emma expressed excitement at the thought of Nolan donning a purple and gold Pirates uniform. "I bet I watched you play. My dad and I used to go to a handful of games every season."

"Oh, really," he said glancing up at her.

"Yeah, I knew your name sounded familiar, I bet that's why."

"So you like baseball?" Nolan asked, spinning the spotlight in Emma's direction.

"I love baseball. I grew up following the Braves with my dad."

Nolan wasn't sure if this was good news or not—both the part about her loving baseball and the fact that he was breaking bread with a Braves fan. "That's cool," was all he decided to say.

"What position did you play in college?" Emma asked.

"Pitcher."

"Did you play any other positions?" she probed.

"Nope."

"When you pitched, did you hit as the designated hitter for your position, or did you have another player bat for you as the designated hitter?"

It caught Nolan by surprise that Emma understood the rules of college baseball well enough to know that a designated hitter must bat for the pitcher; however, the coach could opt to allow the pitcher to be the designated hitter if he was a good batter. The rule could become quite confusing even to an avid fan, and it also added an element of strategy to the college game. "I didn't hit," Nolan answered without any further explanation.

Emma found his lack of response unusual, but she just nodded and carried on with the conversation. "I bet I've seen you pitch. Were you good?"

"I was decent."

She pursed her lips. "If you were just decent I doubt the Red Sox would have drafted you."

Good point, he thought, but she didn't know the whole story. *I was a decent "pitcher"* were the words that came to mind, but he decided to keep them locked up. "Sometimes things change," he said instead.

"Did you have an injury that caused things to change, like Tommy John surgery?"

Tommy John surgery had become a near epidemic amongst both college and professional baseball players in the past twenty years. Nolan's dad had always blamed it on youth baseball teams that traveled around playing weekend ball, often saying things like: "A kid should never play a handful or more of games on back to back days. There's way too much throwing, especially for the pitchers. When a player's throwing arm warms up and cools down over and over, it wears on the joints and muscles," he would tell Nolan when he asked if he could play on a traveling team. "I'm not allowing you to potentially damage your arm while it's still growing." At the time, Nolan thought it was nonsense, just an excuse for his parents not to travel on the weekends and have to pay the fees associated with being on the team. Now, he knew his dad had a valid point. In college, Nolan studied youth sports and discovered the number of elbow injuries had risen in recent years.

"Thankfully I never had any major injuries," Nolan confirmed.

Emma just stared at him as if lost in thought.

"What are you thinking?" he eventually asked.

"I want to show you something."

10

Emma grabbed Nolan by the hand and led him out the back door like two kids rushing outside to play after being excused from the dinner table. As they'd eaten their home-cooked meal and talked about life, the sun had slowly sunk on the horizon and the moon had eventually taken its spot up in the sky—now as dark as Nolan's memories of the last time he'd seen his mama. He had been trying to shake such thoughts from his mind, but all this baseball talk had brought her to the forefront of his memory. He finally forced his focus to shift to the spontaneous woman attached to his fingers. He wanted to kiss Emma again like he had on the porch, but they were walking too fast, almost skipping, and she apparently had other things on her mind.

"You're going to love this," she vowed.

"What is it?" he inquired while the outline of the barn faded into the background as they followed a dusty path between two cornfields. The stalks stretched head high and wore a shade of green, although at the moment, Nolan couldn't make out color. The distance between human-made light and where they were headed continued to fade.

"Words can't explain what you're about to experience," Emma assured.

Words can't explain what I am experiencing, Nolan realized. He loved this, all of this. Being out here in the middle of nowhere with Emma Pate. Having dinner with her, talking about things he hadn't shared with anyone in years. In a way, he felt a burden had lifted off his shoulders this evening even though the fact that the two of them had reconnected was a burden in itself. In a way, though, knowing he shouldn't be here with her made it more exciting, and he let the downside of the thought slip away like the first slimy fish he'd caught as a kid with his dad.

Emma hadn't ever brought a man out here with her before. The spot where she and Nolan were going was *her* place, a special place. Even though Emma wasn't sure why he was the first person she'd decided to share this unique phenomenon with alone, she somehow seemed to know the moment was perfect. It was like something inside her was telling her that Nolan needed this—just like she had needed this at certain times in her life, especially throughout the time since her father had passed. Since then, she had spent countless nights out here alone with the critters and the quiet and her own wandering thoughts.

As they made their way deeper into the fields, Nolan couldn't see the ground beneath his feet; he could only feel it. Loose dirt in some places, packed dirt in others, and the occasional root or rock or something hard that altered his step. He definitely wouldn't want to be walking barefoot since there was sure to be snakes out here. He wasn't afraid of them, though, never had been. In fact, he used to love picking up garden snakes. "He might bite you," his mother would say when he would let them dangle from his fingers. "It's okay; it's not poisonous, Mama," he'd counter. She'd been the one who'd taught him which snakes were venomous and which ones weren't—he recalled the fact that most poisonous snakes had diamond-shaped heads and slits for pupils.

"We should have brought a flashlight," Nolan mentioned.

"Why? We have moonlight," Emma pointed out, literally using

her finger to remind Nolan of the moon hovering above their heads.

Nolan had noticed that the darkness had begun to lessen as his eyes adjusted. He could hear the wind blowing the cornstalks on either side of the path as they walked, and in the distance, he could make out the outline of trees.

"Plus," Emma added, "I know where I'm going. Trust me."

He did. For some reason, he trusted Emma completely. Not just with this venture into the dark but also with their big secret.

"How much farther?" he asked out of curiosity rather than impatience.

"You sound like a kid on a road trip!"

Nolan smiled in the darkness. "And you're like the parent that won't tell the kid where you're taking him."

"I told you where we're going."

"No, you didn't," he laughed.

"Somewhere special."

"It better be worth it." It was already worth it—he just liked giving her a hard time for some reason.

"It will be, I promise," she encouraged. "You can thank me later."

Emma could feel the warmth of his fingers around hers, tightening at certain times—probably when he stepped on a broken cornstalk that had fallen or a rut in the path. She knew he was giving her a hard time about the dark because he thought it was funny. She could tell that Nolan wasn't afraid out here. He hadn't jumped when a raccoon scampered away up the trail or when the cornstalks, dancing in the wind, sounded like something or someone walking nearby—things that had freaked her out as a kid. The two of them were getting close to the field she wanted to show him, and she felt like a giddy schoolgirl all over again. Before they reached the last turn, she slowed their pace and eventually stopped and faced Nolan.

Nolan could see Emma through the dark—the outline of her jaw, her hair falling over her shoulders, the whites in her eyes. He gazed at her as they stood still. She appeared to be breathing a scant heavier than normal but not as much as if they'd been on a jog. He wondered why they'd stopped, and he waited for her to tell him.

"I need you to do something," Emma requested.

"Okay," he replied hesitantly yet willingly.

He watched her reach to her waist with both hands and untie the cotton belt wrapped beneath the loops on her blue jeans. Then, with one hand she slid it out and her head tilted in his direction. Until this moment Nolan's heartbeat had remained relatively normal, but all of a sudden, he realized he was breathing much heavier than Emma.

"Is it okay if I blindfold you with this?" she asked. "It will make the experience much better, I promise."

Nolan searched for a fitting response, but he couldn't imagine saying anything but *Sure.* Suddenly, his mind shot back to all the college parties he'd attended—where he'd complied with some risky stuff, but he'd never had a female ask to blindfold him.

"Sure, why not," he finally agreed. He didn't get the feeling that Emma would leave him out here in the middle of nowhere just for fun. That thought sparked a memory. He'd once known a guy that had been dating two girls behind each other's back. Somehow both of the girls found out about it, and one of them went parking with him somewhere down a dirt road and ended up tying him up in the car naked. The guy had assumed he was buckled in for an exciting night of passion, but then the situation took an about-face when he heard the second girl's voice. Of course, she hadn't been visibly present at the onset—she'd shown up on cue once the blindfold covered his eyes. Then the girls snapped inappropriate pictures of him, seized his clothes, and left him there all alone. Eventually, the guy maneuvered his naked body to where he could reach his phone and called some of his buddies to rescue him. Needless to say, he'd never lived down that story.

Emma folded the thin piece of cloth over to make it thicker and then reached toward Nolan's eyes. He felt her body brush up against his as she wrapped the belt tightly and then slowly tied it behind his head. Once again he felt the urge to kiss her, but he didn't want to risk altering the ambiance of whatever it was she had planned.

"There we go," she commented, sliding her hand down his arm before reaching around his elbow and locking their arms together like two vines in a jungle. "Come with me," she urged, pulling him gently in the direction they were going earlier.

Emma was much closer to Nolan now. He could feel her hips whisking against his, and their steps seemed to be in unison like soldiers marching down a street. They walked slowly around a bend, Emma on his left, and Nolan could feel her pushing him in the direction that the path curved. As they moved forward, the air seemed to change slightly, and suddenly Nolan could feel a steady breeze as if their surroundings had become denser.

Emma looked ahead, then glanced at Nolan. His lips were together, and his body was steady. She watched him off and on as they walked, making sure he remained comfortable. Trees lined either side of their pathway now, and Emma began to catch glimpses of the surreal phenomena she had brought Nolan here to witness. Slowly walking into this wonder was an unreal experience, but she knew that it would be much more of a spectacle if Nolan could take in the full effect all at once. Both ways held their own magical sensation, and she had a feeling that this wouldn't be the last time she and Nolan would wander through the fields and the trees and end up here with their arms intertwined.

Nolan felt the path end, and at first, he couldn't make out the new texture beneath his feet. As they walked through it for another fifty or so steps, he decided that it must be grass. The breeze had picked up slightly, and he could hear trees dancing around him. It was amazing how when one of the body's senses became shut off, the others seemed to intensify. He could smell pine and grass, and he could hear a chorus made up of crickets and cicadas.

Emma brought the stroll to a halt in the middle of the field. "We're here," she informed Nolan.

Neither of them had spoken a single word since Emma had blindfolded Nolan. Now, Nolan waited for her to say or do something.

Emma glanced around the field and smiled from ear to ear. "I'm going to take off the blindfold now," she said. "Try not to pass out."

Nolan wondered the same thing he'd been wondering for the past ten minutes. Where were they and what was he about to see? Would it be as magnificent as Emma had made it out to be? He sure hoped so, but he knew how women sometimes sensualized certain things more than men, so he prepared himself to act more astonished than he might be, just in case.

Suddenly, Nolan felt the cotton belt swish against his skin. At this movement, he opened his previously closed eyes.

Emma's gaze remained fixed on Nolan, and she could tell it was taking his eyes a few moments to adjust. She wanted to see him the instant he saw *them.*

As he stood in the middle of a field in the warm summer air, Nolan's entire body froze for a period in which life seemed to stand still. He had no idea his eyes were bulging, and his lips had fallen apart as he breathed in the most stunning spectacle he had ever witnessed. Emma had been right, this was special, and he found himself utterly speechless. She was standing right there next to him, but he couldn't take his eyes off of *them*—thousands of *them*, maybe millions.

11

A field of fireflies swarmed the outskirts of the open area in which Nolan and Emma were standing. Very slowly, Nolan allowed his body to rotate three hundred and sixty degrees, taking in the magic of the moment as if it was something that might only happen once in his lifetime. Emma moved with him as if the two of them were dancing while the creatures' lanterns twinkled on and off to a piece of music all their own. What amazed Nolan most is how the lightning bugs completely surrounded him and Emma, but the field in which the two of them were standing seemed to be off-limits to the fireflies, a no-fly zone so to speak.

"Welcome to Firefly Field," Emma whispered warmly.

It was in that moment that Nolan was finally able to let his eyes drop from the horizon, off the glow that illuminated the airy field in which he and Emma were present. When he realized that he truly was standing on grass, he was mesmerized, but not because there was anything special about grass in particular. This grass, however, was articulately manicured, and as he glanced around he took in the rest of the most natural-looking baseball field on which he'd ever laid eyes. Sand outlined the base paths, foul lines had been drawn in, and a pitcher's mound adorned the middle of the infield. There was no fence, though, just a small cornfield inside the tree line that was as perfectly shaped as any baseball field on which he'd ever played.

"This . . .," Nolan stammered. He couldn't find words to sound out the thoughts in his mind.

"Just take it all in," Emma suggested. "This is probably one of the oldest baseball fields in North Carolina. No one knows for sure, and we haven't invited any historians out because, well, this place is kind of a secret."

"I can see why," Nolan acknowledged, wide-eyed like a kid at Sea World. "Who wouldn't want to see this place? People would definitely swarm here if they knew about it."

Nolan hadn't picked up a baseball since college, but suddenly he felt the urge to have one in his hand—to feel the laces, the leather, the grits of sand embedded in the skin. Standing on this field reminded him of his childhood in some way, and that feeling made him wish he could have played baseball on this field back in those days. As these memories flashed through his mind and as he took in the whole field, he also couldn't stop glancing out at all the fireflies.

"They show up every year around the beginning of the Major League Baseball season, and they usually hang around until it's almost time for the playoffs."

"Where do they come from?" Nolan wondered aloud.

"They breed here. The environment is just right for them. You see where the tree line lies," she pointed out, "which is where that wooden bridge is that we walked over?"

Nolan nodded his head, remembering how he had wondered what the deal was with the wooden structure beneath their feet a few moments before arriving here. Prior to crossing it, he had no idea that they were merely a bridge apart from such an incredible view.

Emma continued. "There is about a one hundred yards wide

cluster of trees that surround this entire field, and within that area, a shallow creek runs all the way around this field before reconnecting on either side. There is a lot of damp soil in that area, which fireflies like because they feed off of slugs and snails and yucky bugs like that."

Nolan snickered just a hint when Emma said the word *yucky*, but then he honed in as she continued to enlighten him on the subject of fireflies.

"They also love the warm, humid weather here in Eastern North Carolina," she explained. Emma could go on and on with facts about lightning bugs, but she decided she didn't want to bore or overwhelm Nolan with too much information at the moment, plus she figured she should save some for later.

Nolan smiled. Upon arriving at Firefly Field, he had barely noticed that when Emma had loosened her arm from his, her hand had slid down and their fingers had once again intertwined. With their hands still wrapped together, as the fireflies danced around them, Nolan leaned in to feel the warmth of her lips once again.

Their second kiss ever was slow and rhythmic . . . smooth and sweet. Nolan imagined kissing her would never get old, nor would walking with her to this field to enjoy the display of the tiny flying lamps that surrounded them as far as the eyes could see.

Emma could feel traces of Nolan's tongue brushing against hers, gently and repetitively. She had hoped that he would be the one to kiss her this time since she had been the one to initiate the embrace on the porch. Kissing him made her feel happy, inside and out. In all the years she'd been coming out here she'd never kissed a man here at night, surrounded by fireflies and stars and all the simple pleasures of a Southern night in the arms of a gentleman. It seemed that electricity was flowing through her veins, and Emma felt more vulnerable wrapped in the warmth of the man holding her than she ever remembered feeling. At this moment, she knew that she would give in to any place that the intimacy between them led, but Emma hoped that one of the reasons she felt that way was because she expected Nolan would be respectful enough not to take advantage of her in this moment of susceptibility.

12

Nolan wasn't sure how long he and Emma kissed in the middle of Firefly Field. One moment it felt like it had lasted an hour, and the next it felt like only five seconds. He guessed that was why their lips just kept moving as the fireflies kept hovering, the stars kept glowing, and the crickets kept singing. However long their kiss ended up lasting, it seemed just right. Somehow, he found himself completely satisfied. He didn't need anything more, and it surprised him just as much as it pleased him. He could remember nights with other women in college, hoping for things to escalate as quickly as possible. Wanting one thing to lead to the next until they made it around all of the bases—a reference that at this moment literally surrounded him.

This evening, Nolan had definitely enjoyed the company of Emma Pate, yet their night wasn't quite finished. She had just asked him if he would like to throw baseball. No female had ever asked him to throw baseball. They'd asked him to dance, to play a board game, to watch a movie, to do other things . . . but never to throw baseball.

Before Nolan realized what he was getting into, he felt a glove slide onto his fingers. Emma had fetched two of them from a small wooden trunk near the edge of the woods. He hadn't even noticed it until she walked in that direction, and then he spotted a long wooden bench next to the bin. She tossed him a baseball that glowed in the dark, and they walked in opposite directions. He'd seen similar balls in sporting goods stores, but he'd never thrown one with this feature. When he reached back to let the ball fly toward Emma's open glove, the motion came as natural as riding a bike, just like it always had.

Emma caught the ball with ease and quickly returned a throw to Nolan.

The first dozen or so throws they exchanged were soft. Nolan went easy because he was throwing to a girl, and Emma went easy because she hadn't thrown a baseball in quite some time. Her dad had been her throwing partner on this field for as many years as she could remember, and his glove had caught the last ball she'd thrown. She had a feeling that Nolan figured she would probably throw like a girl all the time, and that was fine. Most boys thought that.

"Do you want to back up a little bit?" Emma asked.

"If you'd like me to," Nolan responded.

She expected him to say something sarcastic like, *If you think you can throw that far*, but he hadn't. She sped up the next throw a little bit, and it felt good.

Nolan's eyebrows raised in surprise, but he was glad that Emma couldn't see his expression due to the distance between them. He threw the ball a tad bit harder the next time, yet it still had an arch on it like he was throwing with a twelve-year-old boy. Nolan had relaxed some now that he knew Emma could catch well enough that he didn't have to worry about accidentally giving her a black eye. He would feel horrible if that happened, especially out here at night.

Emma sped up her next couple of throws even though Nolan barely changed his velocity. She knew he was just trying to be nice, and she also knew that since he'd played college baseball, she wouldn't be able to throw a ball that he couldn't catch with ease.

Nolan was impressed with the rate of speed at which the balls were slapping his glove. The next one he received, though, caught him completely off guard. It came fast and straight and shot the sound of a loud pop of leather into the air like a gunshot. The echo lingered for a moment and so did the sting on his palm. He wished he'd been paying a little closer attention and caught the throw in the webbing of the glove. Impressed, he grinned in the dark.

"Can I throw one hard?" Nolan teased.

"Sure," she invited.

His next throw zipped through the air with a little more velocity, but not even as much as Emma's previous throw.

"I think you can throw harder than that," Emma acknowledged. "But thanks for remembering that it's dark out here."

The glow of the moon somewhat lit the field, and the pure volume of the light from the endless sea of fireflies seemed to brighten the area even more, although that seemed nearly unfathomable.

"You have a good arm," Nolan pointed out.

"I've heard that before."

"I bet." He paused as he caught her next throw. "You throw harder than some of the guys on my college team did."

Emma found that funny, and she didn't hide it. "Really?"

"Seriously. Some guys hit way harder than they throw." In the water near the creek, a bullfrog called out in agreement, and both Nolan and Emma laughed in unison. "Now if you can hit as far as them I might have to ask to see your birth certificate."

Emma laughed. "I doubt I can hit anywhere near as far as them, but if I grab a bat will you pitch me a few? It's been forever since I've hit a baseball."

Nolan contemplated Emma's request. He wanted to say *No*. He hadn't expected even to pick up a baseball let along pitch one, but for some reason, he couldn't tell Emma *No*. "Sure," he finally agreed.

He watched her silhouette as she walked back to the trunk beside the bench, and he felt entirely lucky knowing she was the woman he'd been kissing just a little while ago in the middle of this field. She struck him as nothing shy of amazing. Emma was a great kisser, she could throw the heck out of a baseball, and she was the most beautiful woman he knew.

"Is that a wooden bat?" he inquired as she stepped up to the plate with fireflies swarming in the background.

"Yes sir," she said. "Real baseball players use wooden bats, not those pansy composite bats that college players hit with," she jabbed with a joking tone.

Nolan chuckled. "Hey, I didn't hit in college, so I'm not guilty of that," he reminded her. He highly doubted he would ever choose to hit a baseball the rest of his life.

"Just don't pitch it hard because if I miss it we don't have a catcher and the ball will end up in one of those rows of corn back there." She pointed in that direction with her bat.

There was no backstop like on a typical baseball field—the wall of corn made up what would otherwise be a fence.

"Deal," Nolan agreed.

He tossed her the first pitch slowly and watched her swing and miss. He didn't say anything, and Emma just turned to retrieve the ball. He threw the next pitch right down the middle about forty miles per hour. He watched her left leg stride toward the ball as it neared the plate, and when she connected, the sound of the wooden bat making contact with the ball produced an echo that circled the field like a boomerang. Nolan grinned from ear to ear. He loved that sound. Every baseball player and fan loved that sound. There was no other quite like it. It was quick and crisp and a thing of pure beauty.

Emma watched the glow of the ball fly through the air, much faster and much larger than the fireflies but similar in color. Eventually, it landed about fifty feet into the outfield grass, a decent hit by any standards.

"Nice line drive," Nolan acknowledged as he turned to jog for the ball. He threw her twenty or so more pitches at the same velocity, and she connected on all but one. She offered to chase the balls down, so Nolan didn't have to, but he wouldn't let her go alone. After he'd retrieved a few for her, she began walking with him out to where each ball landed. They took their time and talked about baseball and the fireflies and the history of the field on which they were playing. Nolan learned that a cornfield once covered this entire area, but that in the mid-1800s Emma's ancestors plowed most of it under—leaving a thin line to tend between the wooded area—and erected this baseball field. "The slaves that helped work the fields back in those days helped create this even though many of them had never even stepped foot on a baseball field," Emma said. "My family wanted them to experience the game firsthand so they built a field all their own, and on summer evenings as the sun went down, they would all leave the working fields and venture to this field for a game of baseball." She continued telling the story the same way it had been passed down from generation to generation with intentions of never being forgotten. "They didn't wear uniforms or have umpires or arguments, they just hit and threw and ran . . . and laughed a lot. My family believed that all people were created equal and that's how they treated everyone. The family worked just as hard as the slaves, and the slaves had just as much fun as the family." She paused, and it caused Nolan to think she was imagining herself playing on the field with the people who'd thrown the first pitches and hit the first home runs here. "Legend has it that some exceptional ballplayers played on this field, and legend also has it that the fireflies showed up the first evening a game took place here."

"I love that story," Nolan acknowledged. It really warmed his heart as it caused him to think about his dad and all of the conversations they'd had about the history of baseball and the roles that race played in the sport. His dad had always said that there were probably more bad stories about slavery than good ones, but that the good stories should be the ones we highlight and the bad ones should be lessons learned for all of humanity. This thought led Nolan back to the conversation he'd had earlier with Emma about his brother, and he assumed that Emma's raising had something to do with why it hadn't phased her when Nolan had mentioned that Norman was black.

"I wish I could tell the whole world," Emma said.

Showing understanding, Nolan nodded his head. "My dad is black," he then said out of the blue.

Emma just kept looking at him. She wasn't sure how to respond. Not because she'd just discovered that a white man's dad was black, but because the statement left little room for a response. It would be like her saying *My dad was white*. She had a good idea why Nolan had made mention of the fact—most likely because he simply wanted her to know. Emma started just to say *Okay*, but then instead she said, "My dad was white."

At the same exact time, Emma and Nolan both started laughing hysterically. It was as if the two of them had just heard the funniest joke ever told, and they found themselves buckling over and nearly in tears.

When they pulled themselves back together, Emma asked a very debatable question. "Why do you think racism still exists?"

Nolan pondered the question for a moment. "My dad used to always say it's because some people are ignorant." Nolan paused, then added his own thought. "I think that now there is a small majority of people who are ignorant, but this small majority happens to be extremely loud and our society keeps handing them megaphones and microphones."

Emma noticed that he said *people*, not *white people* or *black people*. "So, since you grew up with a black father and brother, I'm sure you encountered your share of racism from both sides of the fence." She paused for a moment, hesitating whether to ask the question that had randomly popped into her mind. There were so many places this conversation could travel from Nolan's last statement, but for some reason, this particular thought sometimes set heavy on her heart. "Do you think one race is more racist than the other?"

At first, Nolan was a bit shocked by her candor, but then he recognized the concern over this issue in her tone. "I wouldn't want to put more blame on any particular race," he started. "Norman and I have actually talked a lot about this over the years. Growing up, he would mainly notice the white people that were racist, and I would mainly notice the black people that were racist."

Emma dissected the thought. "That makes sense."

"We were friends with black people and white people, though, so we often witnessed it from both. There were times when we'd be in a predominately white crowd and other times where we'd be in a predominately black crowd. One of the unfortunate things we discovered is that kids just repeat a lot of what they hear their parents say. Norman and I always tried to prevent racism on both sides of the fence because he saw how much it hurt me when someone called me a *cracker* and I saw how bad it hurt him when someone called him the N-word." Nolan stopped to consider what he wanted to say next. "You know, it's not really the actual words that hurt because in the predominately black neighborhoods most of the kids and even a lot of the adults call each other the N-word constantly, and it doesn't seem to sting most of them one bit. I can remember wondering why white people didn't go around calling each other *crackers* or *honkeys*. Norman would say that when a white kid called him the N-word it made him feel as though he wasn't accepted. Flip the page, and I felt the same way when black kids called me *white bread*. Ironically, some white kids called me the N-word because of the color of my family. So, ultimately, it's about acceptance more than linguistics or anything else."

Strangely, Emma all of a sudden found herself wondering if the mother who raised Nolan was black or white. He still hadn't mentioned her specifically, she had noticed. He'd said things about his parents in general terms, but nothing about just his mother. There were so many possibilities of how Nolan had become part of the family he was telling her about a little at a time. Obviously, his biological mom was white, which most likely meant that she'd had Nolan and then later married a black man. Emma thought about asking but decided to let him bring up that part of the equation when he felt ready. "I bet that was tough on both of you," she ended up acknowledging.

"It was," Nolan admitted. "We got into a lot of fights over such things, some verbal and some that escalated to physical altercations. I didn't want anyone one calling my brother a name, and Norman didn't want anyone calling me a name. Our parents always taught us to kill people with kindness, but Norman and I made a pact early in our lives that we'd never allow the other to be bullied."

"I love it when brothers stick together like that, especially in a case like yours. My dad and grandad told me stories of our ancestors that came to know many of the slaves that worked our farm like brothers, and they didn't want anyone talking down to them because of the color of their skin. Of course, it was much more accepted in those days, but I heard lots of stories about members of my family taking beatings from others for sticking up for the slaves."

What a sacrifice, Nolan thought to himself. He'd always thought that he wouldn't have wanted to live in those days, but at this moment, Nolan hoped that if he had, he would have embodied the courage to be like Emma's ancestors. Sometimes living in a predominately black neighborhood had made him feel like the outcast so Nolan had a very twisted yet ironic idea of what it might have felt like to be a slave. Being called names, beat up because of the color of his skin, spit on, told to leave and go back to the suburbs where he belonged. Along the way, though, Nolan had learned that taking a beating for standing up for who you were and what you believed in meant more than giving a beating to someone who disagreed. Nolan preferred not to relive the hard parts of his life any more than he had to, so he chose not to mention specifics to Emma but rather share some of the positives. "Norman and I would always defend one another, but we never started anything. There were many times when one of us would say to another person, 'Hey, please don't call my brother that name,' and the person who'd said it would apologize. Looking back, I would like to think we had a positive influence on those around us."

"I'm sure the world is a better place because of both of you," Emma uttered with true sincerity.

"Based on everything you've told me about your family and your feelings on this subject, I would say the same about you."

Emma and Nolan talked on and on about this issue and how they both preferred hearing the positive stories about people like them and their families who truly wanted to make a difference in the world, both now and for the future of society. They agreed that in recent years the media and politicians had played a role in stirring up racism out of greed—namely political and financial gain. Politicians pointed fingers to gain votes rather than connecting them to strengthen relationships. The media sought out conflict because it was more entertaining and it sold more advertising than did heartfelt stories.

Before Nolan and Emma said goodbye to Firefly Field for the night, Emma made sure to remind Nolan about the furthest ball she'd hit off his pitching—the one that went all the way to the cornfield in left field. They'd even had to search through a couple of rows before Nolan plucked it out from the soft soil behind a stalk. Granted, it just barely made it into the rows of corn, and it had rolled to that point on the ground rather than landed there in the air, but Nolan figured she'd probably hit it a good two hundred and seventy feet in the air before it touched the grass. It was a superb hit, one he would have taken any day back when he used to hit.

After her last swing, Emma had reached the bat toward Nolan and said, "Your turn, slugger."

Nolan held his hands steady by his side. "No, thanks."

"Come on, are you afraid you won't be able to outhit a girl?" she teased.

He shrugged. "Maybe."

She held the bat up again. "Just hit. I won't strike you out, I promise," she jabbed.

Nolan didn't reach for the bat. "I would rather just pitch to you if that's okay."

Something in his tone told Emma that he wasn't going to hit whether it was okay with her or not, so she decided not to ask him a third time even though she really wanted to see him hit a baseball. She wondered if he was afraid of having a girl pitch to him. Or maybe he was nervous that he might accidentally drive a ball back up the middle that she wouldn't be able to handle. She respected that, especially since it was dark out.

Nolan stared at his feet instead of looking Emma in the eyes. He never wanted another human being to know the real reason why he no longer wanted to hold a bat in his hand—the reason he'd moved across the country rather than staying close to home. The reason he'd become a pitcher in lieu of a hitter. The reason he'd never played professional baseball. The reason he had distanced himself from his father. Bats could hit things other than just baseballs. Bats could be dangerous. Very dangerous. Even deadly.

13

It was well past midnight when Nolan's vehicle coasted out of Emma's driveway with the headlights off and the windows rolled down so that he could see well enough to keep the car out of the ditches on either side of the road. As his tires carried him past Clay Bell's driveway, he glared at the house and wanted to turn the steering wheel to the right and give the guy a piece of his mind. Nolan's better judgment led him to the first paved road where his headlights guided him home.

Over the next week, this became a new routine for Nolan. He would cruise into Emma's driveway after dark, spend time with her until they could no longer hold their eyes open, and then leave as inconspicuously as he had arrived. He considered inviting Emma to his house to make things a little simpler, but then he realized that this idea would be just as complex, if not even more challenging. The first obstacle had popped up in his mind immediately. Just after Nolan had been hired at the community college, Jerry Small had been kind enough to tell him about an available house right next to his family's home. A week later, Nolan had moved in and ever since then he would cross paths with Jerry when Jerry was out mowing the lawn, checking the mail, or walking the dog. The next obstacle presented itself when Emma informed Nolan that she no longer had a vehicle and that she literally rode her bicycle everywhere she went: to work, the grocery store, the bank, and so on. As soon as Nolan discovered this, on nights when Emma worked at the restaurant, the two of them began meeting in a dark parking lot behind a doctor's office just outside of the downtown district. "You don't have to worry about me riding my bike home after work, I've always done it," Emma had said to Nolan when he first mentioned loading her bike into his trunk and driving her home after her shifts. Then she found it extremely sweet when he said he didn't just want to make sure she was safe, but that he also wanted to spend the extra time with her that it would take for her to pedal home. She enjoyed Nolan's company much more than Alan's, so she gave in to his request. Some nights Nolan stayed over so late at Emma's house that he barely made it home before sunrise. They would fall asleep watching a movie on the couch or sit at the kitchen table telling stories or take a walk out to Firefly Field to throw baseball. Emma continued to notice that Nolan never expressed any interest in hitting, but he was always willing to pitch to her. They loved to watch the fireflies float through the air as they experienced a nightlife way better than that which any city filled with bars and clubs had to offer.

During college, Nolan had spent more than his share of nights in downtown Greenville, the area that had helped put East Carolina University on the map as one of America's top party schools. Now, Nolan found out the hard way that having to wake up as a responsible adult and teach college classes was way more difficult than being one of the students sitting in a sea of desks trying to keep his eyes open after partying too late or too hard the night before. He selfishly looked forward to Emma dropping her classes so that she would no longer be an official student at Beaufort County Community College. Nonetheless, he searched for options that might allow her to stay in college. He looked into a few scholarships that were offered. As he perused the lists he was surprised by some of the offers. There were scholarships for academics, which was fair because every student had the opportunity to work hard and make good grades. There were scholarships for women, which didn't sound quite fair because he couldn't find any scholarships for men. There were scholarships for minorities, which didn't sound quite equal because he found no specific scholarships for non-minorities. The afternoon he'd spent thumbing through the list, he'd called Norman to get his thoughts on the subject. The two of them tossed out the pros and cons, and eventually ended up talking about black colleges. Both of them recalled their father saying that he understood the idea of black colleges, but that he thought that colleges shouldn't have such labels even though people of other races were accepted into black colleges. "I don't think society would go for a white college," Norman said, pointing out the imbalance. Nolan agreed but then reminded Norman that from his understanding the reason black colleges started was because blacks either wouldn't be accepted into colleges that at the time were white only—whether it was specified or not—or were having a more difficult time getting in, which was wrong, but society had, for the most part, fixed that form of racism. Based on what Nolan understood, there were actually scholarships for minorities at black colleges, which again just didn't seem right. A white person being a minority at a predominately black college didn't seem like a valid reason for him to receive a scholarship. Nolan understood the purpose of all of these ideas, but at the same time, he felt like it defeated the purpose of the attempt to end racism and injustice. "A man or woman should be accepted into a college based on an equal set of standards, and they should have equal opportunity for every scholarship," he said just before he and Norman finished their phone call, and Norman agreed. In the end, perusing the list of scholarships just irritated Nolan.

It was too late for Emma to apply now that the semester was underway anyway, so he'd somewhat wasted his time. The window for her to drop classes was also diminishing. College policy stated that if a student missed more than a certain percentage of her classes she'd be dropped automatically. Nolan had internally become bothered by the fact that Emma hadn't dropped her classes. She claimed that with the two of them staying up so late on a nightly basis she didn't have time to make it to the college in the morning to officially drop her classes. She'd been clocking in at the restaurant at noon to pick up extra hours. "All of my instructors will eventually just drop me," she'd once said, but then Nolan reminded her that if this happened she wouldn't receive a tuition refund. After that conversation, she promised to drop by the college the next day, and she did. To Nolan's surprise, however, she texted him that morning saying, "I'm coming to your class today. I'll explain later." He became ridiculously nervous upon reading the message, although he felt he had gotten to know Emma well enough to be nearly certain she wouldn't knowingly do anything that would put his job in jeopardy.

That day she helped with clearing the trail behind the college—the ones Nolan's classes had been collectively working on since a few days after Emma quit showing up. This was the big idea for which he had needed Jerry's approval. When he first approached his dean, Jerry had said he liked the idea but that they'd have to get approval from the president of the college. Nolan figured this process would take time, but to his astonishment, he'd received an email the same day stating that the president and a few other staff members wanted to meet with Nolan to discuss his plan. The following day they'd walked through the woods together to see the trail Nolan had mapped out, and when they went back to the president's office, he had his secretary type a formal letter to Nolan stating the college's approval of the project. Nolan was relieved that Clay Bell wasn't one of the additional staff members that had shown up for the walk-through. For some reason Nolan had feared such would happen, but in hindsight it didn't surprise him because he'd barely seen Clay at the college at all recently. Emma had mentioned to him that Clay had shown up at her house two more times and that he'd mentioned to her that he was busy working on real estate deals so his college courses were taking a back seat for the time being. That's when Nolan learned that Clay was an adjunct instructor, and this news only verified Nolan's thoughts about colleges needing to invest in more full-time instructors. Nolan had asked Emma if Clay had made mention of anything suspicious, but to his surprise, she said Clay seemed to be absolutely clueless to the fact that Nolan had been coming and going recently.

When class time expired, Nolan and the students returned all of the tools to a small white-blocked building near the head of the trail. It was in bad shape with busted windows and broken doors, vines growing on the inside and outside, and no working electricity. It was an advantageous place to store all of the equipment that Nolan had been able to have donated by the local hardware store. At the end of each day he tried to secure the building as best he could, but today he remained inside with the last student to leave as the sun sliced in through a hole in the ceiling.

"What are you doing here?" he asked Emma quietly.

"I found a way to stay in college and keep the farm," she shared with enthusiasm.

He wanted to be excited, and in a way he was, but if this news held true it meant they would be right back to square one. Nolan had to admit that the time they'd spent sneaking around, like a couple of teenagers hiding a relationship from their parents, held a certain sense of excitement that he'd thoroughly enjoyed, but at the same time it was stressful. It was taking a toll on his body, his mind, and his emotions. This became immediately obvious by the sharp tone of his next statement. "That's great, but why in the world did you just show up for my class? We were together last night—this morning, actually," Nolan stated, reminding Emma that they'd basically spent the whole night together. They'd woken up in her bed with their arms draped around each other when the alarm that they'd set to sound off thirty minutes before daylight reminded him that it was time to skedaddle.

"If my coming to your class was such a big deal, why didn't you call me as soon as you received the text I sent you this morning rather than wait for me to show up here?" Emma shot back, irritation lining her voice.

"Because I literally didn't see your text until about five minutes before you showed up at this building for class. There were already other students here, and I didn't want to risk them overhearing our conversation." He almost asked her how she even knew they were meeting out here for class now rather than indoors, but then he remembered that the two of them had talked about it one night in her kitchen, and she'd also mentioned that Lisa had been giving her updates. Nolan had to admit that Lisa hadn't acted any differently around him nor had she spoken a single word to him about Emma while on campus. He had somewhat expected her to make mention of the situation covertly, but he was thankful she had been mature enough to realize the risk. "Plus I thought you were going to show up and tell me that you'd dropped your classes and that we were no longer breaking the rules."

"I thought you would be happy about this, Nolan. You've made all those comments about how I should stay in college, how it's more important than anything else in my life right now."

"It is," he said sharply, his voice echoing inside the near-empty building—much louder than he'd anticipated.

"More important than us?" she fired back. As soon as she said it, though, she wasn't sure why. The comparison wasn't fair.

"Please don't go there, Emma," he said, shaking his head, heavy from lack of sleep caused by late night conversations and peanut butter and crackers in bed. Sharing snacks with her in bed while they watched TV had been one of the many highlights of their nights together. It was a simple thing, but it was fun nonetheless, and he cherished it.

Somewhat reluctantly, Emma stepped toward him and gave him a big hug. She wasn't nervous about him forgiving her for what she'd just implied, but because he was right, her being here put his job in jeopardy and her embracing him doubled the risk. How would they explain this if someone were to walk through the open door this very moment?

Nolan pulled back after a brief embrace. "Look," he said, "we're both on edge. Let's step back, literally and figuratively." In response to his words, he watched Emma take two steps back toward a wall covered with spidery vines. He folded his arms and turned his body slightly, looking through the particles of dust illuminated by a beam of sunlight. "First, I am happy that you found a way to stay in college."

Emma stared at him with her lips pursed together. He had a way with words. He could cut her one moment and heal her the next. She had a good feeling, though, that if their relationship were normal he wouldn't cut her in the first place. He wouldn't be sleep deprived and stressed out. The same rang true for her. They'd had several misunderstandings in recent days, but they'd always been able to work through them smoothly. In that way, she was glad things were the way they were. It was good to know they could figure out life in the midst of a difficult situation. Lisa had advised her to slow down and be careful, but she had shrugged off the advice. It was easy for someone on the outside looking in to question her relationship with Nolan, but she knew things that no one else knew. She knew how she felt about him.

"Second, I am eager to hear how you figured out a way to make this work?"

Emma jumped directly into answering Nolan's question. "I was riding my bike to the college this morning to meet with my advisor to have her drop me from my classes when I remembered something. It was odd how it occurred to me—I was watching the wheels on my bicycle spin when I thought of how kids used to insert baseball cards in their spokes so they'd make that clicking sound like the one the *Wheel of Fortune* wheel makes when a contestant spins it."

Nolan smiled, recollecting the exact sound in his mind. He'd never attempted placing cards in his spokes during his childhood, mainly because his father would have beaten his butt if he found out he was abusing baseball cards.

Emma continued her spill. "I think baseball cards were on my mind because the other night you and I were talking about the cards you and your dad collected. This morning it hit me, my granddad used to tell stories about how his friends would stick their cards in their spokes, but he always kept all of his cards, and he ended up with valuable cards like Babe Ruth, Mickey Mantle, and other greats. You were talking about how much old cards are worth—his are all up in the attic, collecting dust, Nolan."

Knowing where this was leading, Nolan furrowed his brow.

"Nolan, I can sell these cards, they're worth a small fortune," she confirmed.

Nolan hesitated before replying. He didn't want to ruin the smile on Emma's face. "But those are your granddad's cards, wouldn't he want you to pass them down? Weren't they special to him?"

"Of course they were special to him, but they're in the attic," she emphasized again. "He stashed the cards away like the old timers used to do with cash—they would bury it out in their fields or backyards for a rainy day because they didn't trust bankers. The cards were more like an investment to my grandad than a collection. He didn't treat them like art that needed to hang on the wall."

Nolan found that hard to believe, maybe because in his mind baseball cards *were* like art. They should be appreciated and enjoyed and sifted through and stared at often just like a painting by Monet or Van Gogh. He wanted to challenge her, talk her into keeping the cards, but it wasn't his place he finally decided. She was right, too, he had to admit—if her grandfather had the cards she'd just mentioned, then selling them would most likely allow her to stay in college. Such cards were highly sought after by collectors around the world, and he'd prefer her to sell them opposed to losing the farm or giving up her education.

Later that night, after Nolan picked up Emma at the doctor's office parking lot, he climbed into a dark attic with her and a flashlight. The air up there smelled like it had been bottled up since the date on most of the baseball cards they found in a dull gray tin container about the size of a tissue box. The first card to take away Nolan's breath, as he held it under a lamp in Emma's living room after brushing off cobwebs from his clothing, was a 1959 Topps Bob Gibson rookie card. He'd already come across a Harmon Killebrew and a Ted Williams, but the Gibson card was way more valuable. He found a few cards with names that he'd never heard of and some of players that he recognized but that weren't household names. His favorite card in the bunch was a 1964 Topps Mickey Mantle card. It displayed a photo of Mantle from about the waist up, gripping a wood bat and donning the famous New York pinstripes. The word *YANKEES* was in bold lettering across the top of the card in red letters. In the background, a teammate was visible, standing near the batting cage, and beyond that, a blur of stadium seating could be picked out.

Emma recognized the names on many of the cards, but she had no idea how much any of them were worth. She quickly realized

Nolan did, and his knowledge of each card amazed her as she listened to him go on and on about not only the players but the conditions of the cards. As soon as they'd opened the box and pulled out a few cards, he began rambling about ratings and talked in numbers and symbols that sounded like they were from the periodic table of elements: MT, NM, EX, VG, FR, PR. There were others, too, but too many to remember as they rushed from his mouth like water bursting through a dam. Thankfully, in time, he dumbed things down for her. "MT means Mint, NM means Near Mint, EX means Excellent, VG means Very Good, FR means Fair, and PR means Poor," he explained when he recognized the puzzled look on Emma's face. "Each card should be graded by a professional authenticator. The cards will be more reputable and in turn more valuable if graded," he expounded. She found out that the numerical grades he'd been talking about were set on a one to ten scale and that they would be attached to the symbols to clarify the rating. She was pretty sure she understood that GEM-MT 10 was the highest rating a baseball card could receive. When Nolan told her that cards could also earn half a point, she called him a *baseball card nerd*. He laughed, and she found herself scooting closer to him on the couch as he continued to show enthusiasm about helping her with the cards. It seemed as if God had sent him here partially for this very reason.

"So what's the most valuable card here?"

"Probably the Bob Gibson, but the Mantle card is worth a lot, too."

There was also a 1955 Topps Don Zimmer, a 1954 Bowman Ted Williams, and more cards of Hall-of-Famers like Hank Aaron, Willie Mays, and Roger Maris. Nolan's mouth remained gaped open even when not speaking. Emma's grandfather's baseball card collection was much smaller than his and his father's collection, but the value was very respectable.

"How much?"

"It's difficult to estimate without inspection and research, but it wouldn't surprise me if your grandfather's baseball card collection is worth $50,000."

Emma's eyes bubbled. "Are you serious?"

"Yes, and that's just a rough ballpark figure, I could be off in either direction." He paused, holding the Maris card in his hand. "It's a good thing a durable case has protected each card, that's helped keep them in good condition."

"I remember seeing cards listed online when I was selling other items in the past." Emma had hated having to part with many of the other items, and she didn't necessarily want to sell her granddad's baseball card collection either, but it seemed like the best option given the circumstances. "Can we start listing some of them tonight?"

Nolan suddenly exhaled and made a face that reminded Emma of a warning sign. "We could, but I don't recommend it. Remember earlier when I mentioned having the cards rated by a professional?"

"Yes . . ."

"We need to have that done."

"So how does that work?"

"Well, there are options. A lot of people these days mail off their cards to a sports authenticator. Of course, then you would want to buy insurance on a secured package just in case anything were to happen to cards of this particular value. Some people research the closest authenticator and personally drive their cards to this person. Either way, you have to pay a fee for each card that you wish to have professionally rated."

"How much is the fee per card?"

Nolan shrugged. "It often depends on the declared value of each card, so it can differ, and honestly it can get relatively expensive."

"So I need money to make money?" Go figure, she thought with a heavy sigh.

"Technically, yes, but—" Nolan paused, not sure he wanted to suggest the other idea that had entered his mind.

Emma watched Nolan closely. As soon as he'd held his tongue, he had turned his head and was now staring at the floor. Since meeting him, she'd already learned not to try to force him to talk but that if she was patient, he'd end up talking when he was ready. Realizing something was bothering him, she reached to his shoulder blade and rubbed it gently. "We can talk about this tomorrow if you'd rather," she suggested.

Nolan spoke almost immediately. "There's only one man I trust to grade baseball cards," he said shifting his lips after he spoke. "He works with a team of experts that will collaborate to grade the cards."

"Who is he and how much will he charge us?"

"He won't charge anything," Nolan whispered, "and he's my father."

14

When Nolan left Emma's house around two o'clock in the morning, she nestled back in on the couch where the two of them had been sitting. Just like earlier, the computer screen provided the only light in the room. Before leaving, Nolan had been showing her some reputable baseball card websites where they could eventually list her grandfather's cards. Now, there were some other things she wanted to search for, things that had been on her mind lately. Tapping the tips of her nails together, she hesitated for a few moments before typing the name Nolan Lynch into the search bar.

A list of links appeared, and as her eyes wandered down the screen she realized that most of them led to social media pages of various people named Nolan Lynch. There was way more than one person by the name, which Emma had figured would be the case before ever starting the search. She wasn't sure what she was looking for, or if she would even come across anything worth her time, but she had a feeling that Nolan was hiding something. She scrolled down the page a bit, and one of the headlines immediately screamed out at her, loud enough to temporarily paralyze her mind and body: *Star Baseball Player Nolan Lynch Involved in Tragedy.*

Emma yanked her fingers away from the keyboard and held her hands over her mouth. Part of her wanted to click on the link, and another part of her suddenly felt a sharp stab of guilt. She had to admit that she wanted to know what happened, and she wanted to know right away. Why hadn't Nolan told her himself, though, she couldn't help but wonder. This was something she would have rather learned from him. Emma closed her eyes, half hoping that when they reopened the words on the screen might not be there anymore. When she opened her eyelids, though, they were still there, and eventually, she moved the cursor and stared at it while it hovered over the link. Instead of clicking it, she decided to scroll down.

Out of the next dozen or so headlines at least half of them were about Nolan Lynch—the Nolan Lynch that had been in her house less than twenty minutes ago.

The entire ride home Nolan had been contemplating how to approach the phone call he promised Emma he would make. Obviously, calling his dad at this hour of the night was out of the question. He wasn't quite sure why he'd been so quick to say that he would involve his father in this ordeal. Maybe it was because he'd secretly been hoping for a reason to reach out to his dad. All of this baseball related stuff lately had brought back so many memories—good and bad—and he realized how much he missed the man that had raised him.

Thinking these thoughts caused Nolan's stomach to twist into knots and eventually it felt as if the pressure burst a water line. Tears began streaming from Nolan's eyes, and he couldn't stop them nor could he dull the awful bellowing sound that was rising from his stomach and exiting his mouth as he sat idly in the driveway. He'd been sitting here in his vehicle for at least ten minutes, and for an instant, he thought about starting the ignition and heading to Arizona. He cried a little longer and then realized a trip home wasn't feasible. Honestly, he didn't even know what his dad would say to him if he showed up on his doorstep. The last time they'd spoken was at the funeral.

Emma stared at the other headlines in disbelief. Along with Nolan's first and last name, there were other words: Baseball Bat, Woman Killed, Death. One headline, in particular, caused chills to shake Emma's body: *White Baseball Player Nolan Lynch Kills Black Woman.*

Nolan didn't feel like going inside his house right now. He didn't even want to be alone, and he found himself wishing he could talk to someone. His brother had been trying to get him to see a therapist for years, but Nolan hadn't been interested. "I'm not sharing the most personal details of my life with someone I don't even know," he would tell Norman.

"Our team has a professional sports therapist, I can probably get him to meet with you," Norman had offered.

Norman had made their dad the proudest father in the world when he was drafted into the NFL in the second round by the Miami Dolphins as a linebacker. Nolan had been extremely proud of his brother, too. All of the training the two of them had put in together growing up had paid off. The long runs on cold mornings. The late nights in the gym lifting weights. They'd also always been each other's accountability partner when it came to strict diets and staying out of trouble. They hadn't partied much in high school, they'd steered clear of drugs and excess alcohol, and both of them had managed not to get anyone pregnant. Yet Nolan's path had deviated drastically on a rainy Monday, and he'd felt all of his dreams come crashing down on him.

"Norman, I'm fine," Nolan promised, but he wasn't. "Plus, I don't have the money to fly down to Miami to lay on a couch and talk to your therapist."

Norman always offered to foot the bill, but Nolan didn't want to accept his money. He'd been adamant about that ever since his brother had received his first paycheck—equivalent to many people's yearly salary.

Nolan reached for the gearshift. Thoughts . . . these thoughts . . . they ate at him. Devoured him at times. He tried to keep them hidden. Tried to mask his pain and anger. Maybe a drive would make things better. Maybe.

A little bit later, Nolan ended up talking to God in the gravel parking lot at Asbury United Methodist Church, where tombstones almost completely surrounded the old white, wooden structure that perfectly captured the essence of a traditional Southern church.

With dried tear lines streaking down her face, Emma closed the laptop screen, and the entire room around her went completely dark. She thought about the time she'd been spending with Nolan. They'd been hanging out a lot, and Emma had felt like she was getting to know him, but in a matter of moments, she found herself questioning everything. She now realized there was so much about Nolan Lynch that she didn't know.

The entire house was pitch black when Emma stood to walk the familiar path toward her bedroom. She'd made the trek hundreds of times, but this time she nearly jumped out of her socks when a loud thump echoed through the living room. Instinctively, she let out a shrill, and her immediate knee-jerk reaction was to turn toward the source of the sound. For a moment she stood there in the quiet, frozen like an ice sculpture. She couldn't think of one single logical reason to answer a knock at her front door in the middle of the night.

As she wondered who might be standing on her porch, she waited another moment to see if a second stream of knocks would follow. Her hands were now shaking by her side, and her heart raced as fast as possible without blowing through her skin. Maybe if she remained motionless the person would just go away, she considered.

The porch light illuminated the area outside the front door, and she could see the shadows of tree limbs dancing through the window, then all of a sudden a dark figure appeared. With her mouth gaping open, she watched the person move slowly across her porch. Her fear seemed to intensify at that moment, especially when he drew nearer to the window and appeared to cup his hands to peek in through the glass. She felt confident he couldn't see her since not a single bulb in the entire house was glowing, but this fact didn't seem to relieve her anxiety even a bit, especially when she began to wonder how long he'd been out there. Had he been watching her?

She should call 911, she decided. Now. The trouble with that idea, though, Emma quickly realized is that she couldn't even remember where she'd left her phone, and now she was afraid to move an inch. It hadn't been on the couch next to her when she'd turned off the lamp. She knew that because she had looked for it when she found herself wondering if Nolan had sent her a text to let her know he'd arrived home safely. Had he come back for some reason? She didn't want to answer the door to find out. Maybe she should find her phone and call Clay, she suddenly considered. He could be over in a matter of moments to check out things for her.

The dark figure seemed to pull back from the window and then all of a sudden she realized she could no longer see his silhouette. Finally, she decided to move. She needed her phone.

Somehow Emma made it all the way to her bedroom without tripping or knocking over anything like the helpless victims in scary movies. Ironically, that's exactly who she felt like right now. As soon as Emma secured her phone from the nightstand, which thankfully had been plugged up to the charger where she often left it, she focused as best as possible on the bright screen in her trembling hand. The first thing she noticed was that she hadn't received a text from Nolan, which was odd. He always sent a message as soon as he arrived home and he should have made it there a while ago.

With the lights still completely out, she opened her closet door, grabbed a baseball bat, and headed back toward the front door. On the way there, she nearly dropped her cell phone when the ringer completely startled her. In that instant, her heart skipped a beat or two. Maybe three. Pulling herself together momentarily, she glanced at the screen and immediately answered the call.

"Clay," she whispered, his name rolling off her tongue with much more excitement than it had in a long time, "someone is at my door. Can you please come over?" she requested with urgency.

In that moment, she prayed that the person on her porch wasn't Nolan, although in a way it would freak her out even more if it was anyone else. If it was Nolan, that would cause a scene for sure when Clay arrived and who knows what would come of it now.

"It's me," Clay said. "I'm at your door."

Emma nearly threw the phone through the window at the dark figure that she now knew to be Clay. She didn't even respond on the phone; she just marched to the door.

"What in the heck are you doing, Clay Bell?" she demanded as she opened the door. "You scared the crap out of me!" she shouted.

"I thought I heard a car go down the road a little while ago, so I've been outside looking around."

She squinted her eyes. "Outside where? In my yard?" she queried.

"No." He paused, glancing back toward the tree line between

their houses. "Well, not at first. I looked around on the road; then I thought I'd walk up your driveway and check on your place."

"Why didn't you just call instead of beating on my door in the middle of the night?"

"Well, I didn't want to wake you, but then I noticed a light shut off when I was walking up the driveway, so I figured you were awake."

"Uh, you still could have called instead of knocking."

"Sorry," he said, sounding like he meant it. "Are you okay?"

"Now I am," she acknowledged. "I was about to call the police."

"Do you know who drove down the road?" he asked.

Emma suddenly felt like a teenager being interrogated by a parent. She wanted to say, *Yeah, Nolan, the guy I am seeing*, but she couldn't. "I have no idea," she answered instead. "It was probably some teenagers out joyriding," she offered, hoping to ease Clay's mind.

"Yeah, maybe," he said. "I just don't like strange cars riding down our road late at night," he added, staring at her as if she was hiding something.

She didn't like the way he was looking at her, and she didn't like the way his tone had come across—more like a warning than a concern.

"I'm going to bed, Clay."

"What are you doing up so late?" he inquired, standing in the way of her doorframe.

"Who are you, my dad?"

He smirked. "Why so defensive?"

"Why I am up late is none of your business."

"You act like I am accusing you of running guys in and out of here at all hours of the night or something."

Again, she didn't like his tone. "Goodnight, Clay," she said, pushing the door with him in it.

He stepped back. "I'll make sure to keep a closer eye out at night. Maybe even put up one of those video cameras with a motion detector."

"That's a great idea," she responded. "Goodnight."

Clay shuffled down the porch steps with a smirk on his face. He felt terrible for scaring the bejesus out of Emma, but he knew she hadn't been completely honest with him. The lights inside her house had been on much later than normal quite often recently. He didn't want to pry into her business, but before her dad passed away, Clay had promised him he would keep an eye on his daughter. As Clay kicked across the dirt road with his hands in his pockets, he found himself wishing that Emma had invited him in to comfort her following tonight's traumatic experience. It hadn't been his intention to frighten her, but since it had happened, he wished it had worked in his favor. He didn't understand why she would want to be with any man other than him. Emma knew him better than anyone. They'd grown up together. They'd had intimate moments and shared special memories. He'd always thought they were meant to be together. Many women wanted him; he knew that. He had money and land and connections. Sure, he didn't have all of his hair anymore, but women still found him attractive. He'd had three different females at the house in the past couple of weeks, which had been somewhat of a distraction with him trying to figure out what Emma had been up to lately. He wondered if that Alan dweeb ever rode by her house late at night—he seemed like the stalker type. Clay had taken note that Alan had given Emma a ride home from work at least a couple of times in the past. He doubted a fine-looking babe like Emma would be interested in such a dork, though. She had probably just taken advantage of the poor guy to catch a lift home from work so she didn't have to pedal that rinky-dink excuse for a bicycle.

The following morning Nolan scrolled through the contact list on his phone and then clicked *call.* The phone rang once. He sat impatiently up against the headboard of his bed. A second ring echoed in his ear. Nolan glanced toward the nightstand where a photograph of him and Norman with their parents set in a thin metal frame. The third ring began, then stopped. Nolan could hear an emptiness on the other end just before a familiar voice spoke.

"Hello."

"Hey." Nolan wasn't sure what to say next.

"It's early, what's going on?"

If there were an alarm clock next to the photo, it would have reminded Nolan that it was six o'clock in the morning. He'd barely slept at all last night.

"Can I ask you a question?"

"You just did," the sleepy voice replied.

"Norman, I'm serious."

"Of course you can, bro."

"What do you think Dad would say if I called him?"

For a moment, the line fell quiet, then Nolan heard Norman yawn.

"I'm not sure what he'd say, but I know he'd be ecstatic to hear from you. Are you going to call him?"

"I need a favor."

"What kind of favor?"

"From Dad."

Nolan explained to his brother that he needed to talk to their dad about Emma's baseball cards, then he heard a woman's voice in the background on the other end of the phone.

"Who's that?" Nolan asked.

"A friend," Norman answered.

Nolan snickered, thinking of a conversation he'd had with his brother the other day. "Oh, is she your 'or something' friend?"

he asked. What made the question funny is that Nolan had told Norman about the first night he'd ended up stuck at Emma's house until dark, which ended up being much later. He had mentioned how Emma had asked him if he wanted to stay for a movie *or something*. "I hope you chose *or something*," Norman had reeled off before laughing all over himself.

"Something like that," Norman answered this morning, too sleepy to joke around with his brother.

The two of them chatted for another minute, then Nolan let his brother get back to his friend.

Emma had woken up with the sunrise this morning, and she had been thinking about Nolan ever since—thinking about the articles she'd seen last night. She waited until seven o'clock to give him a call, hoping not to wake him up but wanting to talk to him about his past before she went to work today. She didn't think it was too much to ask. She deserved to know what happened and there was no way she was going to pull a double at the restaurant today with this eating at her mind. His phone rang, but he didn't answer. It went to voicemail. "Call me as soon as you get this message," Emma requested, her tone rushed. She set the phone next to her cup of coffee on the kitchen table. She forced down a couple of sips then picked up the phone once more. For a moment she stared at the screen, then she sent Nolan a text: *Call me, please*!

Nervous about how this conversation might go, Nolan held his phone close to his ear. He didn't even know how to start the talk or if he would be able to find adequate words to answer questions that were sure to arise.

"Hey, Dad," he said, feeling like he'd spoken the word *Dad* for the very first time.

The air fell as silent as a library for a short moment. Nolan waited anxiously for a response, but he didn't expect what he heard next—the sounds of gasps for breath and muzzled groans grabbed ahold of him like a clamp. For a moment, he worried, then those sounds morphed into the reality of a grown man wailing so hard that he couldn't even force out the usual sound of crying. Nolan could actually feel the vibrations streaming through the speaker and falling into his ear.

"Nolan, is this really you?" his father finally uttered in a broken voice.

"Yes—yes, it is, Dad." He repeated the word Dad, realizing now just how much he had missed saying it to the man who'd been his rock for so many years.

"It's so good to hear your voice, son," he heard his father express as his words obviously continued to battle his emotions.

15

Nolan realized he'd had more time to prepare his emotions for this phone call than his dad had. Nolan had cried his tears last night and even felt a lump in his throat this morning. Even now, he could once again feel the emotions rising up inside of him. Somehow, he was able to hold it together as he spoke to his father for the first time in six years.

"Dad, I've missed you so much."

The plan Nolan had initially had in mind hadn't gone as expected. His first words were supposed to be about the baseball cards. He figured he'd use that as a segue into a deeper conversation, but as soon as Nolan had heard his father's voice, he'd realized that no amount of planning could have prepared him for this phone call.

"I've missed you, too, Nolan."

The difference, Nolan realized, is that his father had tried to reach out to him. Countless times. He'd called. He'd sent letters. He'd relayed messages through Norman. He'd done everything but show up at Nolan's door while he was off at college.

"I'm so sorry," Nolan apologized, holding back tears.

"For what, son?" his dad asked as if nothing had ever happened.

"Everything," Nolan said simply, yet realizing his apology was overwhelmingly complicated. There was no way he could ever make up for what he'd put his dad through, and Nolan knew he didn't even deserve to be having this conversation with his father. He deserved a verbal scolding. Maybe a hung up phone.

"I forgive you."

The words hit Nolan like a splash of cold water. He stared at the photo in his hand—the one of his family. The item he would probably grab first if his house ever caught on fire.

"You do?" Surprised, Nolan paused. "But I didn't even say what I was sorry for . . .," Nolan trailed off.

"You did, you said *Everything*." His dad paused to clear his throat. "I forgive you for everything, son. That's what father's do. You've always been forgiven. Grace covers everything—past, present, and future. I love you no matter what."

"How can it be that simple? I haven't talked to you since . . ." Nolan didn't want to speak the words.

"I know, but you're talking to me now. Yesterday doesn't matter. Six years ago doesn't matter. Today matters. I am talking to my son today."

Nolan didn't even realize that tears had been steadily streaming down his face like rain on a dusty window pane. These same tears seemed to somehow have the power to clean his soul. He had begun to feel a huge burden lift off his shoulders as his dad's voice reminded him of the sound of . . . unconditional love.

"I am so sorry for what I did to Mom."

Emma lifted her right leg over her bicycle seat and climbed on. She had dialed Nolan's number two more times before pedaling away from her house, but he hadn't answered, nor had he returned her text messages. Last night, he'd never texted to let her know he was home. Worried, she began the trek toward his house.

When Emma closed in on Nolan's driveway, she spotted his car even before she eyed the number on his mailbox. This visit would mark the first time she'd ever come to his house, and before turning off the asphalt road and onto concrete, she made sure that Jerry Small wasn't raking his yard or picking up his newspaper. She surveyed his well-manicured yard and the entire area multiple times as her bike coasted, her feet stationary on the two pedals.

The handlebar on Emma's bike dug into the ground when she dropped it at Nolan's steps and knocked on the door.

Inside, Nolan had his face in one hand and the phone in his other hand when he heard a heavy knock at his front door. He wondered who in the world was here this early in the morning. Maybe Jerry needed to borrow a tool or something, he considered, or perhaps his other next door neighbor was looking for her cat again. She seemed to lose the feline often. Regardless of who it was, Nolan wasn't planning to answer. He stayed exactly where he was and kept talking to his dad.

Emma intentionally kept her back turned to Jerry's house as she stood on the porch. She only knew which house belonged to Jerry because Nolan had described it to her as the two-story brick house with a small iron-framed balcony on the front side of the second story. She waited impatiently for Nolan to answer the door, but he didn't come. She tried to occupy her mind by watching the gray cat in the next yard over. It had been clawing at the tires of one of the cars in the driveway ever since she arrived. After a few moments of standing on the concrete porch, Emma tried Nolan's phone again.

Nolan momentarily pulled the phone from his ear to glance at the screen, where the name Emma Pate appeared again. The only reason he hadn't added a photo to her profile was in case someone at the college was to catch a glimpse when she called. He began to wonder if everything was okay. She'd called several times while he'd been on the phone with his dad. Nolan had thought briefly about asking his dad if he could call back but then decided there was absolutely no way he was ending this conversation that way. He'd spent the last ten minutes catching his dad up on his life, and he couldn't believe how proud his father seemed that he'd finished his master's degree and secured a position at the community college. Although Nolan figured Norman had probably told his dad these things, if he had, his father didn't let on that he knew any of the information Nolan was sharing with him. He received the news as if it was breaking news on the front page of a newspaper.

When Nolan didn't answer the door within a reasonable timeframe, Emma knocked hard enough that it stung her knuckles. She even shook her hand as if it would help dull the temporary pain. If Nolan was home, she wasn't leaving until he answered either the door or his phone. Emma wanted to call out his name, but she didn't want to attract the attention of the neighbors. The cat was already looking her way. If Nolan wasn't home, she contemplated the idea of sitting on the front steps until he arrived.

Something in his gut told Nolan that Emma was the person knocking at his front door. When he pinched the curtain between his thumb and pointer finger and pulled it back just a sliver, he saw her standing there in a pair of black leggings and a gray top with her hands on her hips.

"Dad, I hate to ask you this, but can you hold on one moment?" he asked, and then he opened the front door, holding his finger over the speaker as he motioned for Emma to come inside with his brow somewhat furrowed.

"I am on a very important phone call," he said in a whisper. "It's kind of private, too," he shared.

Emma immediately assumed the person on the other end of the line must be his dad. She stepped in slowly and pulled the door to behind her. The first thing Emma noticed was how puffy and red Nolan's eyes looked. When he gestured to the couch, she walked toward it and watched him wander off into another room. This was the first time she'd been in his house, the first time she'd slid onto his leather sofa.

Nolan spent the next ten minutes in his bedroom. Emma surveyed the living room as she waited with her legs crossed and hands folded. There was barely any furniture, she noticed. No coffee table. No recliner. No knickknacks. No magazines. Just a couple of stray books sitting on a small lamp table. A square mirror on the wall. An average size flat screen television directly in front of the couch.

When Nolan touched the red *End Call* button on his phone, he took a few moments to gather himself. He would have preferred to have some time to himself to process the conversation he'd just had with his father, but Nolan knew Emma was waiting for him and he wasn't quite sure why. When he entered the room, she stood and gave him one of her signature hugs. Nolan could feel her entire body, warm and settling, pressed against his. He let his head rest on her shoulders, and he could feel her smooth face pressed up against his. He hadn't shaved this morning, and he wondered if she noticed.

Eventually, Nolan pulled back, Emma let go, and they both ended up on the couch with their bodies turned to face one another.

Nolan spoke first. "That was my dad."

Emma let her lips expand outwardly but kept them closed for a moment before speaking. "I figured it might be."

"I'm sorry I missed your calls," he said. The instant he apologized was the first time he realized he hadn't texted her last night. "And I'm sorry I didn't let you know I made it home last night."

"That's okay," she said. "But I was worried about you." Of course, that wasn't the only reason that she was worried about him.

She still hadn't been able to get the articles she'd found on the Internet off her mind.

"There's something I need to tell you," Nolan said staring at the outline of her kneecaps through the skin-tight pants.

Emma watched his movements. His fingers were shaking slightly. He'd been moving them ever since they'd sat down. Touching her, then the couch, then his arms, then his knees.

Nolan picked up his head and looked directly at her, taking notice of the color of her eyes. Blue. Very blue. A beautiful shade of ocean blue that complimented her ginger hair quite nicely. There was no doubt that she was the most attractive woman he'd ever seen, and he imagined that this fact would always hold true. He would love her the rest of his life as much if not more than he loved her right now, regardless of what happened when she heard the words that he had to speak.

The four words sitting on the tip of Nolan's tongue had never exited his mouth before, and the idea of sharing them with anyone scared him more than death. He'd spoken them inside his mind thousands of times over the past six years. So many times that he would wake up in a cold sweat with them running through his dreams. He could remember the scene of the tragedy vividly, just like it had happened yesterday. He'd been standing there with a baseball bat in his hand. He remembered swinging it as hard as he could, then everything went completely quiet. There could have been a million people around, and everything still would have been eerily silent in those moments that changed his life. Sometimes in his mind, there were a million people watching him swing that bat. Even now, he could still feel it in his hands—the leather grip, the wetness from the rain that had been falling since well before he picked up the bat. The next thing he knew there was blood everywhere. Blood running like rain down the side of a road in a thunderstorm. When he looked closer, he realized where the blood was coming from. Who the blood was coming from. He remembered feeling guilt as soon as he saw her laying there, motionless with her eyes closed and a gash across her forehead. The thump of the bat against her skull had been so loud that he knew he'd made the biggest mistake of his life. The last thing he remembered seeing was the bat laying in the pool of blood that he fell into the moment he passed out.

Nolan stared into Emma Pate's ocean-blue eyes and spoke what he assumed would be the last four words he'd ever speak to her. He had already imagined the scene in his mind. Emma's face would turn pale, and she'd stare at him blankly until reality kicked in. Five seconds later he'd be sitting alone on his brown couch staring aimlessly at a wide-open door that she'd run out of without saying a word.

"I killed my mama."

16

Emma felt as though the color in her face had begun to ooze out rapidly. As she stared blankly at her shoes, she didn't even realize that her hand was rubbing the legs of her pants like sandpaper scraping off a coat of paint. She wasn't sure how to respond to the statement Nolan had just made. To her knowledge, she had never met a person that had killed another human being. Now, however, she would never be able to say that again. It also hit her abruptly that she had slept in the same bed with a person who had taken a life, and the other night she had admitted to Lisa that she was falling in love with Nolan Lynch.

Questions immediately began to take over Emma's thoughts, similar to last night when she had discovered the articles. Why? How? When? Those were just a few broad ones that rattled around inside her brain. Oddly, Emma was almost glad she had come across the information that she had discovered online. Otherwise, if Nolan had dropped this bombshell on her entirely out of the blue, she might have either taken off in a dead sprint out the door or laughed out loud. It would have been hard to take him seriously, but the stoic look on his face at this very moment told her that he was completely serious.

Nolan watched Emma. As he figured, she hadn't said anything.

At least not yet. He was surprised, however, that she hadn't run out like she had the day in his classroom, even faster. He'd purposefully scooted a few inches away from her on the sofa in case this shocking news caused her to be afraid of him. Nolan didn't want her to think that she was in any danger, even though he suspected if he were in her shoes, he would be very unsettled right now. Sitting next to a person who was directly responsible for another person's death was frightening, to say the least.

"I would understand if you don't want to see me anymore," Nolan finally admitted.

Emma glanced up at him, her eyes squinted. "Nolan, I don't know what to say." She felt bad for him. *This* tragedy, whatever it entailed, was the source of his pain, the hurt she'd seen in his eyes and heard in his voice at random times since they'd met. "What happened?" she asked. "Let's start there," she suggested as calmly as possible.

Honestly, Emma had no idea what had happened to Nolan's mother. She'd wanted to hear the story straight from Nolan's mouth. That's why she'd come here this morning, although she had expected to have to try to force it out of him rather than hear him blurt it out as he had. She still wasn't exactly sure why he'd decided to tell her when he did and how he did, but she suspected that it had something to do with the phone conversation he'd just finished with his father. Regardless, she felt relieved that she hadn't read the articles online last night. She'd sat there staring blankly at the headlines for who knows how long, but she couldn't force herself to click on the links. It just didn't seem fair to find out that way—to hear other sides of the story before she heard Nolan's.

Nolan searched for the right words. He wished now that he hadn't just blurted out what he had, but at least so far Emma had stuck around to hear him out. "I've never told anyone what happened that night." He paused. "Other than the police."

Emma didn't respond; she just kept her gaze on him as he continued to speak.

"It happened at my last high school baseball game—the state championship. Mom, Dad, and Norman were there to watch." Nolan swallowed the lump in his throat. "Mom and Dad came to every single one of my games from when I was a little kid all the way up until that day. They always sat in the front row, and they always cheered me on no matter how well or how poorly I played." Nolan paused, attempting to gather his thoughts and himself. "We were playing at a college stadium, not far from where I grew up, so the atmosphere was electric. The stands were full even though it was drizzling rain. Scouts were watching, reporters were buzzing around, and my friends were scattered all over the stadium. I had one of the best games of my career that night. Coming into my last at-bat, I had three hits: a double, a triple, and a home run." Nolan paused to catch his breath.

"All you needed was a single to hit for the cycle," Emma interjected, hoping to show support by commenting on baseball instead of the incident where his story was leading. She knew that in the game of baseball when a batter hit a single, double, triple, and home run in the same game it was regarded as hitting for the cycle. The feat was rare, so much that many of the baseball greats had never achieved it.

"Yeah," he said. "But I didn't hit for the cycle."

Suddenly, Emma felt kind of bad for making the comment.

Nolan continued. "Actually, wanting to hit for the cycle was my first mistake. The pitcher had thrown three balls and no strikes. He was trying to pitch around me on purpose, and that would have loaded the bases because we had a runner on second and third. The game was tied, and it was the bottom of the ninth inning. My second mistake is that I wanted to be the hero in front of all those fans. I wanted to be the guy that knocked in the winning run instead of doing what I should have done and let my teammates have my back. We didn't have any outs so I am almost certain we would have won the game." Nolan paused. "But that doesn't matter. I couldn't care less if we won or lost. It was a stupid game. It didn't mean anything."

It was the state championship, Emma wanted to say, but she knew better based on where this story was moving.

"The fourth pitch was a foot outside, but I thought I could poke it into right field. I began my swing just like any other swing, but I had to really stretch to reach the ball. As I was finishing up my swing something went wrong. I could feel the bat beginning to slip out of my fingers and before I knew it the bat was flying end over end through the air. At first, I didn't know whether to watch the ball I'd hit or the bat, but when I heard a collective gasp throughout the stadium, and then everyone became suddenly silent, I swiveled my head to watch the trajectory of the bat." Nolan closed his eyes and dropped his head into his hands. His voice became nearly muzzled, congested sounding. "I shouldn't have swung. I should *never* have swung at that pitch. My bat flew into the first row of the crowd . . ."

Emma moved one of her hands from her knees and placed it on Nolan's thigh. She had an idea where this tragic story was heading.

"My mom," he whaled, letting out a cry that erupted from the pit of his stomach. "My bat hit my mom in the head."

Emma couldn't see Nolan's eyes, but she could see tears dropping faster than any she'd ever seen. Each one landed on the brown leather sofa and began to make a small puddle that eventually started flowing down the cushion beneath Nolan. She didn't say anything, she just reached for his shoulder and rubbed it slowly.

"I killed my mama," he said again.

Emma's teeth were clinching now. Part of her was telling her to bite her tongue, and the voice of her dad within her was telling her to tell Nolan what he needed to hear. The words "It's not your fault," spilled out of her mouth without notice.

Nolan's head jerked upward, startling Emma.

"How can it not be my fault?" he combatted with an accusatory tone. He'd tried to convince himself for six years that his mother's death wasn't his fault. "It was my bat. It was in my hands. It hit her."

"It was an accident, Nolan. It could have happened to anyone who's ever played baseball. The bat gets slippery when it's wet. A lot of baseball players have lost their bat during their swing. I see it happen often when I'm watching games on TV, even when it's not raining."

"But swinging at that pitch wasn't an accident," he argued.

She understood that, and she realized that he'd put all the blame on himself all these years, but he didn't need to. He didn't have to. "Nolan, you were just trying to win the game. There's no way you could have known what was going to happen. If you had known, then obviously you wouldn't have swung at that pitch. You would have taken a walk. But that's not you, Nolan. I know I don't know you as well as I like to think I do, but I know you well enough to know that you don't take the easy way out." She paused for a moment, wondering if she should relate this to their relationship. It seemed silly, but it also seemed fitting. "Take us for instance; you could have just walked away. Taken the easy road out, but you didn't. Now we're here, and you're telling me something that you've never told a single soul," she pointed out. "Things happen for a reason, and I know that you don't want to hear that your mom died for a reason just like I don't want to hear that my dad died for a reason, but they did. Death is a part of life whether we like it or not. We have to grieve, but we don't have to hold ourselves accountable." She stopped talking long enough to catch her breath. She still wasn't sure why she was saying all of this to him, but probably because she knew that if he hadn't shared this part of his life with anyone else, then no one outside of his family had ever said any of this to him. "Nolan, you didn't kill your mother. You should never say that again. Not to yourself and not out loud."

Nolan sighed. "You sound like my brother."

"Good," she said. "Your brother is a smart guy," she added with a faint smirk.

"My dad just basically told me the same thing you did as well." Nolan looked her in the eye. "Can you believe I haven't talked to him since my mom's funeral?"

"I can't imagine, honestly. I'm glad you talked to him today though. How did that conversation go?" Emma asked.

"Very well, actually," he said, seeming surprised.

"That's great. It makes me happy to know that you talked to your father."

Nolan couldn't believe that he'd faced two of his biggest fears in the same day. He'd often wondered if he would ever talk to his dad again. As for sharing the story about his mother's death, he'd always doubted that he'd ever tell anyone. Ever. He wasn't quite sure why he'd chosen to confide in Emma, but the way she had responded appeared to answer that question. He needed to hear the truth, and she had point blank told him what she thought. Her blunt yet gentle way of putting things was a character trait that made her shine. He still didn't believe that he wasn't responsible for his mother's death, but maybe in time, he would.

"Oh, my dad said he would be happy to rate the baseball cards for you," Nolan said, somewhat changing the subject. "He said he wouldn't charge anything since you are . . . my girlfriend is what he kept calling you."

Emma smiled real big. "I'll be your girlfriend if you want me to be."

He could tell by the tone of Emma's voice that she was thinking along the same lines as was he—the actual act of asking someone to be your girlfriend or boyfriend as an adult just seemed strange. It seemed to be more fitting for middle and high schoolers. In the adult world, it just happened. You started dating someone, and over time you just started calling them your girlfriend or boyfriend. There typically wasn't a letter passed to them that had a box to check *yes* or *no*.

"Oh, yeah?" Nolan laughed.

"I kinda like you, Nolan Lynch," she confirmed, wrapping her arms tightly around his neck.

"Even after what I've told you today?" he asked into her shoulder.

"Even after," she promised. "Maybe more so," she added.

"And you're not mad at me for forgetting to text you last night?"

She lifted an eyebrow. "I wouldn't go that far." She thought back to the way things had unfolded last night and into this morning. "I was quite irritated with you last night."

"I imagine, and I'm sorry. Last night when I was thinking about the idea of calling my dad, it just really threw me for a loop. I didn't even want to go home. I rode around for hours thinking and praying. It somehow completely slipped my mind that I hadn't messaged you." He paused, wondering why she hadn't checked on him last night after some time had passed. She'd probably just fallen asleep, he figured. "You should have just sent me a message."

Emma didn't want to tell him why she hadn't messaged him. "I ended up falling asleep thinking about you," she said. It was the truth, at least the part about thinking about him. She wasn't quite sure if she'd ever really fallen asleep. She felt like she'd seen every hour on the clock all night.

Nolan let his head rest on her shoulder, and within a matter of minutes, they both fell asleep to the steady rhythm of their hearts beating against one another.

17

The month of September brought ups and downs for Nolan and Emma. If they weren't already in love, they fell so deeply for each other that it became emotionally painful to be apart. Although with Emma back in college, their relationship continued to create strenuous moments since they had to hide everything from everyone. The only people who knew they were an item were Norman, Nolan's father, and Lisa. Each of them knew that for the sake of Nolan's position they needed to keep this knowledge private.

Mr. Lynch had been able to grade the cards quickly, and the same day Emma signed for the returned package from the delivery driver, she and Nolan listed the cards on the website he recommended. Rather than list each card singly, which Nolan suggested might eventually bring in more money, they listed the cards as a collection to hasten the sell. To Emma's surprise, the set sold the next morning for more than enough to cover her expenses until she could graduate and find a better paying job. Nolan thanked his dad for helping them, and he began talking with him on the phone regularly.

Nolan continued to drive down Emma's dirt road every evening after dark. Some nights he rode his bicycle, and the two of them would slip out for a late night bike ride into downtown when hardly anyone would be out and about. Some nights they raced from one point to another, and Nolan started calling her Lizzie Armistead—a female cyclist he'd googled to take the place of him calling her Lance Armstrong. Nolan chuckled when Emma pointed out that the two cyclist's first and last names even started with the same letter.

One night Nolan and Emma stopped at the riverfront near the boat slips so Emma could finish the story she had started to tell Nolan on their first date when the helicopter interrupted. She pointed out to a sailboat that belonged to an older man who liked to walk around naked at night. She had never personally witnessed the naked man, but all the locals knew about him and a handful of people she knew had seen him in all his glory. Nolan burst out in laughter at the mere thought of stumbling upon a wrinkly old guy on one of these late nights when he and Emma ventured out incognito, her wearing a Braves hat and him sporting one of his Red Sox caps. They rarely ever saw anyone, but in the event they came across another person or a group of people, they would lower their heads like two bandits on the wanted list in the post office. They found humor in situations like this for the most part, but then there were times when it bothered them, especially Emma. She wanted to be able to go out on real dates with Nolan. She wanted to eat at the downtown restaurants on Friday evenings, watch a show at the Turnage Theater, and walk around the waterfront afterward with her fingers intertwined in his. It's not that she needed the whole town to know that Nolan Lynch was her man, but she longed to have a normal relationship. Nolan understood her feelings, and he tried to show her that he cared by listening and reminding her that at the end of the spring semester they would have the freedom they both dreamed about.

After one of these conversations, he surprised her with a weekend in Virginia Beach. This destination was less than a three-hour drive from Little Washington, and once they arrived there, Emma felt like a queen. They ate every meal out, walked down the beach holding hands in plain daylight, kissed in front of anyone that might be watching, and neither of them wore a hat all weekend. The only time they spent indoors was at the hotel when they needed sleep after their long days had worn them out. Emma's boss had almost ruined the much-needed vacation, though, when he tried to alter his decision to let her have the weekend off. He'd initially been fine with the idea, but then as the time grew nearer and the schedule became tight after one of the waitresses quit, he asked Emma to stay in town to work. She battled with it internally for a day or two before discussing the situation with Nolan. He talked her into standing her ground with her boss, and in the end, she was glad she did. Doug had given her the cold shoulder the following week and made work-life a little more hectic, but she decided the trip had been well worth the agony. The only other downside to the Virginia Beach trip was that Nolan and Emma had to come back to reality.

At the college, the day after they returned, Emma was reminded that Nolan was an instructor and she was a student. They passed in a crowded hallway, and their only exchange was a simple hello. She had to admit that having to hold back from touching Nolan or talking to him made her want him even more at night. That Tuesday they were out in the woods with Emma's classmates working on the trail, which was shaping up quite nicely, but they couldn't talk alone, and Emma couldn't show any jealousy when one of the other women flirted a little with Nolan. She never actually worried about those moments, but it did bother her slightly. It was no secret that the female students thought Nolan was sexy. Emma thought he did a fairly good job of ignoring that fact, but the one situation that had begun to bother her involved her advisor of all people. Ever since the day that Mary had taken a trip to Nolan's office out of concern for Emma, she had been coming around more often. Emma figured that Nolan either didn't recognize it or he didn't want to admit that the woman liked him. It frustrated Emma that Nolan couldn't just tell her he had a girlfriend so she would leave him alone. One day Emma spotted the two of them sitting together in the cafeteria, and she just walked out and ate her lunch alone at the picnic tables under the oak trees. Nolan had seen Emma out of the corner of his eye with a lunch tray in her hands, but he couldn't just get up and follow her out the door. So that night Nolan and Emma had a conversation about Mary which didn't go so well. He accused her of being jealous over nothing more than a friendly colleague. It drove Emma crazy that she couldn't just go sit on the other side of Nolan and give him a kiss on the cheek. She asked him to be careful, but she didn't say much more to him the rest of the night.

A few days later, Nolan played his own jealousy card after a conversation with his least favorite person in the world these days. He tried to avoid Clay Bell as much as possible, but during a lunch meeting one day Clay had cornered him near the punch bowl and began a meaningless conversation. Eventually, though, Clay randomly made a comment about being over at his neighbor's house late one night when they thought they'd heard a vehicle drive down their dirt road. He didn't mention Emma by name, but he kept saying *we*—implying he and Emma—and Nolan got the feeling that Clay knew he realized who Clay was talking about. Initially, it freaked Nolan out because he was concerned about his job, but the stronger emotion he felt was jealousy. When Nolan approached Emma about it later that night on her front porch, he could tell the question caught her off guard. Emma ended up being completely honest about the night that Clay had landed on her porch after Nolan had left—the same night that Emma never heard from Nolan. Nolan didn't come out and accuse her of being too busy to check on him that night, but he might as well have. She didn't mention that she'd been searching Nolan's name on the Internet and that was the real reason she hadn't checked on him. She felt guilty about that night altogether, although she knew she hadn't done anything wrong. Other than keeping it from Nolan, maybe. But in doing that she was only trying to protect him.

As September rolled along, the sun started sinking in the sky above the cornfields earlier and earlier which meant Nolan was able to come over sooner, and ultimately he and Emma had more time to spend together. On nights when she didn't have to work, they would hang out in the kitchen and make an event out of preparing dinner. They discovered that they both liked many of the same foods, and Nolan loved that she would eat healthy with him and that many of the ingredients they used came from right there on the farm. Emma had small gardens near the house that produced nearly every fruit and vegetable possible to grow in the region. She had been pleasantly surprised at how well Nolan knew his way around a garden, especially when they'd venture out there in the dark. Nolan still cheated from time to time by drinking a glass of sweet tea, but most nights he reverted to water or green tea. Emma drank a cup of coffee nearly every night after dinner. The two of them often ventured out to Firefly Field to throw baseball. Emma could tell that Nolan was becoming more comfortable throwing with her, but he still showed zero interest in picking up a baseball bat. He wouldn't even hand one to her when she wanted to hit. He pitched to her often, and every time they would walk or jog or run out to collect the balls together. Nolan had picked up a whole set of glow-in-the-dark balls earlier in the month and surprised her with them one night. When Emma opened the package, she smiled real big, and in a matter of minutes she changed into a pair of yoga pants and a sports bra, and hit baseballs for an hour that night as the fireflies hovered in the imaginary stands above the cornfield and amongst the trees. Nolan laughed all over himself later that night when Emma told him that firefly flashing is a mating display. She explained how the males send signals to the females, and in return, the females respond with their own signals. In response to her comment, Nolan hustled from the pitcher's mound to the wooden bin with the baseball gear, snatched up his cell phone, and started flashing his flashlight off and on at Emma. When he'd headed in that direction, she'd been standing at home plate balancing herself with the bat touching the ground, but she ended up hunched over with her mouth covered as she laughed at his antics. Then she jumped up into his arms and kissed him like she never had before.

Not only was Nolan a great lover, but Emma had discovered that he was a great gift giver. He didn't buy her the normal presents that a man systematically gets for a woman: flowers, jewelry, stuffed animals, and such things. His gifts were thoughtful, even practical, and she appreciated that. A couple of weeks ago, she'd received the first gift that made her tear up—a Kryptonite bike lock. Retiring the old rusty chain had been bittersweet, but it had also been a time saver. Since Nolan could no longer be her knight in shining armor to come along and help untangle the chain, and lock that ancient contraption—that she thanked her dad and God for every day because it had brought her and Nolan together—she really needed a new one.

Nolan wasn't the only one giving gifts, though. Just before he and Emma headed out to the movie theater when they were visiting Virginia Beach, he smiled from ear to ear as she handed him a basket filled with a bouquet of Junior Mints boxes. That night they both ended up with a sugar high and sensational breath, which made for a memorable make-out session. That happened to be the same evening that Nolan told Emma he loved the freckle on her nose. She flashed a crooked smile and said, "Awe, thank you." She then shared the story with him about how as a kid she hated the mark because some of the other children made fun of it. With it being round and raised just enough to notice, the mean kids sometimes called it a booger. She mentioned how over the years she had grown to appreciate the freckle as God's way of making her unique.

Another gift Nolan had given Emma had come as a complete surprise. One random night in her bedroom he handed her a box, inside which she found a mask. When she held it up and asked what it meant, he reached into his back pocket and pulled out a pair of tickets to a masquerade ball. The following week Emma draped a gold dress over her head and let Nolan zip her up. Nolan wore a black suit with a gold bowtie to match Emma. Dressing up fell on the outskirts of their comfort zone, but the opportunity to be at a public event together made it tantalizing. It ended up being one of the most romantic experiences of Emma's life.

The party took place in a historic home in downtown Greenville where the decorations in each room included flickering candles, lights dangling from the ceilings, and silk drapes covering the furniture. Glass vases were filled with feathers and sequins had been scattered everywhere. Nolan and Emma danced for hours amongst strangers to the sounds of classical music. Neither of them had a clue which piece belonged to Mozart or Beethoven, but the entire night they overhead guests showering one another with these names and others such as Tchaikovsky, Puccini, and Stravinsky. Standing near the punch, Emma nearly made Nolan spit the swig he'd just taken into the crowd when she said the people they were hanging out with tonight sounded like him talking about baseball card ratings. One of the aspects that made the night even more fun was that they made up names and careers for each other. Emma became a psychologist named Hope, and Nolan pretended to be a lawyer named Forrest. The night nearly took a wrong turn, though, when Emma spotted one of the accounting instructors from their college. Other than him, they hadn't seen anyone that they recognized, although many of the costumes hid identities well. They decided that no one could pick them out by appearance alone, so as long as they didn't talk around Nolan's co-worker they'd be okay. Nolan highly doubted that he'd recognize either of their voices anyway. Emma mentioned that she had taken his class during her second semester and had said nothing more than *hey* to the man since, and Nolan figured he'd probably had less than a handful of conversations with the guy.

The dust settled behind their getaway car very late on that last Friday night in September. Nolan had hired a driver from Greenville to pick them up at Emma's and drop them off there, too. That way they could both enjoy wine at the masquerade ball and not worry at all if Clay noticed the car that dropped them off. Emma still chose to be cautious and had the driver drop them off behind the house. Nolan spent the night that night and woke up with Emma in his arms as the sunrise slowly swept through her bedroom curtains. He hated that she had to go to work, but they decided for him to stay at her house all day while she spent the day waitressing. He had been promising to work on some projects around the house for her so it worked out perfect.

He spent the day on tasks such as spraying for bugs, sealing cracks in the walls, touch-up painting, and stabilizing loose chair legs. His last project of the day was to install a new drainpipe in one of the sinks. Thankfully he hadn't pretended to be a plumber at the masquerade ball because after a few minutes under the sink he realized he was going to have to search the Internet for a how-to video on the install. He was having trouble with the connection on his phone so he opened Emma's laptop and began to type in the search bar. Then he abruptly stopped. His breathing grew a little heavier, and he felt a lump building in his throat. He couldn't believe what he saw—Emma had searched his name. He clicked on it, and it led him to the same page she had seen the night before he told her about his mother's death. He scrolled through the articles—articles he'd read over and over during the past six years. Some true, some false. Most somewhere in between. One said he'd been arrested. Another said he'd been sentenced to ten years in prison. Some said it was an accident, others murder. The one that had always outraged him the most was the one that read: *White Baseball Player Nolan Lynch Kills Black Woman*. He knew why the source had used the headline—because drama sells. It was all about money. His mother, the woman that he loved more than anyone on this earth had died, and all that concerned this particular media outlet was ratings. One of the unfortunate aspects of the timing of the accident was that it had happened as the country was facing tough race relations and headlines all over the country were dividing blacks and whites. It could have just as easily read *Baseball Player Nolan Lynch Kills Woman* or more appropriately, as his dad, Norman, and Emma had been telling him over and over throughout the past month, *Baseball Player Nolan Lynch's Mom Tragically Dies.* Unfortunately for him and his family, only a small percentage of the people that clicked on the race-related link would have clicked on the latter link titles.

It was sad that this is where the country had been led. Led by people who wanted to divide blacks and whites rather than bring them together. Nolan felt tears falling from his eyes. His parents—black people—had been the epitome of what it meant to close the race gap. They'd adopted him, a white baby abandoned for who knows what reason—they'd raised a boy who'd become a man who still wondered if he would ever meet his biological parents. Nolan wished someone would hold the media accountable. He wished they'd quit pointing fingers at white people or black people or any other race of people and just present the news about people. *Rogue Police Officer Shoots Innocent Man. Criminal Shoots Police Officer. Hero Police Officer Shoots Man with Gun*. Leave race out of it, at least until a full investigation has been completed and a cause determined. But no, the media had to jump to conclusions and cause riots and more deaths. Police officers were shot for wearing a badge. Innocent people were killed. His father was beaten by an extremist white group because they read the article about his mother's death and didn't like that he had adopted a white child. Nolan himself was chased out of his own neighborhood by a group of thugs because they'd read the article about him killing a black woman. They didn't even take the time to learn that the black woman was his own mother. Jumping to conclusions seemed to be one of the roots of the problem once the media ran the story. Reality was and most likely always would be that there are some really crappy white people and black people, but Nolan knew the truth—there were way more good black and white people. He believed wholeheartedly that only a small percentage of people were actually racist.

Thinking about all of this unwarranted drama once again, Nolan wanted to punch the screen in front of his face. Then he considered throwing the laptop through the window where Emma had told him she'd seen Clay's outline that night. This article is the one that had driven him out of Arizona. Nolan couldn't stay there and let his family be in harm's way. He felt that if he moved far enough away, people would quit talking about him, and hopefully, racist groups would leave his father alone. That's one of the main reasons why Nolan up and left—to protect his dad. That's why he hadn't talked to his dad until just this month—because not only had he killed his dad's wife, but he had also caused people to hate his dad.

Why had Emma searched his name? Why? He'd looked at the search date, and he knew she'd discovered this information the night before they talked about his mama. Which meant that the entire time he'd been telling her the story—balling his eyes out like a spoiled child losing London Bridge Is Falling Down—she already knew what had happened. Emma already knew that he was to blame for his mama's death, but she said nothing. Not then and not this entire month as they'd grown closer. She'd had plenty to say about how he should forgive himself, but now who needed forgiving? She did. But he wasn't sure if he could forgive her. She'd lied to him. She'd said that she hadn't checked on him that night because she fell asleep. That was a lie. She hadn't fallen asleep because she'd been searching him online until the wee hours of the morning. She'd also lied about Clay. Clay had been at her house. What had really happened that night? Had Emma called Clay over to comfort her?

It didn't matter, he told himself. It was time to run . . . again.

18

Emma hated working doubles at the restaurant. Other than the additional tips and the increase she'd find on her next paycheck, she regretted telling Doug that she would cover an extra shift. Doug had been his usual self today. He'd complimented her for busting her butt to keep everyone in unison through a busy Saturday lunch. An hour later when she had taken a break to eat her own lunch, Doug complained about a few crumbs beneath one of the booths and asked if she would sweep them up immediately. One of the downsides of restaurant work was that employee meals often ended up being an hour or two different than ordinary people's mealtimes. Today she had been absolutely starving, so much so that her stomach had been growling as she'd been dancing from table to table until the crowd dwindled. She'd wanted to tell Doug where he could stick the broom, but instead, her food became cold while she did someone else's job. On top of that, the task had no significance at that moment. Not a single seat in the restaurant held a paying customer. She didn't understand why Doug felt the need to be at the restaurant all day every Saturday. Why wasn't he with his wife? The man might as well be married to the restaurant—throughout the years Emma had worked for him she'd encountered this thought many times. He basically lived in the place, which made Emma feel bad for his wife. They had plenty of money and instead of the two of them enjoying their small fortune together, his wife frequented a variety of shops in town and out of town to make up for the emptiness in their relationship. *Whatever*, Emma decided, what Doug chose to do with his time wasn't her business.

The dinner rush ended up being even heavier than the lunch crowd. Emma and Nolan had exchanged texts throughout the day, but she hadn't heard from him recently, she realized, as things began to settle down. All day long she had felt a certain comfort about him being at her house. She couldn't believe how much he'd been able to accomplish, and she couldn't wait to ride her bicycle home and see his handiwork firsthand. More so than that, she wanted to fall into his arms, maybe even take a relaxing bubble bath. She was just about to text Nolan when she noticed Doug lurking around the near empty restaurant. Instead of walking out back and pulling out her cell phone, she grabbed the broom. After a few swipes across the floor, she heard the bell on the front door jingle. The broom nearly fell from her hands when she saw him walk in.

"What are you doing here?" she mouthed as Nolan caught her staring at him.

Nolan ignored her and walked to a booth in a corner on the opposite side of the restaurant and sat down. Emma rolled her eyes and followed him, but not before one of the younger waitresses made it to his table.

"How are you this evening, sir?" the young girl with bleached blonde hair asked Nolan.

"It's been a long day," he said as Emma neared.

"I'll take care of this gentleman," Emma announced as she made her way to the table.

The other waitress lifted her eyebrows where only Emma could see them and walked toward the kitchen.

"What's going on?" Emma asked, obviously concerned.

Nolan had picked up the menu the waitress had dropped on the table, and at the moment, he pretended to study it. "I'm just here for dinner," he said. "What's good?"

"What's wrong, Nolan?"

"You knew," he said with an accusatory tone. "You searched my name online."

Emma sat down across from him. "Can we have this conversation at home?"

Nolan lifted his eyebrows and looked at her for the first time since she'd arrived at the table. "Home?"

"Yes, at my house . . . in private."

"We could have."

"What does that mean?" She reached for her pocket. "Did I miss a message from you?"

"Nope," he said. "We could have had this conversation anytime within the last month," he uttered. "Preferably we could have had this conversation the night you read the articles about me killing my mama. But it appears you chose to have this conversation with Clay Bell instead of me," Nolan said in a hushed, yet enraged tone.

"Nolan, please don't say that about what happened to your mother."

"Why?" His right eye squinted as he lifted his cheek and shrugged his shoulder. "Oh, that's right, you don't like telling the truth?"

Emma could feel his eyes accusing her of lying. Why couldn't he have waited for her to come home?

"Nolan, you don't know what you're talking about. I didn't—"

Emma was about to tell Nolan that she didn't read the articles that night. That she didn't invite Clay over and that she and Clay hadn't talked about Nolan at all that night. In fact, he hadn't come into the house, and she'd told him to go home. But then Doug interrupted her and Nolan's conversation, and her face turned as red as a brick.

"Emma, I know you're tired, but we probably don't have time to sit around and chat. As soon as you get this customer's order can you sweep up the other side of the restaurant?" he asked, or basically demanded. Emma hated when he talked to her like a child.

Nolan peered up at Doug then eyeballed the broom Emma had rested up against the wall next to the booth where the two of them were sitting. He'd heard countless stories about Doug throughout the last month, and even though Emma talked highly of the man's charitable efforts and about how much the community loved him, Nolan didn't care for him one bit. He'd caught on to far too many comments from Emma that revealed the man's true character. Nolan didn't like that Doug sometimes cussed at her and the other employees, especially younger ones like the sixteen-year-old waitress that had brought the menu to the table. He'd noticed her nametag and remembered Emma saying that Doug had made her cry one night not so long ago. Nolan didn't find it very charitable that Emma's boss hadn't given her a raise in quite some time even though she deserved well more than she made. Her tips rarely made up for her relatively low salary because she spent a fair amount of her time managing the other waitresses. He thought the idea of not assisting with or outright providing healthcare or retirement benefits for full-time employees seemed like a slap in the face of loyalty. Tonight, Nolan wasn't in the mood to hear this man talk to Emma this way, and tonight might be the last chance he had to give this guy a piece of his mind.

"This woman right here has been working hard all day, sir." Nolan looked at him sideways. "She worked a double and treated your customers much better than you treat your employees. What kind of boss doesn't provide benefits for his managers? What kind of boss gets irritated when his most dedicated worker asks for one weekend off out of the entire year?"

Astonished, Doug took a step back.

Emma's face appeared frozen, but still red. She hadn't looked at Doug; she'd kept her focus on Nolan as he reacted. He was mad. Really mad.

Nolan continued. "So why don't you take that broom right there and walk over to the other side of your restaurant and clean the floor yourself. Emma's food got cold at lunch because she spent her break cleaning the floor that someone who'd already had their break could have cleaned."

"Who are you?" Doug asked, seeming to unearth a boost of confidence.

"I'm one of your customers who doesn't like you talking to your staff the way you just talked to Emma."

"Sir, I think you need to leave," Doug suggested.

Nolan rose from the wooden bench that had been holding up his tense body. Emma thought for sure that he was about to punch Doug in his face, but then Nolan glared back at her.

"Leaving is what I came here to do," were the last words out of Nolan's mouth before he started toward the door, and Emma realized that they possessed a double meaning.

19

Emma scampered after Nolan as he exited the restaurant. He hadn't made a scene, and she doubted any of the customers or employees had even heard a word he'd said to Doug. Nolan had said what he'd said very respectfully, yet breathing fire. As mad as she was with him showing up at her work tonight, it felt quite good to hear someone tell off Doug finally. Most all of the employees were scared to death of the short man.

"Nolan, wait, please wait," she begged as her feet met the asphalt in the parking lot.

"Yeah, Nolan, please wait," another voice echoed sarcastically.

Nolan had kept his stride steady as Emma called out to him, but then when he heard the belittling tone of a man's voice, he whipped around. He somewhat expected to discover that Doug had followed them outside, but he immediately realized the voice belonged to someone else.

"What are you doing here?" Nolan challenged as he peered at Clay Bell.

"Just looking out for the integrity of the college," he shared with a divisive grin.

"Clay, leave!" Emma howled.

"No way," he said. "This show is way better than I anticipated."

Wearing an untucked button up shirt and a loose hanging tie, he walked toward and leaned against his large SUV, parked a few empty spaces from Nolan's vehicle. "You two finish up, and I will wait my turn to offer my proposal."

"Clay, this is none of your business," Nolan roared.

"This is definitely business," Clay responded with a smirk.

Emma didn't like Clay's choice of words nor the way he was acting. She'd had a bad feeling that he would eventually realize what was going on between her and Nolan.

"What are you talking about Clay?" Emma inquired.

"I think it's wonderful that the two of you are dating," he said as he watched Nolan take a step toward him. "Don't worry, Nolan, this doesn't have to end with you losing your job." Holding his hand up toward Nolan, he paused. "I'm sure you know college policy shuns what's been going on here," he added glancing back and forth from Emma to Nolan, wiggling his finger all the while. "Emma, I know you know," he added with sarcasm.

"What makes you think we're dating?" Nolan asked, standing his ground one parking space away from Clay. "Emma works at this restaurant, and I just came here for dinner, that's it."

"Right," Clay laughed. "But you forgot one thing."

"What's that?"

"Where you came from—"

Nolan knew that leaving Emma's house in a hurry with his headlights on so he could see down the dirt road to drive faster could turn out to be a mistake.

Emma butted in. "Clay, this isn't what it looks like."

Clay furrowed his brow. "It's not? So y'all aren't dating?" he said pointing at one then the other.

An hour ago Emma would have had no problem pretending that she and Nolan weren't dating, but after what happened inside the restaurant she didn't want to play this game. Her biggest fear right now was that the two of them truly were no longer dating.

That Nolan was leaving her just like he'd suggested a few moments ago.

Clay crossed his legs at his ankles and waited for a response.

Emma scuffed her shoe against the asphalt but didn't say anything.

"We're not dating," Nolan confirmed bluntly.

Clay chuckled. He turned to Emma for a reaction.

Emma wanted to crawl under a rock and weep. The words Nolan had spoken had erupted from his mouth so effortlessly, and they splashed onto her skin like lava from a fiery volcano.

"I have pictures that suggest otherwise," Clay offered, holding up a manila envelope that had been in his hand the entire time. He stepped slowly toward Nolan and held out the package. "Here, you can have the copies in here; I have the originals in a safe place. Maybe these images will remind you who you've been dating."

Nolan opened the package and carefully removed the contents. Emma, with her fingernails in her mouth, ambled slowly toward him and stood by his side as he thumbed through the photos: Shots of Nolan's car driving down the dirt road, which proved nothing. Images of Nolan and Emma on her front porch, which opened the floor for questions. Pictures of Nolan and Emma embraced and kissing, surrounded by a field of fireflies, which were relatively incriminating. There were even pictures of the two of them at the waterfront on their very first date.

"Why did you take these?" Emma asked, especially curious about the one of her on the handlebars with Nolan pedaling her bike, since it was the first time she'd been out with Nolan.

"Did you hire a private investigator or something?" Nolan added.

"Well, it all started out when you two lovebirds were in the right place at the right time. You see, I was minding my own business, flying over downtown in a helicopter—you remember, the one that was blowing everyone's things all over the park." Clay laughed out loud as if replaying the memory for himself. "I just happened to have a camera in my hand when I spotted an instructor with a student. So being the faithful employee that I am, I felt it was my duty to snap some pictures."

Nolan couldn't decide what to say or do next. He wanted to punch Clay Bell in the nose. Just one good time. Knock that cheesy smirk right off his contentious face. He also considered throwing the photos on the ground, opening his car door and leaving. He could just put all of this behind him. Offer his resignation Monday morning at the college, leave this town, and never look back. He'd done it before; he could do it again.

"You're a jerk, Clay," Emma clamored. "I'm sorry, Nolan," she said, turning her focus to him momentarily, feeling bad because she knew Clay was doing this because he couldn't have her. It had very little to do with Nolan.

"Listen, let's not get all emotional here," Clay suggested. "This is an opportunity for all of us to walk away happy. Emma, all you have to do is sell the farm to me at a reasonable cost, and these photos will disappear. No one will ever know our little secret."

Nolan stepped in close enough to Clay that he could smell the hint of alcohol on the man's breath. "Emma isn't signing the farm over to anyone, especially you."

"You two are more serious than I realized," Clay responded, tilting his head to look around Nolan's shoulder at Emma. "Mr. Lynch is making decisions for you now, I see."

Just as Nolan was about to put his hands on Clay and before Emma could input her two cents, she heard Doug call out from the restaurant entrance. "Emma, I need you in here," he said in a flustered tone. She wondered how long he'd been standing there with his hands on his hips.

Both Nolan and Clay turned their heads just in time to watch Emma march toward Doug, throw her apron into his face, and shout, "I quit!" Then she walked back to where Nolan and Clay were standing, tears running on her face and the appropriate sounds accompanying them. "As for you, Clay, you're a dirty weasel. I'm not selling you the farm. Ever." She snatched Nolan by the arm and turned him toward her. "And you, Nolan Lynch," she declared. "I love you!" She paused for just a short moment, and no one else even considered making a peep. "I didn't read a single one of those articles that night, and I still haven't."

Emma didn't wait around for a response from any of them. She just said what she needed to say and walked to her bicycle.

20

Emma pedaled fast, then slow. The sky was dark, the streets empty, and her face filled with tears and tear stains. She hadn't cried this much since her father passed away, and she found herself wishing that he would be at home when she dropped her bike off at the back steps. She wished she could collapse into his arms and just bawl. In a situation like this, he would have listened if she wanted him to, talked if he needed to, or just sat with her until she left his fatherly arms and crawled into bed alone.

Losing Nolan would take many nights to sleep off, she realized. She would probably eat through a dozen cartons of ice cream in the next month and watch a handful of romantic movies every week. Emma thought about calling Lisa, but as a cool breeze slapped her in the face, she knew that being on her phone would slow her down. She would call her when she got home, she decided, as she rode the white line. Emma knew Lisa would be willing to come over even though she would tell her that it wasn't necessary. Lisa would show up anyway.

A couple of cars passed by Emma as she headed up River Road. One stopped. She didn't.

"Emma, let's talk," he said as she pedaled faster and rode right past the SUV.

She had nothing to say to Clay Bell, and thankfully he got the message because a few moments later she watched his vehicle whiz past her. She knew he was mad because he hadn't gotten what he wanted. A short time elapsed, and another vehicle drove by Emma and then pulled onto the shoulder of the road just ahead. Before she had left the restaurant, Alan had found out what happened and had come out to check on her just as she hopped onto her bicycle. She appreciated the offer he'd made to take her home, but she'd said, "No, thanks," and pedaled away. She felt kind of bad that she had been so short with Alan since his words had seemed so sincere this time around.

Now, as Emma rolled up to Alan's open window, he called out, "I know you said you don't need a ride, but I just wanted to come check on you. I wanted to make sure that Clay or that other guy weren't harassing you."

Emma tried to smile. "Thanks, Alan," she said. "Neither of them are that type of guy, though." She thanked Alan one more time for checking on her then began to pedal again.

The dust from Clay's vehicle had settled by the time Emma rolled down the dirt road and ended up at her back steps. There he sat—not Clay, but Nolan. Emma was surprised to see him. Didn't even know if she wanted to see him, or talk to him, or listen to him.

"I overreacted," Nolan admitted as she laid down her bike slower than she had envisioned.

Nolan had been sitting in the rocking chair for almost ten minutes. He had purposefully taken the long way to the farm so that he wouldn't pass by Emma on her ride home. He wanted her to have that time to think. Truth be told, he'd needed some time to think, too.

Emma crossed her arms. "You think?"

Nolan looked her in the eyes. "You seriously didn't read the articles?"

"Not a single word," she promised.

"Why?"

"I decided I wanted to hear your side of the story first," she said. "Then once you shared it with me, I decided that I *only* wanted to hear your side of the story," she added. "I didn't want to know what anyone else thought."

"That means a lot to me," he said. "If I were in your shoes I probably would have read the articles." Twiddling his fingers, he paused. "Will you be honest with me about something?"

"Of course, Nolan." The boards on the back porch creaked when she stepped on them and then she leaned against the wooden column closest to Nolan.

"Did you ask Clay to come over that night?"

"No. I told you the whole truth about why Clay showed up at my house that night."

"Thank you," he conveyed. "I won't say another word about what happened that night," Nolan promised.

"Does that mean you want to stay?"

"If you'll still have me?" he wondered aloud.

Nolan and Emma spent the rest of the weekend trying to figure out the best way to move forward. Come Monday, Nolan would most likely lose his job. Maybe not that exact day, but within a short period of time. Emma had abruptly quit her job, and she wasn't quite sure how she felt about the hasty decision. She had envisioned that moment for years, and right now she had the money from selling the baseball card collection, but soon enough she would need a regular income again. The only positive from tonight's craziness was that the two of them would most likely no longer have to hide their relationship. Emma was confident that in addition to turning Nolan in at the college, Clay would announce the news to everyone on social media with pictures to support his case.

Monday came and went, but nothing out of the ordinary happened. Nolan didn't receive a visit from Jerry nor anyone in the front office. No email. No phone call. Nothing. Neither Nolan nor Emma had heard from Clay, which was fine but odd. Tuesday, Nolan and Emma went about their normal routine of pretending to be student and teacher. It felt even a little more awkward because both of them were just waiting for the news to come out at any given moment. Nolan expected that if Clay hadn't run straight to the president of the college Monday morning, he must be waiting for an opportunity to embarrass him publicly. Maybe at a staff meeting—Nolan imagined a slide show produced by Clay that started with business statistics then turned into a photo display of Nolan and Emma.

As October began to move along, such speculation didn't come to fruition. Nolan and Emma continued to hide their relationship. At first, they were even more careful than ever in case Clay was trying to gather more evidence. Then one day Nolan mentioned that tiptoeing around even more than they had previously seemed ridiculous. Clay had retained all the evidence he needed, and Nolan was willing to let the cards fall where they may. So eventually he and Emma fell back into their regular routines like eating dinner together every night possible. One evening, Nolan picked up hotdogs from Bill's Hot Dogs to finally fulfill his promise to Emma. They ate them at dusk on a checkered blanket in the middle of Firefly Field and ended up spending the entire night under the stars. Nolan had started coming over earlier in the evening since there was no reason to hide from Clay anymore. They still didn't go out in public together, though. The following night Nolan made his trademark zucchini pasta with grilled chicken. Emma loved it enough to have two helpings, and she had to admit that she had grown to like eating healthy with Nolan. Postseason baseball began, and even though the Braves didn't make the cut, Emma watched the games with Nolan.

Nolan's Red Sox did make the playoffs, but they ended up losing in the first round. The two of them enjoyed watching the games together nonetheless, so they continued to watch the games and picked a team to root for in each series. Before the games each night, they'd usually venture out to the ball field and throw ball since they were in the baseball mood. Some nights Emma would hit, and other nights she didn't. Of course, Nolan still expressed no interest in touching a baseball bat. The fireflies had begun to trickle away as of late September, and as October moved forward, only a few stragglers were floating around. It indeed was one of the most amazing natural spectacles Nolan had ever seen, and he found himself looking forward to the field being filled with fireflies again next spring.

Nolan felt guilty about Emma quitting her job, but she wouldn't let him help pay the bills even though he offered every time she opened one. He made sure to bring more groceries than normal, continue to give Emma practical gifts, and cover the cost of anything extra they did together. Emma seemed fine with that arrangement. Weekend trips became their new thing since Emma was out of work and had been unable to find a new job. This was partially because the opportunities were limited, but also because when she wasn't in class or working on homework, she and Nolan were together. They spent their free hours during the week at the farmhouse, and on three consecutive weekends, they ventured out of town, visiting the Outer Banks, Bald Head Island, and Boone. They cherished being able to get away where they could openly act and feel like a typical couple. They spent the first weekend in October on the pristine beaches of the Outer Banks, where surprisingly warm temperatures made it feel like summer had returned. Eastern North Carolina weather between October and December tended to fluctuate anywhere between twenty-five degrees to eighty-five degrees so regularly checking the forecast came recommended. The nights and mornings were often cool or cold and the afternoons could feel mild, warm, or hot. At the beach, Nolan and Emma laid out some and Emma joked that it might be her last chance to add a layer to her gradually disappearing tan. Even though Nolan had been dating Emma for a couple of months, he still found himself checking her out in her white bikini outlined with black straps. When other guys would walk by, he would jokingly throw a towel over her body. Emma laughed, but it made her feel good inside to know that Nolan had been ogling over her and that he was a tad bit jealous. He tried to hide it but Emma, like most women, had a knack for noticing such things. She had to admit that she'd taken a few peeks at his body, too. He was lean and toned, and although not muscular in a bulky way, his muscles were outlined with a visible definition. The first time she'd seen his body she'd noticed that he had very little hair, almost giving the appearance that he waxed. Of course, she hadn't asked that day, but later she did and he laughed at her. In the mornings, they jogged a few miles down the beach, leaving their footprints in the sand for latecomers to follow. They rented bicycles from a local shop and cruised around the island day and night until time to head back home.

The following weekend they drove to Southport and took a twenty-minute ferry ride over to Bald Head Island. The forecasted temperatures were low enough that they didn't even bother packing their bathing suits for this trip. They toured Old Baldy—North Carolina's oldest lighthouse—which had recently celebrated its 200th birthday. The town had literally thrown a birthday celebration, or at least that's what one of the locals they'd met while dining at Mojo's on the Harbor told them. The menu reminded Emma of the one from Central Pork, and she and Nolan laughed out loud when the waitress informed them that the restaurant had recently started serving honey barbecue.

"Do you miss the food from Central Pork?" Nolan asked Emma after the waitress had taken their order.

"Not at all," Emma declared. "Don't get me wrong, the food there is delicious, but I ate it nearly every day for all those years."

That evening while overlooking the waterfront at Mojo's, Nolan and Emma chatted like two teenagers on their first date. While they watched boats come and go, they held hands and nearly sat on top of each other.

"Maybe one day we'll have a boat," Emma said as she sipped from a glass of red wine.

Nolan had begun to like the little comments that each of them would make about a future that pictured them together. Upon moving to Washington, he'd had no idea that he would meet someone with whom he would even consider settling down. Nolan had imagined he would date around as he had in college, and if at any time he felt a relationship beginning to get serious, he'd planned to wiggle his way out of it. With Emma, though, he always wanted more. More weekends like the one they spent in Bald Head Island. More romantic moments like the one in the whirlpool that evening after dinner at the house they'd rented. Nolan could close his eyes and remember every moment—her wet, dark hair draped over her shoulders. That freckle on her nose—the one that he loved so much—as she climbed on top of him and settled in while the bubbles in the tub danced around them. The way her lips found his and the way her body moved, and the way he seemed to become temporarily paralyzed when she decided she wanted all of him.

Similar intimate memories were made the next weekend in a hot tub on the back porch of a remote log cabin in Boone. The view featured a valley with a creek snaking through it and rolling mountains climbing the horizon. Emma spent more time looking at the man kissing her neck and shoulders and making her feel like the luckiest woman in the world than she did taking in the colors of the leaves. Fall was the best time to visit the mountains of North Carolina. The air was crisp and cool, and the foliage really was to die for, as promised by *Our State* magazine. To Nolan's and Emma's surprise, this particular weekend they spent more time at the cabin than they did out in the town amongst other people. They hiked through the woods, took more than enough selfies together, and had acorn wars.

The downside to the romantic weekend getaways was always Monday. It was the day when reality hit the hardest. Instead of hiding out in a remote spot in the mountains, Nolan and Emma hid out in plain sight, separately, at the college. Other couples would walk the halls together, share a picnic on the lawn, and attend functions. Emma continued to be bothered by how Mary always seemed to find a way to be around Nolan. He would mention her stopping by his office from time to time, but the reason rarely warranted a visit. Mary had even brought Nolan a jar of local honey one day. She'd told him that her neighbor had given her more than she needed, but Emma knew Mary was just craving Nolan's attention. Emma somewhat regretted asking Nolan to please tell her when he spent any time with Mary. She hadn't asked as much because she wanted to keep tabs on him but because she didn't want to hear any gossip that made her question his intentions. She still didn't think he liked Mary, but when Emma walked by one of the conference rooms and through the large window spotted the two of them sitting next to one another laughing, she felt a sudden pang of insecurity. Emma realized jealousy wasn't attractive, but she didn't know any woman that wouldn't be jealous of another woman pursuing her man. She had said very little to Nolan about the situation, but she wondered from time to time if he noticed how conversations about Mary altered her mood.

Nolan had sensed that Emma continued to let their hibernation at her house bother her, and he knew that Mary had become more than just a sore subject. He considered not telling her about the times that Mary came around, but he preferred knowing his conscience was clear. Ever since he'd shared the secret about his mother with Emma, he had found it easy to talk to her about everything, even the touchy subjects like Mary. He didn't quite know how to break the news to her that Mary had invited him to the annual college Halloween party, though. He waited an entire day, and it ate at him like he had been eating at the candy Mary had been randomly bringing him. Finally, as they sat on Emma's couch watching a movie, he blurted it out.

"Are you freakin' serious?" Emma all but shouted as she pressed the pause button. "I told you she likes you!"

Nolan just shrugged his shoulders as the air around them became silent. He would have rather just talked as the movie played in the background. He'd had a pretty good idea that Mary liked him, but he'd always convinced himself that she was just being nice. She had an easy going personality, and he enjoyed talking to her, but every time he was around her, he felt a little guilty even though he hadn't done anything wrong.

"I can't believe she's been bringing you candy," Emma fumed. "Do you eat it?"

Nolan tried not to laugh but failed. "Why wouldn't I?" he asked. "It's not like she injects it with some special potion that's going to make me like her."

"You rarely even eat candy, though," Emma pointed out. "Other than the basket of Junior Mints that you snack on every once in a while, I'm not sure I've ever seen you eat another piece of candy."

Nolan furrowed his brow. "Are you asking me not to eat the candy she brings me?"

"No."

Nolan stared at Emma, waiting for her to say more.

Emma's gaze had become fixed on the frozen television screen.

"What did you tell her?"

"About the candy?"

"No, about the costume party . . . did you tell her you'd go with her?"

Nolan's eyebrows nearly lifted to his hairline. "Are you serious right now?"

"Yes."

"I told her I already have a date."

Emma felt a sudden sigh of relief, coupled with confusion. She knew she'd come on strong, but this bothered her. A lot. What she already knew had now been confirmed. "Wait, what do you mean you already have a date?"

"Well," Nolan hesitated. "I guess I don't technically have a date . . . but if you'll agree to go with me, I would love to have you as my date."

"Really?" Emma asked, making a face that caused her nose to scrunch. "I mean, of course I want to be your date. But are you willing to take that risk? Think of all the people that will be there that know us."

Faculty, students, and their families all received an invitation to this annual event held on the college's campus. Emma had attended every year since she'd started taking classes. There would be bouncy houses, cakewalks, pony rides, pumpkin carving contests, and other festive games and attractions.

"Sure. We'll just dress up in costumes that won't reveal our identity."

Emma bit the tip of her fingernail. "What do you have in mind?"

"I figured I'd let you choose since I picked out the costumes for the masquerade ball."

Emma batted her eyes. "I have a perfect idea."

The Chicago Cubs beat the Cleveland Indians to win the organization's first World Series title since 1908. Nolan and Emma watched game seven in their pajamas on her couch and jumped up and down when the Cubs made the final out. Over the course of the playoffs, they had become self-proclaimed honorary Cubs fans. When Emma would hit balls at Firefly Field, she would pretend to be Kris Bryant or Addison Russell like a kid on the sandlot dreaming about being her favorite players.

At first, Nolan found the concept corny, but eventually he discovered himself pretending to be Jake Arrieta pitching to her. It reminded him of countless evenings spent on the baseball field with his dad as a young boy. While his dad worked, Nolan would spend the afternoon concocting a batting lineup of Major League Baseball players that he would write on a sheet of paper and take to the field with him later. His dad would pitch to him and let him pretend to be every batter on the list. Nolan would hit, run, and even pretend to steal bases. His dad would play along like a big kid, and Nolan remembered it being the absolute best time of his life. He loved baseball. Then. Now . . . now . . . now he felt trapped. He was supposed to hate baseball. During college, he had started hating it. After college, he'd decided he would never play again, but being surrounded by a field of fireflies with Emma Pate on warm evenings in North Carolina had somehow gradually changed his life. He had slowly and unintentionally fallen in love with the game of baseball all over again. Never in his wildest dreams would he have imagined that the most attractive red-haired woman that he'd ever met would be the one to remind him that it was okay to love this game. As he pitched to her, an epiphany suddenly hit him, and it completely changed his way of thinking. One day he wanted to have children. Right then, in that very moment, standing on the pitcher's mound at Firefly Field, he imagined being on this field with Emma and their children and being able to teach them the game of baseball with his wife.

Emma watched as Nolan stepped off the rubber mound and walked directly toward her at home plate. He didn't say anything, and neither did she—he simply wrapped his arms all the way around her and kissed her passionately beneath a million twinkling stars. Then he did something that she had imagined would never happen.

21

Nolan slid his hand down Emma's arm and let his fingers fall over her fingers—still gripping the handle of a wooden baseball bat. With his eyes closed and his heart racing a thousand beats a minute, his fingers slowly took the place of her fingers on the bat. Emma opened her eyes and watched him closely as he pulled back and eventually gripped the bat with both hands. He held it in front of his face and looked it over from top to bottom studying the grain pattern in the wood.

"Will you throw me soft toss?" he asked, turning his feet in the white-chalk outlined batter's box.

Nolan hadn't even considered the idea of asking Emma to pitch from the mound. He would be way too afraid of accidentally hitting a ball back up the middle that she might not be able to catch or dodge. Having her throw him soft toss—a drill where a person squats down a few feet off to the side of the hitter and tosses up balls underhand for the batter to hit—would be much safer.

Emma simply shook her head yes. She didn't ask if Nolan was sure he wanted to do this or why he had decided at this particular moment that he wanted to swing a bat. She just grabbed a few balls from a nearby bucket and knelt down. When she threw the first ball, she was so nervous that it nearly hit him. Nolan began to stride but didn't swing.

"I'm sorry," she shrieked, afraid the bad toss might cause him to think twice about holding the bat.

"It's okay," he said, his focus remaining steady on the area above the plate, the space between him and Emma.

His stance looked so natural, she noticed, that it was hard for her to believe he hadn't stepped into a batter's box in over six years. She tossed the second ball into the air over the plate and watched the bat in Nolan's hands fly through the zone with more force than she'd ever witnessed. She'd seen a lot of grown men hit a baseball, but she had never heard the whip of a bat make a swishing sound quite as powerful as the one that traveled into her ears and caused chills to rise up her spine. When the barrel of the bat connected with the ball, it sounded like it had disintegrated the object. One moment the ball was right there floating in front of her face above the plate, and then it completely disappeared. In that instant, Emma felt her head whip and her eyes began to search the air above the field as if pursuing the flight of a bumblebee that had just buzzed by her ear. She spotted the ball in the sky about halfway into its voyage over the outfield, and in a matter of moments, she watched it disappear through the tree line and into the cornfield. In her entire lifetime, no one had ever come close to hitting a ball that far on this field. She honestly doubted they would even be able to find it.

"Holy cow!" she exclaimed.

"Toss me another, will you?" Nolan asked as if the distance was no big deal.

Emma figured the ball had traveled at least four hundred and fifty feet. Still shocked, she tossed another ball in Nolan's direction. His second hit was a line drive into centerfield, hit just as hard but not nearly as far. She tossed him the third ball, then the fourth, and then the fifth and final ball she had brought to the spot where her knee was digging into the sand.

"Will you throw me the rest of the balls in the bucket?" Nolan asked, his feet remaining steady, his insides still rattled.

Emma fetched the bucket and tossed ball after ball over home plate until she was afraid Nolan's hands were going to start bleeding. As she watched him hit, he appeared to be in some sort of mental zone that made it seem like he was in an entirely different world. When Nolan first told her that he had played college baseball for ECU, she had been impressed, and when he said the Boston Red Sox drafted him right out of high school she'd been even more impressed. However, watching him here, live, hitting ball after ball with so much power seemed absolutely unreal. He'd belted a dozen or so that she guessed traveled between four hundred to five hundred feet. The grounders he hit skipped across the field so fast that she couldn't imagine an infielder trying to stop them, and it seemed he could hit a ball to any part of the field he wanted with ease.

When the last ball fell somewhere in the cornfield, Nolan gently laid the wooden bat flush on the sand beneath his feet.

"Thank you," he said.

Emma realized that those two words were intended to exclaim more than a simple appreciation for her taking the time to throw him soft toss. She noticed a pure and deep meaning behind them that explained to her that he might not have ever hit another baseball in his entire life if he hadn't met her and ended up with her here on this baseball field in the middle of nowhere. Something about the fireflies that normally flew here, and even the crisp autumn air that sent cool breezes floating through the trees, made this place magical. Emma had always been able to feel her dad here, and in many ways, she felt that Firefly Field had helped heal the wounds his death had caused.

"How did that feel?" Emma wanted to know.

"Natural," Nolan responded.

Nolan reached for Emma's hand and led her out into

centerfield where they eventually laid down on the grass and stared up at the stars.

"What were you thinking about as you hit those balls?"

"My mama—"

Emma felt tears forming in the corners of her eyelids. "I bet she was as proud as a mom can be watching down from heaven as her son enjoyed hitting baseballs just like you did when you were a little boy."

Nolan stared at the night sky. "She's been watching me the whole time," he said.

Emma smiled with a frown on her face, and as Nolan took in her expression it reminded him of the sun shining while clouds poured out rain.

"I'm sure she has been, Nolan."

"I know she has. You see, I used to have a hard time falling asleep at night, so much so that my parents took me to the doctor for it," Nolan admitted. "No one could figure out why and nothing they tried seemed to help. Then one night my mama randomly brought into my bedroom a mason jar filled with fireflies. I vividly remember watching them swirl around and around inside the glass, their little lights flickering on and off like Morse code. I fell asleep quickly that night and slept more peacefully than I ever had. The rest of that summer, Mom, Dad, Norman and I would go outside before bedtime and catch fireflies. Norman and I would bring a jar of the little creatures inside with us. We always let them go the next morning so that they wouldn't die."

Emma smiled real big. "Dad and I used to do the same thing," she said. "Catching fireflies is like a rite of passage, I think."

"Definitely," Nolan agreed. "One of the best."

"This is sad, but do you know that adult fireflies only live a matter of weeks?"

Nolan frowned. "I think I've heard that."

Nolan had picked up a baseball that had been lying nearby on the outfield grass. The rest of the balls were scattered all around the field as if mirroring the stars above them.

"Did you know that a baseball is made up of one hundred and eight stitches?"

"Really?"

"Yep."

Emma's brow suddenly furrowed. "So, when you were a kid, what did you do when fall came and the fireflies went away?"

Nolan smiled. "My mom ended up making this snow globe-like thing where she used a mason jar filled with tiny glow-in-the-dark balls, and beneath it, a small fan blew them around to make them look like fireflies."

"That's ingenious and sweet." Emma paused, imagining the object. "Do you still have it?"

Nolan smirked. "When I'm at home, I sleep with it on every single night," he admitted.

"That's cute," she said, wrapping her arms around him and settling her head on his shoulder. "You should bring it with you when you stay here—I'd like that."

In a matter of moments, Emma fell asleep, and not long afterward Nolan did the same, right there on the cold outfield grass.

22

A few nights earlier, Nolan and Emma had shown up to the Halloween party at the college dressed as Batman and Catwoman. She'd made sure to order a costume that nearly covered her entire face so that no one would be able to recognize her. The two of them walked amongst friends and strangers that cold night at the end of October, but no one had any idea of the true identity of the couple beneath the black costumes. Nolan and Emma held hands and kissed and frolicked like two puppies in between throwing darts at balloons, eating funnel cake, and sliding down a massive inflatable slide. Emma snuggled up even closer to Nolan every time they crossed paths with Mary, who dressed as a prisoner handcuffed to a police officer—Clay Bell. Nolan and Emma both had a good laugh about that, and Emma hoped that Mary would fall for Clay and leave Nolan alone.

November came and went and brought some cooler weather with it. Nolan continued to talk on the phone to his dad, and for Thanksgiving, Norman flew everyone to Miami to watch his game and celebrate the holiday together. Norman had become single again, and Nolan had been telling him about Emma's friend Lisa, so they invited her to come along for the trip. At first, Lisa seemed hesitant, but she had never been to an NFL game or met an NFL player, so she agreed to give it a shot. Both Emma and Lisa loved their first NFL experience, especially being able to go behind the scenes to meet all of the players and coaches, and walk the sidelines before the game started. The best moment, though, had been when Nolan reunited with his father. Emma felt the tears run down her face and watched tears run down both Nolan's and his father's face as they embraced at Norman's house. The rest of the weekend the two were inseparable, and Emma had no idea how Nolan had been able to go so long without having a relationship with his father.

Nolan's family absolutely loved Emma and treated her like family. Norman and Lisa seemed to get along well and even went out on a date by themselves one night. The entire group ate Thanksgiving dinner when it was eighty degrees outside, which didn't seem quite right. They also swam in Norman's pool, played board games, and did all the tourist things in Miami. Emma made sure to personally thank Nolan's father for rating the cards for her. He told her that he would do anything he could to help someone that his son cared about so much.

When Nolan and Emma made it back to Washington, they decorated her house for Christmas. The following week Nolan had all of the students from his classes meet together on Friday and cut the red ribbon at the entrance of the new exercise trail they'd worked hard on all semester. A small group of faculty members was there to be a part of the celebration as well as local businesspeople and a representative from the newspaper and the television station. Also in the crowd, Clay and Mary were holding hands.

Nolan and Emma were nearly shaking with nervous bones the entire afternoon because it seemed like just the right occasion for Clay to make a scene in front of a camera. Some of the students jogged the trail, others walked, and along with Nolan, Emma, and

Lisa, about a dozen folks rode their bicycles. The path wound through the woods for five kilometers. Nolan had intentionally planned it that way so that it could also be used for 5k charity races. There were some small hills and a short bridge that crossed over Broad Creek, then the trail followed the creek, making it quite scenic.

The reporters interviewed Nolan, Jerry, and some of the other students and faculty who tried out the trail. Nolan watched Clay anxiously, but to his bewilderment, Clay never ended up in front of a camera.

The semester ended not long after the trail christening, and Nolan felt grateful to still have a job. Emma had picked up a part-time waitressing position at another local restaurant to help ends meet. Norman and Lisa continued to talk, and he even flew her down to see him a couple of times during the month of December. Nolan asked Norman if he would please not come to Washington for the time being. He figured the press would pick up on an NFL player being in a small town, and Nolan didn't want the extra attention while he and Emma were concealing their relationship. They had made it through one semester without being caught, and they only had one more to go.

Nolan, Emma, and Lisa flew to Arizona for Christmas and enjoyed the holiday with Nolan's father and Norman. On Christmas morning, Emma tore the wrapping paper from her final Christmas present from Nolan and upon inspecting it didn't know whether to hug his neck or punch him. Inside a wooden box with a baseball carved on the lid, she found the entire collection of her grandfather's baseball cards. She had neither desired nor expected Nolan's charity, but she had to admit that the way he had gone about anonymously helping her was one of the sweetest gestures she'd ever known anyone to make. The idea of Nolan secretly buying the cards online—which his generous father helped him with—had never crossed her mind, and it meant a lot that he waited until Christmas to let her know.

Sentimental gifts seemed to be the theme on Christmas morning at the Lynch's, with the most moving one being a present to Nolan from his father. Nolan unwrapped a leather-bound photo album that contained photos from every baseball game Nolan had ever played. Some of the pictures were of him playing and some of them were of his parents in the stands watching him. He became emotional as he flipped through two pages of photos from the last game his mom had ever attended. They were hard to look at, but they took away his breath in a good way. The next page didn't contain a photo but rather a note that read, *Son, I promised you I'd never miss a game. –Dad.* At first, Nolan didn't quite understand the meaning, but then he flipped the page and the first picture was of him on the mound at Clark-LeClair Stadium in Greenville. Nolan glanced up at his dad then looked at the adjacent page where he found a photo of a man decked out in a pirate costume. He remembered noticing this guy at the stadium–he always stood beyond the outfield fence near the pirate flag. Nolan had never seen the man this closely, though, and he erupted in tears and fell into his dad's embrace when he realized the man in the pirate outfit with concealing make up had been his father. He'd been at every single game Nolan had ever pitched.

23

The New Year started off as rough as a ride on a wooden roller coaster. The one-year anniversary of Emma's father's death hit her harder than she expected. Nolan consoled her as best as possible, but he knew from the firsthand experience of losing a parent that no one could say or do anything to make specific times better. The only positive thing Emma gleaned from making it through the past year without ending up clinically depressed was knowing she'd conquered all of the firsts without her father: his birthday, her birthday, Thanksgiving, Christmas, and so many more memorable days and family traditions. Spending the recent holidays without him had proven to be extremely difficult, but Nolan and his family had been nothing short of amazing. Not only had they kept her busy which kept her mind off how much she missed her dad, but they basically adopted her into their family. They made her a part of their family traditions at Thanksgiving and Christmas. While in Washington, Nolan and Emma had kept each other company through what was the loneliest time of year for people who had lost family members. They'd watched Christmas movies and drank hot chocolate, and at the end of the year, they'd watched the ball drop together on television. After Christmas, Lisa had flown out of Arizona on the plane with Norman instead of coming back home with Nolan and Emma. She was excited about traveling with Norman to his next football game. The two of them were becoming relatively close, and Nolan and Emma couldn't be happier for them. Nolan hoped their relationship would last, but he knew that long distance relationships could be quite challenging. He'd tried that with a girl he dated his senior year of high school, but college life in different states quickly pulled them apart. The thing Norman and Lisa had going for them was that Norman, fortunately, had the means to fly her out to see him pretty much anytime it worked out for their schedules. Lisa's family's farm had done quite well, so she didn't have to be there all the time. Her role with the farm these days mainly consisted of office work such as accounting, handling business contacts, and such, which Lisa could manage from anywhere with a laptop and a smartphone. As for her yoga classes, she had a friend who could fill in for her anytime she needed the help.

Not only did the New Year start off rough, but it also ended in heartbreak. Mary showed up at Nolan's office early one morning in tears. She sat with him and talked for nearly thirty minutes. She apologized over and over and asked him to please forgive her for what was going to happen. At first, Nolan didn't understand, but as she continued to talk, everything began to piece together. After the Halloween event, Mary and Clay had started dating, and over the past few months, Mary had learned all about the secret relationship between Nolan and Emma through Clay. She had seen the pictures, even mentioned watching videos that Nolan had no idea existed. She made Nolan privy to a plan Clay had been working on before she started dating him—the main reason for her visit today.

"Nolan, while Clay and I were together, I talked him out of going through with his arrangement, but now that we have broken up I fear the worst."

Nolan didn't know what to say. Whatever came of Clay's shenanigans would in no way be Mary's fault, and Nolan felt bad that she had been dragged into his and Emma's dilemma, especially since she was a colleague at the college.

"I've had a lot of time to think about Clay's intentions, Mary, and I recognize the chance I am taking," he assured her. He made certain not to confess to anything specific. Even though he realized that Mary obviously knew something was going on between him and Emma, he didn't want to admit it out loud, especially on campus. It wasn't like he feared a wire could be found hiding under her button-up white blouse, but he didn't want to drag her into this situation any more than she already had been by Clay Bell.

"I hope everything works out for you, Nolan," she said, standing and surprising him when she stepped around behind his desk. "You're a sweet guy, and you deserve the best."

Nolan fidgeted in his chair. Not only did he feel awkward with Mary being so close, but he wasn't sure how to respond to the compliment. Then Mary shocked him when she admitted that she had been interested in him ever since they'd first met. Before leaving his office, she wrapped her arms around him and tears were falling down her cheeks again.

Nolan gathered himself and texted Emma soon after Mary walked out of his office. He asked Emma to meet him at the storage building out near the trail entrance. While waiting for her to respond, he fiddled with random items on his desk. Then after a few minutes, Nolan decided to walk the campus to see if he could track her down. He headed for the bicycle rack and found her bike parked there. With it now being cold outside on a regular basis, he'd tried to talk her into letting him buy her an inexpensive car, but she wouldn't agree with the idea. She said that riding in the cold didn't bother her as long as she bundled up. Winter had brought pros and cons as far their relationship was concerned. One day Emma had mentioned that other couples on campus were holding hands with gloves on and wrapped up together in warm clothing. The gloomy sound of her voice explained to Nolan precisely what she meant—the two of them couldn't enjoy such moments. They *could* cuddle up by the old bricked fireplace at her house, though, and they had on many nights. They'd also taken walks and watched their breath travel down the dirt road with them. Nolan could tell how much Emma had enjoyed pulling out her winter wardrobe and being able to wear jeans and boots and sweaters and scarfs. She looked stunning in her cold weather attire, and he enjoyed unwrapping her like a present on evenings when things heated up by the fire.

Eventually, he spotted Emma on the sidewalk, her hair falling over a black scarf on a blue sweater. Then, as he noticed her dark blue jeans and tall black boots, he came to a sudden halt. Standing right in front of her, Mary had her hands on her hips, and Nolan couldn't tell by their body language if they were arguing with each other or if they were venting about Clay Bell. Either way, he figured he better veer off the path and head elsewhere for the time being. Before he turned, he noticed Emma catch a glimpse of him out of her peripheral vision. Her eyes darted in his direction two more times as she continued to carry on a conversation with Mary.

By this time, the clock on Nolan's phone told him his students were waiting for their instructor to start class, so he headed there, a bit nervous. Standing at the podium, he quickly checked off the class roster and started the lesson with his teeth slightly chattering. He played off this embarrassing bodily function to his class as his bones being cold from being outdoors too long, but this uneasiness reminded him of the first day he and Emma had ended up in this same room. Nolan remembered thinking that particular class period would never come to an end. Today, he had two things on his mind. He found himself interested in knowing what all Emma and Mary had talked about, specifically because of how the last few moments with Mary in his office had played out. The phone in his pocket had yet to vibrate, so he wondered if they were still talking. Emma had a class the same time as his, so Nolan doubted she'd skipped it, but then again he figured why not. He probably should have already canceled his class for the day and gone back to see if he could track down Emma again. In fact, in hindsight, he actually should have never let her out of his sight. He should have waited back or maybe even joined in on the conversation with Mary, but he constantly found himself concerned about raising red flags amongst staff and students. Although now it might be too late anyway based on what Mary had shared with him this morning.

As these thoughts bombarded his mind, his phone vibrated. While lecturing, he tried to set it on the podium inconspicuously. It wasn't the first time he'd opened a text while teaching, but when he read the words Norman had messaged, he felt panic settling in. The text read, *Bro, call me!*

Within ten seconds, his phone buzzed again, this time because of a text from Emma: *We need to talk!!!*

Before Nolan could tell the class they were dismissed, a heavy knock rattled the classroom door. At this point, his heart was racing, and he was pretty sure his face had turned as red as the apple he'd eaten for breakfast. He walked to the door, praying silently, and wondering who would be on the other side. Emma? Clay? Mary? Lisa?

When he opened the door, he didn't see any of the faces he had imagined. He saw Jerry Small, and Nolan knew exactly what had happened.

24

Nolan spent the next hour in a conference room surrounded by Jerry, the president of the college, the human resources director, and the public relations director. He hadn't had time to respond to Norman or Emma, and he hated that. On the walk to this meeting, Jerry hadn't said much, just that he would do everything he could to help Nolan, but the situation didn't look promising. Once Nolan sat down and the group started talking, he heard many of the comments he'd expected to hear when this day arrived.

"Mr. Lynch, we expect professionalism out of every one of our staff members," was one of the first statements out of the president's mouth.

The public relations director turned on the television and before clicking play on the remote at her fingertips prefaced what she was about to show him with, "This isn't the kind of press the college needs."

She showed Nolan some of the pictures of him and Emma that he'd already seen and then a video clip he hadn't seen. The thing that shocked him the most was the professionalism in the piecing together of the story. The work itself wasn't Clay Bell's doing; it was the online tabloid to which he had sold the compiled evidence.

Nolan had never imagined this being national news, but the media had their way of spinning stories to make advertising dollars, and it seemed that the online video had gone viral: "The brother of Miami Dolphins player Norman Lynch has gotten himself into hot water this winter in the little town of Washington, North Carolina," the voiceover sounded as images of Norman playing football displayed on the screen. Then came images of Nolan from high school. "Nolan Lynch, the former high school baseball standout once drafted by the Boston Red Sox, is now a college instructor. Maybe not for long, though. Bad luck seems to follow Nolan. His bat is the one that killed his mother at the Arizona High School Championship game . . ." More images, disturbing images—from *that* game. Then came present day photos. "This is Emma Pate, one of Nolan's students." The pictures Clay had given Nolan and Emma reeled through. "We're pretty sure Emma received an A in Mr. Lynch's class last semester." Then came a video of Nolan hitting baseballs at Firefly Field. "But at least Nolan Lynch can still hit a baseball." That's how it ended.

Nolan let his head drop into his hands. He couldn't believe this, even though he could. The human resources director handed him a packet and a pen.

"The college has a particular set of guidelines that we desire our instructors to follow. I am sure you are familiar with the protocol that accompanies an unfortunate situation like this one," she said. "Our office has highlighted the specific rules that are in question in this case, Mr. Lynch." She slid another sheet of paper to Nolan. "This is the document that you signed stating that you understood the code of conduct expected of you."

Nolan glanced at his signature. Then he looked at each of the people in the room. "I am sorry," he said simply.

Jerry spoke up before Nolan could say anything else. "Nolan, I assume you probably would like to hire an attorney," he said, more as a piece of advice than an expectation. He then glanced at his peers. "We're not here to ask you to explain yourself. Much of this is your personal business, but unfortunately, the college is involved now. We know you're a good man," he said.

"Nolan," the president said, "you will be placed on leave while an investigation of this matter takes place."

As Nolan had watched the video, he had expected to get fired on the spot. He realized the relevance of the innocent until proven guilty clause, but the video was pretty cut and dry. He closed his eyes before he spoke again. "I'd like to resign," Nolan declared.

"You don't have to do that," Jerry interjected.

"You do have that option available to you," clarified the human resources director.

Nolan was impressed how each person in the room had handled the situation. He didn't feel judged by any of them, surprisingly. "I would rather not bring any other bad press to the college." *Nor to Emma*, he thought but didn't feel the need to add audibly. He picked up the pen and said, "Where do I need to sign to resign my position?"

Before Nolan eventually walked out the conference room door, he had been prepped on what to expect on the other side. Security would be there waiting to escort him to his vehicle, which he had driven rather than riding his bicycle since it was cold, thankfully. Once they reached the double doors that led out of the building, that's where the local news media would be waiting. Thankfully the national media hadn't had time to make it to Little Washington yet, although he doubted they would waste a trip for this news. If they had been in the other Washington—Washington, D.C.—the vultures surely would have been swarming. As Nolan walked past the cameras and the reporters, he kept a straight face. He didn't hide under his jacket, he didn't stare at the ground, and he definitely didn't smile. The security officers weren't holding his arms or making a big scene; they were just walking alongside him.

This breach of contract issue wasn't a legal matter as far as in the realm of anything he could get arrested for, so thankfully there were no handcuffs involved. The media followed him to his car, flinging out questions the entire way. He didn't answer a single question or respond to any of the comments. He just kept walking as bystanders looked on curiously, then he slowly backed his vehicle out of the space and headed toward his house. While the cameras were on him at the college, even in his car in the parking lot, he had refrained from texting or calling Norman or Emma. When he made it to the nearest crowded parking lot, he pulled over and blended in his vehicle with the others. Thankfully, though, it didn't seem as though anyone had followed him.

Nolan's first call went to Emma Pate.

25

"Nolan, where in the world have you been?" were the first words out of Emma's mouth.

"It's a long story," he said.

"I'd like to hear it," she responded. "There are a lot of stories going around about you," she said, pausing for a breath. "And me."

"I know, Emma, and I am so sorry. I never imagined it would blow up like this." Nolan realized this news would be the buzz of Little Washington throughout the coming weeks. It would be talked about at the Coffee Caboose and the beauty shop and definitely around campus. The local newspaper and television station would run multiple stories. They would interview staff members at the college, and they would be hounding him and Emma for an interview. "Have you seen the video?" he asked.

"Yes, *everyone* has seen the video, Nolan." She paused. "I should have known that Clay would find a way to make money off of this. I kept trying to figure out the reason why he hadn't exposed us sooner, and this is it."

"Of course, but I never even thought about him selling photos and videos of us to a tabloid. I guess somehow Clay figured out my brother plays in the NFL so he figured he could exploit us the most by using Norman."

"Speaking of Norman, have you talked to him? Lisa is the one who first reached out to me about the video, and she said Norman was trying to get up with you."

"You are the first person I have talked to since I learned about the video, other than the leadership team at the college—that's where I've basically been since I saw you in the commons area."

"What happened? Did you lose your job?"

"I resigned."

"You did what?" she responded emphatically.

"Yes, I had to."

"So they forced you to resign?"

"No, they were going to put me on leave during an investigation of the matter."

"So why did you resign?"

Nolan explained his reasoning to Emma, and as he did he wondered why he hadn't thought about talking to her in more detail about all of this before it actually happened. It would have been nice for the two of them to have been on the same page heading into this fiasco that they knew was most likely inevitable.

"I want to see you, Nolan. We need to talk face to face."

"You do realize that's going to be difficult to make happen today without adding fuel to this fire, right?"

Nolan wanted to ask Emma about her conversation with Mary, but he didn't want to open a can of worms that might best stay sealed for the time being.

"Yes, I know," she said, sounding worn down.

"Where are you?"

"I am home. After I finished talking to Mary, I headed to the shed to see if you were there like you mentioned. The next thing I knew I was watching the video Lisa sent me the link to while I was waiting for you. When you didn't show up, I skipped my class and headed home."

"Is there anyone there?"

"At my house? No, why would anyone be here?"

"The media?" he asked specifically.

"Oh, I don't think so," she said, but then when she peeled back the curtain she saw two cars parked on the dirt road. "Wait, there are some cars I don't recognize . . ."

"If they come to your door, don't talk to them. Don't even answer the knock," Nolan advised. "They're probably just waiting to see if I'll show up."

"So, what do we do?"

"Lay low, let this die down."

The next couple of days moved like molasses. Emma skipped all of her classes and hunkered down at the farm as if there were two feet of snow on the ground outside. Nolan hung out at his house and watched television when not talking on the phone to Emma. The two of them racked up more minutes than they ever had, but when Nolan tried to make light of the situation by saying it was a good thing they didn't have limited minutes like when they were teenagers, Emma didn't find it funny. She made it clear to him that she didn't like being forbidden to see him. She said it actually did feel like they were teenagers whose parents had found out they were dating behind their backs and banned them from seeing one another. Nolan understood that, but he kept promising her the media would be chasing another story soon.

After Nolan's phone conversation with Emma the morning everyone had found out about their secret relationship, he had called Norman. The first thing Norman did was laugh.

"I told you that you'd get caught," Norman reminded him.

"It's not funny," Nolan responded.

"Maybe not from your point of view."

"What about for you? Wasn't that story embarrassing?"

"Bro, my jersey sales are up."

"You're as greedy as the media," Nolan teased, half meaning it.

"You have to find the silver lining."

"What's the silver lining for me?" Nolan asked. "I'm out of a job, and now that everyone knows why, I'll have a hard time finding another one. I have bills to pay, Norman. I don't have money stockpiled like you."

"Now you can openly date Emma; there's your silver lining, man."

"True. However, I think it will be best if she and I let things settle down a little here before we hang out."

"That's your call."

"Emma was born and raised here. She knows many people in this town, and the locals are going to judge her over this. So the quieter we can keep it, the better."

"You're both adults," Norman reminded Nolan. "Anyway, who cares what others think about this situation?" Norman paused, waiting for a response but Nolan didn't say anything. "I'll fly in on my bye week, and we'll go on a double date and have some fun with the media and the townsfolk."

Every NFL team received one bye week—a week without a game—during the sixteen game season. Nolan knew his brother was serious about coming to Little Washington during the break, which at any other time Nolan would have loved. "You probably would enjoy that."

"They say there is no such thing as bad publicity."

"Yeah, when you're a football player that might be true, but not when you work in education as I do—or did."

Later in the conversation, Norman told Nolan that he had his back no matter what, just like always. Norman expressed how much he loved him and offered to help him out financially if Nolan needed anything while he searched for a new job. When Nolan told him he didn't need his charity, Norman reminded him that the story blowing up was in large part due to him being a professional athlete, so he felt partially responsible.

"I don't know if I can do this anymore, Nolan," Emma said, fighting tears but losing.

Nolan's jaw dropped. *Was she serious?* The calendar on his phone had reminded him that today was the first day of February, but he found himself wishing it was the first day of April and Emma was pranking him.

"What do you mean?" Nolan inquired, hoping she didn't mean what he thought she meant. Hoping she just meant that she couldn't handle not seeing him one minute more.

"I mean *us.*"

"Why?"

"This is no way to live life."

"Emma, we've made it through the hard part."

"We have?" She paused to let out a few tears. "Are you sure about that? Because over here, it doesn't feel that way. I haven't seen you in days, and when I went back to class today everyone was looking at me funny. They're talking about me, Nolan. Behind my back. In front of my face. Everywhere. The college newspaper wants to write a story on us. They've been hounding me. They've already written a story about how it's wrong for instructors to date students."

"Emma, I'm sorry. I hate that you have to deal with all of this, but the two of us splitting up isn't the answer."

"Then what is?" she asked. "You want to just wait it out a little longer?" she said sarcastically.

"No. I will come over right now so we can talk about this in person."

"Oh, so this is what it takes to get you to talk to me face to face? How about that morning when everything went down, and I wanted to talk to you in person? Or these last few days when I've been stressing out."

"Emma, please, let's just talk."

"We are talking."

Nolan hadn't seen this coming. He hadn't imagined she would consider walking away, especially now.

"I'll come over now."

"No, that will just make it harder, Nolan."

Nolan suddenly felt a million miles away from Emma. He spent the next ten minutes pleading with her, but it seemed like their conversation only went in circles.

"There's a rumor going around that Mary has a crush on you," Emma said spitefully. "Maybe you should go talk to her," she suggested.

"Who cares about rumors, Emma?"

"I do, Nolan, and it's not just a rumor. Mary told me that she liked you. She even apologized to me for liking you while we were dating. *She* apologized, Nolan, not you."

"Why should I apologize for *her* liking *me*?"

"You should apologize for not telling me that Mary told you that she liked you." Nolan froze, and Emma continued. "I had to find out from her, Nolan."

"When did she tell you that?"

"Does it matter?"

"Did she tell you when I saw the two of you talking that morning after we all found out about the video?"

"No, but *you* should have. Because that's the day *she* told you," Emma fumed. "I had to find out from her when I went back to the college. She reached out to me and wanted to talk to me before I went back to my classes."

"I'm sorry, Emma. You're right, I should have told you, and I was planning to, but then the video went viral, and I felt like we needed to deal with that first."

"How many times have we talked in the past few days, Nolan? How many hours have you spent on the phone with me? In all that time, did it not occur to you that you might should share with me that another woman confessed to having an interest in you? That she hugged you and she admitted the hug probably lingered a little too long?" Emma didn't give Nolan time to respond yet. "You've told me all along how much you love hugging me. How special embracing me and looking into my eyes is to you—"

Nolan interrupted, although he didn't have to because Emma's words turned into sobs. "I am sorry, Emma," he said again. "Nothing happened. The hug meant nothing. It felt awkward, and I've never liked Mary other than as a friend."

"Well, now I'm just a friend, too."

The phone conversation didn't end there, but it might as well have. Nothing else that was said mattered. Emma didn't want to be with Nolan right now, and she made that clear. She didn't want him to come over so they could talk things through. He wanted to so badly. He wanted to have the opportunity to look into her eyes and tell her how much he loved her. How much he wanted to be with her. How sorry he was for how things had turned out. There were so many things he wanted to say.

26

That day, Nolan packed everything he cared about into two suitcases and boarded the next flight to Miami. He spent the next month with his brother and not once did Emma reach out to him. When he would text her, she would respond, but she kept the conversations short and to the point. Emma answered his questions, but she didn't ask many of her own. When Nolan said *I love you,* she didn't say it back. That hurt the most. He was accustomed to her saying *I love you* all the time, especially at night before bed. Those were always their last three words to each other. He knew she probably still loved him, but she basically told him that loving him wasn't worth all the drama that came with their relationship. He tried to remind her that they'd made it through the difficult months of hiding their secret affair and that things were sure to be simpler if she would only give them a second chance. Emma expressed no interest in that idea, and it began to eat at him just like his mother's death had eaten at him. Nolan felt depression settling in but wouldn't admit it. He said *No* every time Norman asked him to go out for dinner or a movie or do anything that involved leaving the house. Nolan sat around and ate chips and frozen pizzas and drank sodas—things he hadn't done regularly in forever. Instead of exercising, he watched TV and started gaining weight. Nolan just didn't care. If Emma didn't care about him, he decided he didn't care about anything. He had no job. No girlfriend. No mother. No friends. He couldn't seem to think about anything other than all of the things he didn't have.

The first two weeks were the roughest, most likely because Nolan held on to hope that Emma would come around. The next two weeks weren't much better. Norman's football season had ended before Nolan had arrived in Miami, which meant Lisa came to visit often, and her being around only seemed to make things more difficult. Seeing her reminded Nolan of Emma. When she arrived, he usually went into his bedroom and stayed there. The first time she'd come to visit, Nolan had tried to talk to her about Emma, but Lisa said that she didn't want to be in the middle of the situation. She said she was willing to listen to his thoughts, but she wasn't going to share anything that she and Emma had discussed. That was up to Emma, Lisa told him. He often wondered what Lisa shared with Emma about him when she returned to Washington.

Norman kept telling Nolan that everything would work out for the best. Nolan doubted it. Things never seemed to work out for the best in his life. Every time things started looking up, everything crashed down all around him. He had been talking to his dad less and less. His dad would call, but Nolan wouldn't always answer. Nolan felt like he'd let his dad down—again.

Eventually, Norman slowly began convincing Nolan to leave the house. It started with a trip to the grocery store, then Norman talked him into going out to eat, then they started doing some of the things they used to do when they were younger. They went bowling, zip lining, and spent time out on Norman's boat.

Then one day, Norman came home with news that shocked Nolan.

"*Off the Field* wants to shoot a feature story on our family."

"What?" Nolan inquired, his head tilted and brow furrowed. *Off the Field* had always been one of his favorite sports shows. It aired in prime time on one of the most popular sports networks in the country. The stories were about athletes' lives off the field—hence the name of the show. They were almost always positive, often sad, and Nolan couldn't count the number of times the show had made him cry in a good way. "You serious?"

"Yep. They've been talking to my agent. They want to interview me, you, and Dad."

"Why?"

"Well, they initiated conversation with my agent after your story went viral online."

"So they want to do a story on me screwing up my life?"

"You know that's not what the show is about."

"Well, the timing is impeccable," Nolan said sarcastically.

"It's obvious that our family landed on their radar because of the online video, but that's not what the story will be about."

"Then what will it be about?"

"My agent says the primary topic will be race relations."

"Keyword being *primary*," Nolan pointed out. "Meaning secondary will be about what happened to Mom and probably about me losing my job because of my relationship with Emma." Nolan paused, thinking briefly about how things had ended with Emma, wishing it could have turned out much differently. Then he thought about the accident with his mom and all the media hounds that had chased him for a story. "I'm not interested in exposing myself to those issues again. I haven't had to deal with talking to the media about Mom in over six years. I'm done with all the drama that surrounds the makeup of our family."

"So you're done with being part of a black family?"

"We're not a black family," Nolan shouted. As soon as the words came out of his mouth, he realized Norman had said *black family* just to get him riled up. Their father had always emphasized that they were a family, not a black family or any type of family that came with a label.

"That's right; we're a family. Period. That's the message we have the opportunity to spread to the world. But you just want to run away from it. Like you ran away from Arizona and from Dad."

"You're going to throw that in my face now?" Nolan followed the anger in his voice toward his brother, ending up only a few feet from his face. "I worked things out with Dad. He forgave me."

"How about Emma?"

Nolan stepped so near to Norman that he could smell Doritos on his breath. "What about Emma?" Nolan shot back. "Actually, don't even bring her into this," he demanded, glaring into his brother's eyes.

"She is in it, bro. You ran away from her just like you ran away from Dad."

Nolan shoved his brother in the chest. "I didn't run away from Emma. She ended our relationship," he clarified.

Norman staggered backward but caught his balance. "You keep telling yourself that," he said choosing not to retaliate physically.

"What does that mean?" Nolan inquired, his brow wrinkled with question marks.

"That means Emma needed you. Just like Dad and I did." He let his words sink in before going on. "You worry too much about what people think about you, especially people you don't even know. You should have been there for Emma and not worried about what the media said or what people in her community thought. She knew the chance she was taking with you."

"Is this what Lisa has told you?"

"This is what I know," Norman protested. "This has nothing to do with Lisa. This is how Dad and I felt after you ran away from our family. *Your* family."

Emma leaned her head against the wall behind her kitchen table. Sitting across from her, Lisa watched as tears fell from her best friend's chiseled chin.

"Why did Norman say those things to Nolan?"

"Because he loves and cares about his brother."

"Why did you tell Norman those things?"

"I tell him everything, Emma." Lisa fidgeted with her phone on the table. "I didn't think he would say anything to Nolan."

"But he did, Lisa."

"I know, and that's why I came directly over here to tell you. I'm sorry," she stammered.

"I don't know what to do," Emma admitted.

"Just call him," Lisa suggested.

"It's not that easy." Emma used the back of her hand to wipe her face.

"Why not?"

"Because this has been the hardest month of my life, and now that I'm starting to put the shattered pieces back together, I don't want to risk going through all of this again."

"But you've told me over and over that you didn't really want things with Nolan to end. That you were stressed and you overreacted, and you wish you could take it all back."

"I do wish I could take it back. I also wish Nolan would have just come over that day when things happened at the college, but he didn't."

"Emma, he was freaking out, too. Sure, he made mistakes, but when you broke things off he tried to talk you out of it. He offered to come over then and work things out."

"But he didn't, Lisa. He didn't come over," Emma pointed out.

"Because you told him not to."

"I didn't mean it, Lisa." More tears fell down Emma's cheeks. "If he would have come over I would have jumped into his arms and held him and never let him go." Emma cried even harder. "But he left . . . when I needed him the most, he left me."

Later that evening when Nolan calmed down, he apologized to his brother for pushing him. Then he surprised Norman when he agreed to film the story with *Off the Field.* Norman called his agent, and his agent told him he'd be in touch when the show responded with proposed filming dates. It left Nolan in a near state of shock when Norman came to him the next day and said *Off the Field* wanted to start filming almost immediately.

"Immediately, as in when?"

"As in fly us out to the studio next week."

"What?" Nolan figured the show would want to film months down the road. These things took planning.

"Some big-named boxer flaked out on them, and now they have a film crew available next week."

A week later, Nolan and Norman boarded an airplane to a studio in California. Their father met them on the set, and then the three of them sat down with the producer and the host of the show. They went over a list of questions that the producer had emailed to the family as soon as they'd agreed to the interview. Nolan felt at ease when the producer explained that the family would be heavily involved in the content and that the show wouldn't air anything that bothered them. Nolan now realized why the show had always stood out to him. They tackled the tough issues in life and sports, but they did it the right way.

They spent five days shooting footage in four different cities. The first leg of the trip took them home to Phoenix. There, they visited Nolan's and Norman's childhood homes—one in the projects and the other in the suburbs. They took a limousine to the stadium where Nolan had played his high school state championship game. He never imagined he'd step onto that field again, but he did with tears in his eyes. The second location they flew to was Miami which Nolan found ironic since he and Norman had just flown out from there a couple of days prior. When Nolan mentioned the oddity, the producer said something about the schedule working out better this way. They shot video at the Dolphins' stadium and at Norman's house. Their next stop brought them to Fenway Park in Boston. Nolan had been nervous about stepping onto the field where the team who had once drafted him played. The left field wall—nicknamed the Green Monster due to its height of just over thirty-seven feet—was intimidating to stand next to, Nolan found out firsthand. He couldn't believe he finally had the opportunity to stand on the field where legends like Ted Williams, Carl Yastrzemski, Cy Young, Roger Clemens, and Pedro Martinez had played.

The last leg of their trip had been the one that made Nolan most nervous when he'd first studied the proposed itinerary upon arriving in California. In fact, he almost backed out, but then the producer told Nolan that it was entirely up to him whether or not they filmed at Firefly Field in Washington, NC. Nolan vividly remembered the conversations that followed. Along with the producer and the host of the show, Nolan, Norman, their father, and Norman's agent were sitting on expensive couches in a high-rise building overlooking the city of Los Angeles.

"I'll need to talk to someone first," Nolan announced to the entire group.

"Who?" Norman asked.

"Emma," Nolan clarified, wondering why his brother even asked. "I don't think Emma will be on board with this."

"I think she will," the producer suddenly interjected.

"No disrespect to you, but you don't know Emma Pate. You don't know the history of Firefly Field, and you don't know what it means to her family."

"Let's ask her," the producer suggested, reaching for the phone on the coffee table in between him and Nolan.

Nolan suddenly began to feel uneasy. He stared right through the producer and out the large windows behind the man. Behind Nolan was the door where they'd all entered, and Nolan began to seriously consider standing up, doing an about-face, and walking out.

"I will give her a call in private and ask her myself," Nolan said.

"Invite her to come with us for the entire taping," the host of the show suggested.

Nolan furrowed his brow. "It starts tomorrow; I highly doubt she'd be able to even if she were interested, which she won't be."

"Nolan and Emma haven't been talking," Norman clarified to the group.

Nolan threw his hands up. "That's none of their business," he said, becoming frustrated with his brother.

Finally, Nolan's father spoke up, and everyone else grew quiet. "Alright, I think you all have carried this far enough."

Nolan looked at his father, then glanced around the room and noticed smiles and grins on the faces surrounding him.

Mr. Lynch spoke again. "Your brother has set you up," he confessed. "Emma has heard this entire conversation."

Nolan didn't quite understand. Then, he looked down at the phone on the coffee table, assuming it must be on speaker phone with Emma on the other end, but why?

"Just ask her now if she'd like to make the trip with us," Mr. Lynch added.

"Emma," Nolan said simply, feeling odd and wondering if, in fact, she was on speaker phone.

"Yes," her sweet voice replied.

Nolan's ears perked up, wondering if the phone was connected to surround sound because her voice didn't appear to be coming from the speaker on the phone.

"I'd love to go," Emma said.

Nolan's head swiveled, and he nearly fainted when he saw Emma Pate standing right behind him. He stared into her ocean-blue eyes as he made his way around the couch. He barely noticed that everyone else in the room had stood and began to walk out the door as he wrapped his arms around her neck.

27

On the fifty-first floor in one of the tallest skyscrapers in Los Angeles, Nolan and Emma made their way to a set of window panes overlooking the busy city below. Pedestrians were filing down the sidewalks, cabs were weaving in and out of traffic, and street vendors were selling a variety of items from flowers to food. Life out there moved forward while Nolan and Emma talked about the mistakes they'd made in the recent past.

"Emma, I am so glad that you are here, but what made you want to come?" Nolan took his eyes off the bustling city below long enough to look into her eyes again. He sure had missed them. "I had honestly begun to wonder if I would ever see you again."

"I've missed you like crazy," she answered, stepping in to kiss his lips. It had been way too long since she had felt his mouth on hers, his hands touching her body.

"I've missed you more," he said, wrapping his arms around her waist and wanting never to let her go again.

"I want to be with you, Nolan. That's why I'm here."

"There's no one in the world I'd rather be with," he promised Emma. "I'm so sorry that I left Washington the way I did. I'm sorry that I didn't even tell you I was leaving. I should have done things differently. After I resigned, I should have met you at your house and not cared what anyone thought about me or us."

"We both could have done things differently, but we didn't. Things happened the way they happened for a reason. I don't know why I freaked out that day when I broke off our relationship. I just needed you, and you weren't there, at least not physically, and then I started worrying about the whole ordeal with Mary. I've since talked to her, and she said that she probably weirded you out the day she hugged you in your office. She said she didn't mean anything by it, only that she felt bad for us. I shouldn't have been so jealous, even though you have to admit that I was right about her liking you," Emma said with a grin. Nolan snickered and nodded his head but didn't respond audibly. "I should have trusted you, and I am sorry that I didn't, Nolan. Will you forgive me?"

"Of course," he said. "I hope you'll forgive me, too."

"I do."

Emma went on to explain that she'd found out through Mary how Clay had discovered that Nolan's brother was a professional football player, and then used that and Nolan's past to exploit Emma's and Nolan's relationship. Emma felt terrible about it because the comment she'd made to Nolan about the online articles regarding his past, in the restaurant parking lot in front of Clay, had been what sparked Clay to search for those same articles, which led him to the ammunition he needed.

Nolan simply nodded his head, surprised that neither of them had put two and two together sooner, and like adults, this time, they talked through all of the mistakes they'd made and apologized to one another over and over until they felt like they'd brought everything into the open and made things right.

"So, Norman set this whole thing up for you to show up here?"

"Well, him and Lisa together," Emma clarified. "I think she was tired of me sulking, and she knows that you and I are perfect together," she said with a smile. "She flew out here with me."

"I guess I owe them dinner or something."

"I think we both do."

"When we're in Washington filming we can take Norman to Bill's Hot Dogs. It's the offseason for him, so he'll probably eat a dozen hot dogs," Nolan laughed.

The *Off the Field* story featuring the Lynch family was scheduled to air three months after taping, but the next three months didn't turn out anything like Nolan and Emma would have expected after reuniting in California. Following the completion of the filming, Nolan had planned to return to Washington and hopefully stay there with Emma Pate for the rest of his life. He expected he would find a job at a fitness club as a personal trainer or maybe something in the nutrition field. Nolan knew he probably wouldn't have the flexible schedule he'd enjoyed at the college, but he looked forward to coming home to Emma after working from eight o'clock to five o'clock like the average person. He imagined the two of them would often head to downtown for dinner and a walk on the waterfront. He wanted to ask her if they could move in together, take the next step in their relationship. But that didn't happen because their lives changed forever on that filming trip.

Not long after Nolan and Emma had made up for lost time, their entire group boarded a plane in Los Angeles and made it safely to Phoenix. Emma held Nolan's hand as he stepped onto the field where he'd played his last high school baseball game. He stepped up to the plate with a baseball bat in his hand and explained to everyone and the camera the thoughts that had traveled through his mind that rainy night. Nolan sat in the seat and took in the view from where his mother had watched him play one last time. He cried on camera when he noticed her name engraved on the seat, and the host informed him that no one had been allowed to sit in his mother's spot since that gloomy day.

One emotional filming session led to another as they headed into the inner city, and Nolan found himself walking the streets of his old neighborhood. Most people were respectful, especially because of all the cameras and lights surrounding Nolan and Norman, but some still hollered out profanities and racial slurs as the two brothers walked side by side. Many of the people that hadn't made it out of that neighborhood were jealous of Norman's success on the football field. Nolan had feared that if he ever stepped foot in this neighborhood again, he wouldn't make it out alive. He'd insisted that a police officer escort Emma as he and Norman filmed the interview on the sidewalks, and thankfully nothing dangerous happened.

They visited the other neighborhood where the Lynch family had lived and then they walked the tarmac to another plane and headed for Miami. As planned, they filmed at the Dolphins' stadium. Nolan and Norman raced the entire length of the football field just for fun; they had a contest to see who could throw the furthest and who could kick the longest field goal. Their dad stood by and laughed at them just like he had when they were kids. They'd always been competitive, and that spirit is what had driven them to work hard in life. The camera crew took a little footage at Norman's home, and then they packed up and headed to Boston.

Soon after arriving at Fenway Park, Nolan found himself standing at home plate with a dark-colored maple baseball bat in his hands. One of the members of the grounds crew had handed it to him and said that he was welcomed to hit some balls. At first, Nolan felt hesitant, but then he thought back to the night he'd hit with Emma. He also realized this would most likely be his only chance ever to hit a baseball where the Boston Red Sox play. Just in front of the pitcher's mound, a net shielded the area so that someone could throw batting practice to him. The show had even scheduled a batting practice pitcher, but Nolan asked if his father could pitch to him like old times. A few moments later he was blasting pitches from his dad toward the Green Monster. Emma, Norman, and Lisa were sitting in the front row just behind the plate cheering him on. Even though Emma had seen how far he had hit the ball at Firefly Field, she had no idea how that would translate onto a Major League Baseball field. It took him a few swings, but before she knew it, Nolan was launching balls over the thirty plus foot wall in left field. Some even flew over the rows of stands beyond the wall and ended up landing somewhere outside the stadium.

Once Nolan seemed satisfied with conquering the Green Monster, he began to spread out hits and home runs to center field and right field and everywhere in between. He'd been hitting for about fifteen minutes when he asked Emma if she wanted to pitch some. Even though she wasn't a Red Sox fan, he knew that as a baseball fan she would cherish an opportunity like this. Emma nestled in behind the net and began throwing him pitches, her velocity increasing as her arm warmed up. At one point, Norman hollered out, "Emma's gonna end up striking you out." Everyone laughed, and Nolan kept bruising baseballs. He'd made sure to remind Emma, and his dad when he had been pitching, to stay behind the net. Thank God he had because he hit a sharp line drive right back up the middle when Emma was throwing. It hit the net and bounced back in Nolan's direction. When Nolan eventually handed the bat back to the guy from the grounds crew, another gentleman came walking onto the field.

"We've been sitting up there watching you," he said, pointing to an obscure area in the stands where a few other men waved down to Nolan. "I'm one of the Boston Red Sox coaches," he said introducing himself by name with a handshake.

Nolan felt honored to meet the man. "It's a privilege to meet you, sir. Thank you for allowing me to take batting practice on your field."

"You're welcome," he replied. "I hear you've just recently started hitting baseballs again."

"Yes, sir."

"You pitched for ECU?"

"Yes, sir."

"But you honestly haven't hit a baseball since high school?"

"Yeah, it's a long story," Nolan trailed off.

"I'm familiar with your story," he said, surprising Nolan. "You never left our radar. You're a much better hitter than you are a pitcher, though," he added with a grin. "At least that's what our scout sitting up there said." He pointed at the group of men again. "He scouted a few of your college teammates, and he kept an eye on you when he was at the games. He always hoped he'd show up and you'd have a bat in your hand."

Nolan laughed and looked at Emma. "I told you I wasn't a very good pitcher," he reminded her.

"You sure did," she remembered, giggling.

The other men eventually made their way down to the field to meet everyone, and then they gave their guests a tour of the rest of the stadium, including the locker rooms and training facilities. Boston ended up being the most enjoyable place they filmed. In a way, hitting and throwing in a Major League park reminded Nolan of what he had possibly given up, but at the same time, he had now fulfilled one of the things on his bucket list—hitting a home run over the Green Monster.

The last stop of the trip brought them to Little Washington. No one on the film crew had ever been to the town, but they all seemed to love the slow pace and the friendly people. Nolan and Emma ended up taking the entire group to Bill's Hot Dogs on the day they filmed in downtown. They shot a lot of footage at Firefly Field, some during the daytime but most at nighttime. Nolan hated that the fireflies weren't in season, but the producer assured him and Emma that he could have some added in during editing.

Emma spent some time in front of the camera in Washington, and at the end of the trip, the producer and host told them that this group had been their favorite ever.

Three months after the week Emma had spent with Nolan and his family filming the story for *Off the Field*, she found herself nestled in on her couch—alone. The feature was set to air this evening, but she squeezed the pause button on the remote as soon as the intro for the show began. A tear trickled down her cheek. She didn't want to watch this without Nolan. They were supposed to watch this together—that had been the plan—but things had changed for her and Nolan. Looking back, she realized she had been the one who indirectly convinced him to pick up a bat when he'd made it clear that he never wanted to swing a baseball bat again. She wondered how things would have turned out differently if she had never even taken him to Firefly Field. She wondered if he would have been here these last three months. If he would have found a normal job, taken her out for dates every weekend, and made love to her every chance they had. But fate seemed to have a different course for their lives. Fate brought him to her, fate set the stage for them to fall in love, and fate put that baseball bat back in his hands. She could still remember the swing that changed their lives, and thinking of him at that moment, caused her to bury her head in her hands.

28

The sound of a key slithering into the grooves in the doorknob on the front door prompted Emma to hop over the back of the sofa like a kangaroo. When Nolan Lynch pushed open the door and stepped inside, she pounced into his open arms. Emma kissed him like she hadn't seen him in two weeks. She *hadn't* seen him in two weeks. She loved this. Loved being in his arms—having her man. Her future. Her professional baseball player. Everything in their lives had taken a new direction on the trip to Boston when Nolan hit baseballs for the first time at Fenway Park—after watching him bat against one of the team's pitchers, the Red Sox organization had invited him to practice and play with the team in spring training. Since then, he had spent every single day gearing up for his second chance at playing baseball professionally. He threw. He hit. He ran. He worked out at the gym. Then he went through the routine over and over again. Emma had enjoyed being a part of this process with him. She had pitched to him. Ran with him. Biked with him. Lifted weights at the gym with him. They'd done everything together. They'd even traveled to batting cages in Greenville so he could experience pitches coming in at ninety plus miles per hour—Emma had a great arm, especially for a female, but she didn't have the arm for Major League velocity.

At spring training, Nolan had played well but not well enough to make the Major League roster. No one had expected him to, though—he had a lot of rust to work off as well as lingering emotional scars to battle through. The team had taken note of the progress he'd made during the spring and realized the potential he showcased. Nolan's eyes had bulged out of his head when the team offered him a contract worth seven figures to begin an assignment with the Red Sox Class A affiliate team in Greenville, South Carolina. The agent Nolan had hired told him that the signing amount meant the Sox expected him to play at the Major League level in the near future and hopefully be an impact player. When Nolan held a black ballpoint pen between his fingers to sign the deal of a lifetime, he felt proud to have his father, Norman, and Emma sitting at the table along with him and his agent. Nolan and Emma teased about how they wished the team played in Greenville, North Carolina, but the drive south to the other Greenville wasn't all that bad. It took about six hours from Washington which made it possible for Nolan and Emma to see one another relatively frequently. Her boss at the restaurant—an avid sports fan—had been very supportive of her taking off every weekend that Nolan wasn't traveling with the team, and even some when the location of the opponent was a shorter drive than his home games. She enjoyed driving to spend time with him and watching his games, and when the team practiced, she tackled her college assignments.

Since Nolan had games almost every day of the week, he rarely found time to make the trip to Washington, but this week his team had a couple days off so he'd offered to give Emma a break from driving. He had been somewhat surprised that she had let him buy her a new car so that she wouldn't have to make the trip via bicycle. He'd also talked her into letting him pay for other expenses like gas and food since she'd had to give up so many hours at work to come see him.

"Why are you crying?" Nolan asked Emma, concerned.

"I was just thinking about you. About how fate has intertwined our lives and even though the road has been rough and led us all over the place, I am so absolutely in love with you."

Nolan kissed her lips again and again. "I love you, too," he said between breaths as his lips fell to her neck then traveled toward her shoulder as he pulled her shirt back.

Emma leaned her upper torso away from Nolan, arching her back but leaving her midsection pressed against his as if she were practicing one of the yoga poses Lisa had taught her and Nolan. That was another activity they'd been doing together to help Nolan gain flexibility for baseball. It had proven to have other benefits as well. "Save all this affection for later," she encouraged playfully. "We have a special program to watch, remember?"

A few minutes later, Emma was nestled in on the couch, but no longer alone—she was relaxing on Nolan's shoulder and eager to watch the feature with him. When she pressed play, the announcer's voice began to flow through the speakers. "*Off the Field* presents 'Gray Area' with the Lynch family." A photo of Nolan's parents emerged and then a black and white baby photo of Nolan slid in on the right side of the screen and one of Norman on the left side simultaneously. "Nolan and Norman Lynch were born on the same day. This is just one of the many things they have in common. They are also athletes—Norman, a professional football player for the Miami Dolphins, and Nolan played college baseball at East Carolina University and was once drafted by the Boston Red Sox. On paper, they've lived the life all kids dream of, but in reality, the dream at times has resembled a nightmare." Images of paramedics and ambulances and a hospital flashed quickly on and off the screen.

"Nolan's baseball career took an unexpected turn on a rainy day in Phoenix, Arizona . . ." The announcer gave a brief overview of the tragedy, but didn't yet mention his mother. As that part played,

Emma squeezed Nolan's hand just a little tighter. "The closest tie these two men have is brotherhood. They're not twins, but they might as well be." In a relaxed studio scene that looked more like a living room than a set, the host asked Mr. Lynch a question he'd been asked many times over the course of Nolan's life. "Why did you and your wife choose to adopt a white child?"

Mr. Lynch chuckled. "Why not?" The rhetorical question hung in the air for a moment. "There is no simple answer to that question. Actually, it's very complex. Ultimately, Nolan was meant to be part of our family. My wife was pregnant with twins, but one of the babies died during childbirth. My wife was devastated and I was as well." With his hands folded, Mr. Lynch openly fought his emotions. "One of the first things my wife said was 'What will Norman do without Nolan?' You see, we'd already named the boys. They'd been growing together for nine months in the womb. It just seemed right that Norman would have a twin to grow up with. We soon found out about this little boy who'd been born at the hospital on the same day as Norman . . . and he needed a family. It didn't matter to us if he was black or white or any other color. We didn't even ask. He was a baby boy that needed a home and our little Norman needed a brother."

The camera panned over to Nolan, sitting on one side of his father.

"What was it like growing up with a black family?" the host asked.

"Perfect," Nolan answered. "Our parents taught Norman and me that love is thicker than blood. As we grew up, we realized that we were different colors, but ultimately, we bonded more because of it." Nolan carried on about the things his parents had taught him and Norman about race.

"Norman, how did it make you feel to have a white brother?" the host asked as Norman suddenly joined the picture, sitting on the opposite side of his father.

"Honestly, it seemed natural to me, and I agree with everything Nolan just said. We were best friends from the beginning."

"How do you feel about it now that you're an adult?"

"I can't imagine life any other way."

The host turned to Mr. Lynch. "Did you ever worry about the challenges Norman and Nolan would face with them being different colors?"

"I think every good parent worries about the challenges their children will face in society, but my wife and I prepared these boys for life. We knew Norman and Nolan would find the positive and that they would turn the negative into positive."

The camera focused back in on the host. "We spent some time with the Lynch family in one of the neighborhoods where the boys grew up."

The footage of Norman and Nolan walking on the sidewalks surrounded by projects and low-income housing began to roll, and a voiceover spoke. "Life isn't easy on these streets, but Norman and Nolan Lynch talked to us about how they made the best of their surroundings."

In the video, the host was walking between Norman and Nolan, with their father on the same side as Norman. "What life lessons did you learn living here?"

Nolan spoke first. "That playing together unites us," he said. "I quickly found out that a commonality I had with the other kids was a love for sports."

"Was it tough to be a white kid growing up in a black neighborhood?"

"I never thought of this as a black neighborhood. It was my neighborhood. One of the things our parents taught us was not to label things black or white. As an adult, I've noticed that labeling races seems to be one of the things that divides people. For example, I wish we didn't have white churches and black churches, white colleges and black colleges, and all the rest."

The host turned his head in Norman's direction as the three of them walked past clotheslines with an assortment of clothes flapping in the wind. On a nearby concrete stoop, a black man with a cigarette was talking to a white man drinking from a brown bag and another black man. "Norman, how do you feel about black and white labels?"

"I understand that this neighborhood is predominately black, but I think when we call it a black neighborhood we are doing the community an injustice. The same goes for an area that's called a white neighborhood. People will always label things, but I think we need to do away with officially labeling anything black or white when it comes to race. Even Black History Month is a slap in the face, in my opinion. To black people, it has historically said you get this month, and white people get the other eleven. To white people, it says one of two things: you have the other eleven months, or you don't get a month at all—there is no month labeled white history month. Why can't we just include all history in every month? To explain it further, I think if the United States starts a Mexican history month or an Asian history month it would do more harm than good to race relations. It's all history, just put what is important in the history books and don't label it based on race. We don't need to read about a black inventor or a white inventor, let's just read about inventors. If they're black, great, and if they're white, great. If they have brown hair, that's wonderful, and if they have red hair, that's wonderful. Would we label a section in the history books 'Red Haired Inventors'? It's pointless. Black and white is a feature, just like tall or short or skinny or plump. I think that's how we should see color."

Mr. Lynch interjected. "We segregate ourselves when we label, which is what so many good people—white, black, and other—fought to dissolve. I truly believe that any type of purposeful segregation hinders unity, even that done in the name of equality." He paused for a moment. "When our kids grow up in a labeling society, they automatically begin to segregate themselves in various areas of life."

The scene suddenly changed to the baseball stadium in Arizona, and the voiceover played again. "Nolan Lynch felt segregated after the tragedy at his last high school baseball game." The announcer eloquently described what happened that day and how the media blew up the story by making it into a race issue.

As Nolan watched from the couch, he felt relief in the way that the show honored his mother. Both he and Emma had tears rolling down their faces.

"Nolan, did the article that was titled *White Baseball Player Nolan Lynch Kills Black Woman* change the way you viewed black people?"

Nolan had known that the tough questions would arise, he had received an adequate warning. The earlier frame from the scene in Phoenix had also set the record straight and explained the accident well.

Sitting in the stadium chair dedicated to his mother, Nolan responded to the question. "Not at all," he said simply. "But it caused me to be irate at how the media stirs up racism."

The host looked at Norman. "Do you agree that the media stirred up racism in the accident involving your brother and mother?"

"Most definitely," Norman answered without hesitation. "When the headline of a story says that a white man or woman has killed a black man or woman, or vice versa, it automatically aims to divide."

"What makes you believe this?"

"How often do you see a headline that says a black man kills a black man or a white man kills a white man?"

The announcer nodded his head in agreement. "I'm not sure I've ever seen that."

"Controversy evokes interest," Nolan interjected, "and the media realizes this." Nolan thought carefully about how to articulate the words that followed. "Neither the headline nor the story itself was racist. Also, I do not believe the people who wrote it were racist. I did some research, and I found out that the journalist of the story written about my mom and I was white. So was his editor." Nolan paused. "Earlier you asked if the headline changed my view of black people . . . it would have been very ignorant of me to allow that to happen."

Norman added his thoughts. "The same thing happened when the press went nuts over white police officers shooting black people. The media stirred the pot to make money, and in the end, way too many lives ended up lost—black and white—and I believe their involvement further divided the two races of people. Don't get me wrong, if an investigation is done and a white or black officer shoots a black or white man because of the color of his skin, they deserve to be held accountable. But when the media and politicians start jumping to conclusions, they invite the public to do the same."

The host spoke up again. "Most men wouldn't have the courage to say the things you men are saying on national television about race. What is it that gives you the right and the tenacity to take this stand, knowing that some people will strongly disagree with you?"

"We've lived in each other's shoes," Norman answered. "Nolan has about the best idea of any white man in this world as to what it feels like to be black."

"Nolan, do you think the same rings true for Norman, that he has an idea of what it's like to be white?"

"Yeah, I think so. As we grew up, we watched how people of different races treated each of us. We saw racism from both sides. We know it exists, but we believe the vast amount of people in this country are not racist."

The location on film quickly changed to Fenway Park where it showed Nolan hitting baseballs and then to the Miami Dolphins' stadium where it showed Norman playing on a Sunday afternoon.

"What role do you think sports play in racial equality?"

"A very significant one," Norman answered. "Sports have

always brought people together. I huddle up with black men and white men every Sunday, and we have each other's back on and off the field."

"Do you ever hear any racist comments from players?"

"It happens from time to time, but it's usually in the heat of the moment, and we try not to make a big deal of it."

"Do you think that's wise to just let it go?"

"It's situational, but we all say stupid stuff every now and then. A lot of it stems from things we've heard our parents say. In mine and Nolan's case, we didn't hear an ounce of racism from our parents, so we just don't talk like that."

Nolan added a thought. "I think it's also important to remember that there's a huge difference between a racist comment and a racist person. Growing up, when someone would call Norman or me the N-word, sometimes we'd just ignore it, and other times we'd try to have a conversation with that person about it."

"People called you the N-word, Nolan?" the host asked, somewhat dumbfounded.

"Yeah, all the time. It came with the territory, I guess. That's why Norman said that he and I have walked in each other's shoes. People called him *White Bread* and other similar names."

"What do we need to do in life and in sports to eliminate racism?" the host asked.

"I'm not sure we can ever eliminate racism, but there is a lot we can do to limit it. I think it starts with parents following the lead of other parents like ours," Nolan said. "If kids don't hear racist comments at home, they're less likely to be involved in racism."

"What else did your parents do on this subject?" the host asked.

"They educated us," Norman said. "They taught us about slavery and the Civil Rights Movement and so on—the good and the bad. They didn't point the finger, though. They explained to us that it was history and that people could either use it as a lesson learned or as ammunition."

"Well, Mr. Lynch, it certainly seems as though you and your wife have done an incredible job raising these two young men."

"Parenting is all about raising kids to become adults who will make this world a better place. I believe that my boys are making this world a better place. I am proud of them for taking a stand on race, especially because neither of them stands with just white people or with just black people, they stand with people, as humans with one goal to love one another regardless of the color of our skin. We need our churches to get involved in this agenda. We need our politicians to quit playing sides for votes. We need our media to share stories about love and the positive things that human beings are doing to help one another. Just the other day I was watching a television special about one of the hurricanes that came through last year, and you know what I saw?" he asked rhetorically. "A black man was pulling a white family into his boat, to safety; and the next clip was of a white man dangling from a helicopter rescuing black people trapped in a flooded building. Those are the kind of stories we need to see, but even these don't have to say *Black Man Saved by White Man*. It's one man saving another man because he values life."

"There is nothing I can say that brings more light to the subject than what the Lynch family has shared with us today," the host said. "I thank them for their candidness and for the choices they're making to help dissolve racism in America." The host reached out his hand to each man and shook his hand, then a collage of images from the trip the Lynch's had taken began to flow onto the television screen. It showed Nolan and Norman laughing with their father, displayed photos from when they were kids, and ended with a photo of Nolan crushing a glow-in-the-dark baseball pitched by Emma Pate into the cornfield at Firefly Field. Fireflies surrounded the field, and blended in with the stars in the night's sky as a ball the same color as the fireflies traveled through the air. Then, suddenly, the photo turned into a video and the voiceover began to roll. "Nolan Lynch hadn't touched a baseball bat in over six years following the accidental death of his mother, and he'd vowed never to swing one again. Then he met Emma Pate, a sweet southern gal with a fastball worth clocking on a radar gun. We did that, in fact," the voice announced, and the video showed her pitch crossing home plate at Firefly Field at sixty-six miles per hour. "The two fell in love, and eventually Nolan rediscovered his roots."

Standing on the mound at Firefly Field, Emma began to talk into the camera. "One day when we were out here at the field, Nolan was pitching to me like he had many times over the summer, and then he just randomly walked up to the plate and grabbed the bat. When I tossed him a ball, he hit it into the cornfield."

"Have you ever struck him out?" the host asked.

In the next scene, Nolan and Emma were sitting next to each other on the wooden bench beside the equipment bin. She looked at him and grinned. "I don't want to embarrass Nolan on national television after the Red Sox just invited him to spring training."

The voiceover rolled one last time as it showed images of the family in the quaint town of Little Washington. "Nolan Lynch made the Boston Red Sox Class A affiliate team, and they expect him to work his way into the majors in the near future. As for Nolan and Emma, maybe one day she'll answer that question for us, but for now, Nolan has a question for Emma Pate—"

Sitting in her home with Nolan, watching this feature, Emma furrowed her brow. She had been present throughout the entire filming session, but she didn't remember the scene now playing on the screen. Holding himself up with a baseball bat, Nolan knelt down at home plate on Firefly Field. Fireflies were dancing in the background to the music of summer nights in Eastern North Carolina.

"Emma Pate, will you marry me?"

29

So entranced by the scene on the television, Emma hadn't even noticed that Nolan, who'd been right there next to her on the couch, had slid off.

Propped on one knee, Nolan flipped open a small box, and that's when Emma finally glanced down and spotted the ring.

"Will you be my wife?" he asked with a small stutter.

Like so many other women when asked this question, Emma's first reaction was to cover her mouth and at the same time gasp with excitement. Instantly, she reached out her finger for Nolan to slide on the ring and answered, "Yes! Yes, I will definitely marry you, Nolan Lynch!"

It seemed fitting for the wedding to be held at dusk on a late summer evening at Firefly Field. As Nolan's father walked Emma down the aisle toward home plate—where Nolan stood in wait with an enormous smile—the fireflies were beginning to perform their nightly show. This night, though, it seemed as though they had sent out invitations to their friends and family just like Nolan and Emma had done. There were more fireflies floating around the field than Emma had ever seen, so many that she whispered to

Nolan, "Did you have extra fireflies brought in from somewhere?" It seemed like something sweet he'd do for her as a surprise. Lost in Emma's ocean colored eyes, Nolan smiled and slightly nodded his head side to side as the preacher welcomed the guests.

Fifty white wooden baseball stadium-style chairs were holding people who couldn't believe their eyes. Everyone in attendance watched in amazement as Nolan and Emma exchanged vows surrounded by the twinkling lights of fireflies beneath a clear starry sky. During the ceremony, one of the chairs on the front row remained vacant in honor of Nolan's mother. On one side of the empty seat sat a woman Nolan had met for the first time yesterday. His biological mother had happened to see the *Off the Field* feature and had a hunch that Nolan was the baby boy she had given birth to all those years ago. When she reached out to Nolan, he nearly wrote her off. As much as he wanted to learn why she had abandoned him, part of him thought that chapter of his life might be best left closed. Things had been trending in a positive direction, and he didn't want to muddy up his life especially just as he and Emma were about to embark on this new adventure together as husband and wife. Emma had graduated from the community college in the spring, and they had made plans for her to travel full-time with Nolan who had been promoted to the Red Sox Class AAA team and was expected to be called up to the majors in September. She decided that being on the road with him would give her the perfect opportunity to work on her bachelor's degree. Emma had applied to and received acceptance into East Carolina University's online education program. She wouldn't even have to step foot on campus unless she wanted to, so all she would need was a laptop computer which she already owned. In the offseason, Emma and Nolan would come back to Washington and live at the farm.

After multiple lengthy conversations with Emma, Norman, and his father, Nolan decided to allow his biological mother a chance. When they talked on the phone the second time, the first question he asked was, "Why did you abandon me?" The only reason he hadn't asked during their first phone conversation is because he had been in a state of pure shock. Honestly, it still didn't seem real that he had been talking with the woman who'd given birth to him.

"Nolan, giving you up for adoption was the most difficult decision of my life, but please believe me when I say that at the time it was what I thought to be the best option for you."

For days that answer clanked around in his head like the silver ball in a pinball machine. Ultimately, he decided her answer wasn't good enough, and the next time they spoke, he told her as much. He had no idea what type of relationship he wanted to have with his biological mother, but he decided that if she wanted to have any part in his life, she would have to be completely honest with him. During their next phone conversation, he found out that both she and his father had been in the military, part of a special forces team to be exact. Quite ironically, she explained to him that no one knew about the relationship she had with his father because such a relationship was forbidden in their line of work. He nearly laughed out loud thinking of how that paralleled with his and Emma's relationship, but then she went on to tell him that his biological father had died in an overseas raid sometime between Nolan's conception and birth. Nolan felt his heart skip a beat as his mother explained to him that she became extremely depressed after the loss and while being out of work on maternity leave. She said that for her own mental health she knew she had to go back to work which would have meant regularly leaving her infant son with people he didn't know as she deployed for missions.

After a few more conversations, Nolan got the feeling that she had regretted the decision. He knew firsthand about regretting decisions. He only planned to get married once, and he decided he didn't want to look back ten or twenty years from now and regret not having her at the wedding. He and Emma talked about the idea in depth, and Emma helped him see the positive side of the situation. Nolan's final question to his biological mother before mailing her an invitation to the wedding had been, "Why now?"

"I always pictured you having this perfect life with a perfect family, and I didn't want to interfere. I felt bad that I hadn't given that to you, and I didn't want to show up out of the blue as you were growing up and throw your life into a tailspin." Weeping, she paused. "When I heard your story on the show, I knew. I just knew that you were the grownup version of the handsome baby boy I'd given birth to, and I couldn't walk away again."

She went on to say that if Nolan wanted nothing to do with her, she would understand. He didn't get the sense that she might be after money—a lot of people from his past had all of a sudden begun reaching out to him lately for that reason. It amazed him at how many people just came right out and asked for financial help. He'd heard from former teammates, teachers, and all kinds of people he'd met throughout the course of his life. Some of them he remembered and some he didn't. Most of them seemed happy for him and most didn't ask for anything.

Ultimately, Emma had been completely on board with adding Nolan's biological mother to the guest list. On the other hand, one person that she and Nolan were both fine with leaving off was Clay Bell. He hadn't spoken a word to either one of them from the moment Nolan resigned from the college until the day the Boston Red Sox signed Nolan. As soon as that news spread, however, Clay began making attempts to squirm his way into their lives. He apologized for leaking the photos and videos to the media and said if he had it all to do over again, he would have just burned them, and he even offered to give back the money he'd made from them. Neither Emma nor Nolan believed his intentions to be worthy for one moment, but they decided to forgive him anyway, and in the end, they actually sent him an invitation to the wedding. Emma thought it was mighty big of Nolan to be the one to say that even though Clay had always been a jerk to him, Clay had been Emma's childhood friend and he thought that should count for something. Surprisingly, not only did Clay show up, but he showed up with Mary. Nolan and Emma agreed that Mary seemed to bring out the best in Clay, and they hoped that Clay wouldn't do anything stupid to lose her again.

After Nolan and Emma kissed passionately, the two were announced as Mr. and Mrs. Lynch for the first time ever, and then they walked out to a wooden dancefloor staged atop the grass in centerfield. Their first dance as husband and wife happened slowly and romantically as the song *Thinking Out Loud* by Ed Sheeran whispered through a set of speakers on the corners of the dance floor. The small crowd around them gasped as Nolan and Emma's actions mimicked the lyrics of the song—

Take me into your loving arms
Kiss me under the light of a thousand stars
Place your head on my beating heart
Thinking out loud
Maybe we found love right where we are.

30

The night of their wedding, Nolan and Emma made their way back out to Firefly Field. Their friends and family had trickled away, all decorations and props had vanished, and this is where they chose to spend their first true moments alone as husband and wife. They spread out a comforter on the outfield grass and found a comfortable spot to lay next to one another. For a few moments, they talked about the amazing night they'd just experienced, then they let their conversation dwindle as they held hands and listened to a steady stream of chirping critters—crickets and frogs and who knows what else. The occasional bullfrog let out a melodious groan. An outline of towering trees framed the most beautiful living photograph they'd ever seen. A million tiny lights made up of fireflies and stars twinkled all around them and above them. Every now and then a shooting star streaked across the horizon and eventually appeared to dissolve into nothingness. Each time, Nolan and Emma would make a wish and kiss a little more passionately.

There were no streetlights, no porch lights, and no houses in sight. Just the two of them surrounded by darkness and dreams and living out a reality they'd never imagined possible. They talked about things like how every time they moved their heads it seemed as though the sky rotated ever so slightly. They watched as over time airplanes followed the same paths in the sky between the same clusters of stars. Nolan and Emma wondered how far in the distance they could see as they watched each plane fade out of sight. They asked questions like *Where do you think that airplane is going? How many people are on it? What are their lives like? Are they in love like us or lonely?*

To repel the mosquitoes, Nolan had brought an unscented spray that actually worked—a practical gift he'd given Emma in her honeymoon basket. The soft comforter beneath them had also been in the basket, and on the centerfield grass, it began to collect the first drops of dew of the night. A thin white sheet covered their bodies, and out here it felt like no one else existed—just the two of them completely encapsulated in this moment of time. No cell phones. No television. No distractions. This was the way life was meant to be lived. Slow. Quiet. Real. Two people having conversations that would live forever. Making memories that wouldn't fade in time. It was an incredibly surreal experience. The longer they laid beneath the night's sky, the more stars they could see, and the more the lights of night illuminated Nolan's and Emma's faces and figures. As the two of them began to move in unison beneath the thin sheet covering their bare bodies, a soft breeze danced across the field. This moment—surrounded by a field of fireflies—seemed to define love, happiness, perfection, and everything that was right in the world.

THE END

A Note from the Author

Thank you for reading *A Field of Fireflies*! I am honored that you chose to invest your time in this book. If you haven't yet read my other novels, *A Bridge Apart* and *Losing London*, I hope you will very soon. If you enjoyed the story you just experienced, please consider helping me spread the novel to others, in the following ways:

- REVIEW the novel online at Amazon.com, goodreads.com, bn.com, bamm.com, etc.
- RECOMMEND this book to friends (social groups, workplace, book club, church, school, etc.).
- VISIT my website: www.Joey-Jones.com
- SUBSCRIBE to my Email Newsletter for insider information on upcoming novels, behind-the-scenes looks, promotions, charities, and other exciting news.

- CONNECT with me on Social Media: "Like" Facebook.com/JoeyJonesWriter (post a comment about the novel). "Follow" me at Instagram.com/JoeyJonesWriter and Twitter.com/JoeyJonesWriter (#AFieldofFireflies). "Pin" on Pinterest. Write a blog post about the novel.
- GIVE a copy of the novel to someone you know who you think would enjoy the story. Books make great presents (Birthday, Christmas, Teacher's Gifts, etc.).

Sincerely,
Joey Jones

About the Author

Joey Jones fell in love with creative writing at a young age and decided in his early twenties that he wanted to write a novel. His debut novel, *A Bridge Apart,* released years later, in September 2015. His second novel, *Losing London*, released in October 2016. Prior to becoming a full-time novelist, his day job was in the marketing field. He holds a Bachelor of Arts in Business Communications from the University of Maryland University College, where he earned a 3.8 GPA.

Joey Jones lives in North Carolina with his family. In his spare time, he enjoys spending time with his loved ones, playing and watching sports, reading, and serving others. His favorite movie is *Meet Joe Black*, and his favorite book is *The Poky Little Puppy*.

Joey Jones is currently writing his fourth novel and working on various projects pertaining to his three published novels.

Book Club/Group Discussion Questions

1. Were you immediately engaged in the novel?
2. What emotions did you experience as you read the book?
3. Which character is your favorite? Why?
4. What do you like most about the story as a whole?
5. What is your favorite part/scene in the novel?
6. Are there any particular passages from the book that stand out to you?
7. As you read, what are some of the things that you thought might happen, but didn't?
8. Is there anything you would have liked to see turn out differently?
9. Is the ending satisfying? If so, why? If not, why not, and how would you change it?
10. Why might the author have chosen to tell the story the way he did?
11. If you could ask the author a question, what would you ask?
12. What author(s) would you compare to Joey Jones?
13. Have you ever read or heard a story anything like this one?
14. In what ways does this novel relate to your own life?
15. Would you reread this novel?

Made in the
USA
Columbia, SC